THE FAULKES CHRONICLE

Also by David Huddle

Blacksnake at the Family Reunion, poems, 2012

Nothing Can Make Me Do This, novel, 2011

Glory River, poems, 2008

Grayscale, poems, 2004

La Tour Dreams of the Wolf Girl, novel, 2002

Not: A Trio, two stories and a novella, 2000

The Story of a Million Years, novel, 1999

Summer Lake: New & Selected Poems, 1999

Tenorman, novella, 1995

A David Huddle Reader, stories, poems, essays, 1994

The Writing Habit, essays, 1994

Intimates, stories, 1993

The Nature of Yearning, poems, 1992

The High Spirits, Stories of Men & Women, 1989

Stopping By Home, poems, 1988

Only the Little Bone, stories, 1986

Paper Boy, poems, 1979

A Dream With No Stump Roots In It, stories, 1975

DAVID HUDDLE

THE FAULKES CHRONICLE

Tupelo Press
North Adams, Massachusetts

Library of Congress Cataloging-in-Publication Data
Huddle, David, 1942–
The Faulkes chronicle / David Huddle. -- First edition.
pages cm
ISBN 978-1-936797-45-5 (pbk. original : alk. paper)
1. Mothers--Death--Fiction. 2. Family life--Fiction. 3. Grief--Fiction. I. Title.
PS3558.U287F38 2014
813'.54--dc23
2014016998

Cover and text designed by Ann Aspell.

Cover photographs: *Great Blue Heron* by Matthew Hull, used by courtesy of the artist (www.morguefile.com/creative/matthew_hull). Thanks to Sabrina Alderman, Anne Boyle, and Sally Quesenberry for providing the family photograph that found its way onto the cover of this book.

The author is grateful to the editors of *Blackbird* (www.blackbird.vcu) for publishing the first fourteen sections of this book in their Spring 2013 issue.

First edition: September, 2014.

Tupelo Press
P.O. Box 1767, North Adams, Massachusetts 01247
Telephone: (413) 664–9611 / editor@tupelopress.org
www.tupelopress.org

Tupelo Press is an award-winning independent literary press that publishes fine fiction, nonfiction, and poetry in books that are a joy to hold as well as read. Tupelo Press is a registered 501(c)(3) nonprofit organization, and we rely on public support to carry out our mission of publishing extraordinary work that may be outside the realm of large commercial publishers. Financial donations are welcome and are tax deductible.

In Memory

Of the mothers —

Teresa Jennings Massie

and Mary Frances Akers Huddle

And the fathers —

Joseph Anderson Massie

and Charles Richard Huddle Jr.

THE FAULKES CHRONICLE

Nothing feels better
Than blood on blood.

—Bruce Springsteen,
"Highway Patrolman"

In her last year of life

our mother betrayed us by becoming pretty. We are a homely family. For generations we've been that way. A different idea of beauty evolved among us. Faulkeses looked for plain-faced and chubby mates. Our choices weren't particularly conscious, they were just what our genes told us to do. Now and then a Faulkes boy would be attracted to a cheerleader or a Faulkes girl would get the hots for a pretty boy. Those relationships sometimes quickened, but they could not be sustained.

Our mother had the classic Faulkes features, the small wide-spaced eyes, the negative cheekbones, the too-long chin and nose, the short forehead. When she went into chemo, chemo rearranged her face, thinned her down, installed into her repertoire of facial expressions a grimace that had every appearance of a starlet's smile. Our mother's baldness made her look delicate and vulnerable. A slightly visible blue vein that throbbed along the side her head just above her ear made our father close his eyes to the sight of it. "It looks like a clever painter's brushstroke," he said. "Notice it, and you want to touch it."

Indeed that was generally the case with our mother as she was dying. We wanted to be near her, wanted to be within touching distance of her, wanted to sit shoulder to shoulder with her, so that our arms might brush against her arms. And this was not merely the case with us Faulkeses.

Townspeople and even strangers were drawn to her. People introduced themselves to her — we understood after a while — just to be able to shake hands with her.

"This was bound to happen sometime," said our mother's oncologist. "Mostly chemo ravages people's looks. In your mother's case, the effect has been to beautify." He glanced at us. "I plan to monitor her very carefully." Then he looked back at her with a gaze a sculptor might bestow upon his recent masterpiece. This was in the oncology conference room with all of the immediate family present. It was a month after our first session with Dr. Lawson, when he had stunned us by explaining that our mother's tumor was located too near her heart to be operable. And this "monitor her very carefully" moment was when we first began to suspect that Dr. Lawson was smitten with our mother.

The effect on her was not what we would have anticipated. Though she married into the family, our mother had had the Faulkes character before she even met our father. Faulkeses are first and foremost practical, unpretentious, and straightforward people. You won't find a simpering Faulkes anywhere on the planet. We don't flirt, we don't small-talk, we don't suck up, we don't flatter, we don't shoot the breeze. We have thrived because we are notably competent and dependable. A Faulkes makes an excellent plumber, a skilled commando, a steady airline pilot. But as our mother moved into her prettiness, she evidently thought it worth her while to enter the social fray and enjoy the lower order of human intercourse. After all, what did she have to lose? She actually batted her eyes at her oncologist when he took her pulse that afternoon in his conference room. Our Aunt Beatrice audibly inhaled and left the room when she saw our mother's shameless act. "I didn't know people actually did that thing with their eyes," she said later in the afternoon.

Our mother allowed her oncologist to be evasive about telling us how much time she had to live. We all knew that the only legitimate offering oncologists have for their patients is the life-span estimate, which everyone knows is usually incorrect. But in our mother's case, we were greedy to hear it — six months to a year, five years, whatever, accurate or not, we wanted the time she had with us to be named and quantified. And our mother encouraged Dr. Lawson in his shifty language. "There are too many unknowns in your mother's case," he explained, looking from one to another of us around the room. "And besides, a single day for one person may be the equivalent of several years for another," he pontificated to us that afternoon in the conference room — after he'd taken our mother's pulse for a good two minutes. "I suggest to you all that you try to appreciate every instant of your mother's company. After all, doesn't the fact that death comes to us all eventually make the fact of death a tawdry and useless piece of information? Put death-thoughts aside, I say," he said. "Love your mother completely in each moment you have with her, and both you and she will be fulfilled." Then he patted our mother's hand, stood up, looked us each in the eyes in turn, nodded as if to agree with himself, and walked back out into the corridors of the oncology floor of the hospital.

"That fellow's sort of a turd," our father said, and we were glad for his outburst. A Faulkes virtue is that we are not inclined to use degraded words. And even by Faulkes standards, our father was a taciturn man. Which is not to say that he lacked an emotional life. As long as we children lived in his house, he insisted on kissing us good night, always very late and after we'd turned out our lights, a quick brush of his lips across our foreheads followed by his softly uttered "Night, Franklin" or "Night, Susan." "Night, Tony" or "Night, Carlton." "Night, McKenzie." "Night, Sarah Jean." "Night, Desiree." "Night, Jane." "Night, C.J." There are so many of us it takes him a while to make the rounds, and the syllables of our names might be the only ones he's spoken to us throughout the day. So the gutter word he chose to describe Dr. Lawson caused us to flinch almost in unison but then to look gleefully at each other's faces. Our mother paid no attention to us, but she did look up from her wrist, which must still have been feeling the oncologist's fingers pressing on it. And she scrutinized our father with unusual intensity.

At Goshen High School our father had risen from shop teacher and wrestling coach to principal. If it were possible for a mostly silent and nearly invisible man to become a beloved figure in our town, our father would have been that person. In our immediate family, we believed that he deliberately behaved so as avoid becoming beloved. He was expressive with his hands — and they were his primary teaching and coaching tools. With a quick slicing motion of his extended fingers across the fingers of the other hand, he could show you why it was important to push a one-by-six into the rip-saw in the correct fashion. And you'd remember the lesson forever. He never touched his wrestlers, but he could move his hands and sometimes his legs and his whole torso to demonstrate a certain hold or tripping maneuver or escape from a hold or evasive tactic.

As the high school principal, our father used his physical presence and his singular variation of the Faulkes face to maintain discipline in the hallways, the cafeteria, and the gymnasium. When we Faulkes children saw him in these venues and witnessed how he adjusted his face to suggest hellish consequences for misbehavior, we were grateful that he never brought his "professional" facial expressions into our house or into our own family life. But at home or at school he never resorted to physical punishment. When a teacher sent a problem student to his office, our father often returned that student to the classroom with an improved attitude and a determination to try to live a more constructive life. One such student told of sitting an hour directly across from our father at his desk with our father saying nothing but insisting that the student continue looking into his face.

Faulkeses tend to have large families for no reason other than that we enjoy children and we favor dogs and cats and even exotic pets like possums and hamsters. All Faulkeses like the general chaos of a human- and animal-populated household. Ours, however, is the largest Faulkes family on record. A joke in Goshen is that the Delbert Faulkeses are trying to replace all the townspeople with their own kind. Our mother once told us that it might not be as much a joke as our townsfolk think it is. A Faulkes generally prefers the company of another Faulkes to that of a non-Faulkes. All of which background made our mother's emerging prettiness raise some questions in the minds of each of us. Can there be a winsome or cute Faulkes? If, through no fault of her own, a Faulkes woman loses those physical characteristics that define her as a Faulkes, how should she be treated by other Faulkeses? And how can she continue to view herself as a Faulkes if she no longer looks like one? More disturbing, do we Faulkeses behave the way we do because our looks are not conventionally appealing? Do we subconsciously pay for our homeliness by working harder, being more responsible, and cultivating unimpeachable integrity? Couldn't a beautiful Faulkes — as our mother appeared to be in the process of becoming—simply sit around all day eating chocolates and chatting with the ladies of the Goshen Bridge Club? Or sitting out on her front porch fanning herself and encouraging the attention of lazy and superficial townsfolk? "Would you like to come up and sit a spell and join me in a glass of iced tea?" such a pretty Faulkes might call down to a passing acquaintance, such as her oncologist, who happened to be walking past her house.

Our mother's maiden name was Karen Seifert. She told us that when she was growing up, people thought she was smart but too quiet for her own good. People told her she should smile more often, which she considered stupid advice. "What they missed about me," she told us, "was that I have a really silly side. But evidently I was pretty good at keeping that a secret." Karen Seifert took a degree in American Literature from Georgetown University, then she came north to teach English at Goshen High School. She married our father after her first year of teaching and while he was still the shop teacher. When she became pregnant with our oldest sister, Jane, our mother submitted her resignation and committed herself to what she liked to call "household management." She often said that reading was her addiction, so she'd never stop doing that, but keeping a clean and orderly house and tending to her children's needs was considerably more appealing than trying to persuade country children to appreciate Emily Dickinson. She said she'd never found much pleasure in the classroom. Now and then one of us would hear an old rumor about her —

that she was a teacher without mercy, that she feared no student, parent, or school board member.

"When I stopped teaching, I became a human being again," our mother liked to say. "It's you children who brought me into myself." But we children — and everyone else in the family — understood her to mean that she became a complete Faulkes. Thanks to her, our family life took on energy, humor, soul, purpose, and camaraderie. She liked us. That was the simple fact of her. Of course she loved us, and she made sure that we understood that. But the great pleasure of our mother was that as soon as we were born, she began studying us, discerning our qualities and our inclinations. She began talking with us, joking with us, asking us questions, reading to us, playing music for us, teaching us songs, telling us little things she knew we would appreciate. With each of us, it was as if we were born with our best friend already out there and waiting for us to arrive. We children functioned like a troupe of acrobats.

In one of our late-night conversations about our mother after she had died, our sister Jane described for us how our mother had shown her — and Jane thought this happened when she was about four — how to carry out the end-of-the-day cleaning of the sink and the countertop. "Swear to God, I had no idea this was something anybody else in the world would have considered work," Jane said. "Our mother said, 'Here's what you can do with a sponge.' She picked up the dish-drainer and set it aside, picked up the pan beneath it, poured out the water, used the scrubby side of the sponge to clean it, then the soft side to wipe it almost dry. Then she set it back in place and polished it up with a paper towel before she set the drainer back in its place. She proceeded to move aside all the canisters, the microwave, the coffee grinder, the jars, and she sponged away every speck of food or stain or coffee ground, then dried it all with a single paper towel. She did these tasks neatly, as if she were following a pattern in her mind. The whole time she cleaned, she very softly hummed and scat-sang and murmured to the flour and sugar jars. It was like this amazing adult recreational activity. She'd sit me up on the stool over by the phone counter, and she'd tell me what she was doing while she did it. She'd show me the sponge, let me smell it, show me her wet hands, ask me if she'd got the canisters lined up just right. When she'd finished and arranged everything back in its place, she lifted me up so that I could view the results. 'What do you think?' she asked me and touched the faucet that she'd polished up to look like new." Jane shook her head and even teared up a little bit. "Even now," Jane said, "if I'm feeling wrong with the world or if I'm missing her just way too much, I know what to do."

What Jane said applied to every one of us. We each had our own private ritual our mother had taught us — back when she was the imperial Faulkes mother — that just incidentally installed some order into the world. She gave each of us a way to defend ourselves from discouragement and squalor.

In our immediate family,

we do not lightly use the word *betrayal* when we speak of our mother's evolution into prettiness and away from absolute Faulkesness. Disturbing as the mere fact of her coming death is to us, we're hurt more by the doubt we've inherited from her treachery. If our mother can reject so much of what she's taught us, so much of what she's represented to us as worthwhile, then was there any truth to her teaching in the first place? "We are talking about metaphysical uncertainty here," says our brother, Robert, who's recently taken a course in Existential Literature at Bard.

"She would so totally snort at you for even saying something like that," says our sister Jennifer. "If you use words with more than three syllables, she'll roll her eyes at you."

"Yeah, right," says Robert. "Damn right in fact, if you're talking about before the chemo. But now that she's changed, I'll bet she'd go for these French writers I've been reading. I'll bet she'd say she finally understands what can be cool about philosophical literature."

The ones of us who are sitting around the table this evening nod our heads. A longstanding debate about whether or not our mother is cool went on among us even before the cancer came to get her. Was it cool to wear clothes that nobody noticed? Cool never to drink more than a single glass of wine? Cool to teach your kids the old hymns like "Shall We Gather by the River?" and "Bringing in the Sheaves"? Cool to teach the whole family — including our father — to recite *Goodnight Moon* from beginning to end and to sing "Frank Mills" and "What a Piece of Work Is Man" all the way through? It isn't a debate anybody will ever win, and we children can — and often do — argue either side of it, but we almost always reach the conclusion that cool doesn't apply to Faulkeses in general or to our mother in particular.

In the face of our mother's increasing beauty,

our father becomes helpless. Early on, when none of us quite realizes what's transpiring with her, our mother insists that he take her to the Iron Boots New Year's Eve dance. This is such a radical request that later we surmise that Dr. Lawson must have put her up to it by giving her free tickets to the event. But that information hasn't yet come into the open. It is simply the case that one day our mother has the tickets, she never explains how she got them, and when she and our father arrive at the dance, Dr. Lawson is the only person there who welcomes them and talks with them during the evening. We haven't even met Dr. Lawson yet, because our mother has not told us of her initial visit to him.

The Iron Boots Society is the last organization any Faulkes would ever join. Its members are the kind of people who involuntarily look down on Faulkeses. Iron Boots members hire Faulkeses, do business with them, ask favors of them, speak politely to them, but almost never socialize with them. Which is just how Faulkeses prefer things to be. Iron Boots members are Goshen's social people, and the greater snobbery may be that of the Faulkeses, because we have so little respect for the ones who think they are our local keepers of taste and beauty. Dr. Lawson of course comes from somewhere out West, and so he is excused from the mild contempt Faulkeses feel for Iron Boots members — except that he so perfectly fits into that pompous crowd.

"You know how it is with dancing and this family," our father tells us the next evening after our mother has gone to bed. "If a Faulkes dances at all, it's darned exceptional. And if a Faulkes does dance, it's goofy, awkward, spontaneous, and pretty comical. If he dances at all, a Faulkes will do it someplace where it probably ought not to be done — meandering through the plumbing section of Aubuchon Hardware, putting gas into his car, shoveling snow. So I asked your mother if she and I were going to have to dance at the Iron Boots thing, and she said yes, we were going to have to do it, because that's what you do when you go to a dance. And I thought" — this is our father speaking the truth to us, as he never fails to do but with considerably more passion than we are used to hearing from him — "I thought, this is the love of my life, the mother of my children, and my companion until death takes one of us away. If she wants me to dance with her, then I will dance, even if all of Goshen sees me acting a fool."

Our father is as much a brother to us children as he is a father, and so our hearts go out to him as he gives his account. Of course this is before we know that our mother is ill, and so we have no inkling that we are embarking on the journey of our mother's dying. But since the topic is dancing, we can't help noting that our father's appearance seems more Faulkeslike than ever. His arms are about an inch longer and his legs an inch shorter than is normal for a man of his size. He likes to say that his true calling was to be a brick-layer because he is strong, good with his hands, and an agile climber. He likes to claim that he accidentally fell into his career as a high school principal. Poignancy radiates from him as he tells of accompanying our mother to the Iron Boots dance.

"She'd bought that dress," he says — and of course we know about the frilly deep purple velvet frock in which our mother presented herself to us in the living room that evening just before she and our father left the house. We'd witnessed her brilliance in that dress. It had surprised us all, maybe even slightly bruised our consciousness, because we were never again able to see our mother in quite the same way, and it was days before we could even bring it up for discussion.

"She'd bought that dress, and she'd bought some lipstick and eye make-up, too, and so even though she still looked like a Faulkes, the way she'd got herself up also made her look like a forest queen. She looked like some kind of new and improved human female. I'll tell you, when we walked into that ballroom" — our father is speaking of the Goshen Hotel's dining room, which becomes a ballroom once a year for the Iron Boots New Year's Eve dance — "I was as nervous and proud as I was on the day I married her. She led me straight through the door out into the crowd of people on the dance floor. Then she turned to me, took my hand and lifted her arm up around my shoulder. I forgot about the other people. As far as I was concerned, she and I were just out there by ourselves, dancing to 'Stars Fell on Alabama,' which is a song I've always thought told the biggest lie about a mean-spirited state that ever was told but which sounded, with your mother in my arms — I hate to admit this — romantic and sweet to my ears. So we danced, your mother and I, as if we'd never even met a Faulkes, let alone been Faulkeses ourselves and lived happily among Faulkeses for our whole married life."

Our father goes on to tell us many more details of that evening of his and our mother's Iron Boots adventure. Such as that at the end of their first dance, Dr. Lawson carried out onto the dance floor and presented to them full glasses of champagne. Such as that he and our mother found themselves seated at a little round table with Dr. Lawson and his friend Dr. Prendergast. Such as that when the band played "Burn That Candle," Dr. Lawson asked our mother to dance, and that our mother who'd never even heard of the jitterbug let Dr. Lawson tell her what to do with her feet and even managed to do a kind of semi-Faulkes version of the jitterbug without completely disgracing herself. Our father says that even before she had her second glass of champagne our mother's face began to glow. He says that after they'd been there in the ballroom maybe an hour or so, he asked her if she was having a good time. Our mother's eyes went misty, and she leaned discreetly into his shoulder and told him no, that even though she was trying her hardest to enjoy herself, it wasn't working and all she really wanted to do was go home and peep into her children's rooms to see if they were there where they should be, with the little ones sleeping while the older ones read or worked on school projects.

"This dance is a Faulkes version of hell, don't you think?" our mother quietly asked our father as she leaned into him. Instead of answering her, he asked her if she wanted to go home, and she told him yes, she did. That was exactly what she wanted.

Our mother tells us about the cancer

on a Saturday more or less during breakfast. We're always up at our regular school-day time on Saturday, because most of us have our designated chores or activities. Even the little ones who don't have assigned duties generally get up anyway, because weekend breakfasts are pancakes and bacon and we enjoy being together without having to rush to get to school or work. Saturday breakfast is also merrily chaotic, with one or the other of us standing up from the table for syrup or milk or juice or a book, a teddy bear, a Lego contraption, whatever, and there'll be two or three conversations going on across the table.

"My dears, my creatures." Our mother raises her voice enough to get most of our attention, though her tone is pleasant enough that we aren't alarmed. And her face this morning has begun its changing, so that once we look at her, our Faulkes brains probably can't help tackling the mystery of what's up with her. "My dears, my creatures," she says, "I've managed to catch a little bit of cancer. Or I've accidentally gotten in the way of a cancer when it probably wanted to go visit somebody else. Dr. Lawson thinks we've intercepted it in time to put a stop to it, but he doesn't know for sure. So I'm going to have to go to the hospital once a week for treatments that will make me weak and a little sick and probably make my hair fall out. I will need your help."

That's when we know we have some very bad times coming to us. No Faulkes likes to say he or she needs anyone's help. But the warning is as much in our mother's face as it is in her words. Even though it's Saturday breakfast, which is always our time of talk and laughing and cooking noises, the room—the whole house—becomes very quiet. Our father's head is slightly bowed, which we understand to be because he doesn't want us to see how troubled he is by our mother's news. She herself, however, smiles at each of us in turn and continues looking around from one to another, meeting our eyes. This is the face she had showed us when she presented herself in the purple dress for the Iron Boots dance.

Leopold, who started walking only a few months earlier, flings himself against her, and she takes him into her lap. "We're Faulkeses," she says, patting Leopold's back. "We know how to get through bad times. Your Uncle Quentin over in Stone County got his legs chopped off in a tractor accident, and those Faulkeses kept that farm going without missing more than a day or two of work. Quentin got himself a couple of these new genius artificial legs, bought himself a new tractor, and was good to go the next spring. *A Faulkes will maybe flinch, but a Faulkes persists.*" As if to demonstrate her point, our mother lifts Leopold off her lap, stands, and begins clearing the table. "Also, Faulkeses nowadays have dishwashers," she says. "Which makes a big difference." It isn't an especially funny thing for her to say, but her wry tone of voice is just what we need to hear. We start talking again and proceed with our Saturday. Gradually this Saturday breakfast becomes what it usually is, a ritual that reasserts our common blood by way of riling up the dogs under the table and bickering over who's going to change Leopold's diaper. Also, Eli is starting to put one of the ferrets in the freezer before our father notices what he's up to.

So that's how it comes to us, the news of our mother's cancer. News that we don't realize we are getting at the time is the name of her oncologist. Later we realize she wouldn't have mentioned his name if he hadn't made an impression on her.

Our mother usually takes two of us with her

to Price Chopper for the weekly grocery shopping, and though she prefers that it be a boy and a girl, she doesn't much care which two it is who go. Whichever children are in closest proximity generally dictates the choice. Along with the five pounds that went away during her first two weeks of chemo, she's lost some strength. She's tried to conceal the weakness, but we've been alert to the changes we see beginning in her appearance. When she pulls the gallon jug of milk from the refrigerator, she uses two hands to heft it up onto the countertop. Also in the evening before she goes up to bed, she uses both hands to push herself up from the sofa, and Peter says he heard her panting when she came upstairs one Sunday morning. Peter is the one of us who watches her most carefully, and he volunteers to be one of her shopping assistants this morning, and Emily says she'd like to go, too. These two often pair up for the least appealing of the family tasks, though the Price Chopper errand is ordinarily more of a lark than a chore. Our mother has often said that few places improve her mood the way Price Chopper does — she claims to adore the smells of the produce section, and she is especially fond of the artisan bakery in the back corner of that huge supermarket. "Plenitude is what I like," she says. She claims she never enters Price Chopper without thinking she might encounter Walt Whitman or Alan Ginsberg pushing a cart through the aisles. "I want to see them there together," she once told Katie. "I want to see them holding hands, skipping around, being loud and chanting lines of each other's poems to the other shoppers."

This particular morning, however, our mother picks up a large cantaloupe to smell and press on it to test for ripeness. Halfway up to her nose, the heavy thing drops from her hands and thuds down into an astonishing splattered mess on the floor of one of her favorite places on the planet. Though the spray of pulp and juice on the floor testifies to the accuracy of her judgment of it as probably being ripe, our mother has misjudged both her own strength and the size of the melon. "Oh dear," she says, according to Peter. But then, rather than do what he and Emily expect her to do—what, really, any Faulkes or any other person at all acquainted with her would expect her to do—which would be to go to one of the produce specialists who are always there to help and ask for a trash can and a mop and insist on cleaning it up herself, our mother stands where she is and begins to weep.

"She doesn't just cry," Emily says, "she blubbers like a little kid. Her lower lip goes all trembly, tears stream down her cheeks and she doesn't try to wipe them away, she just keeps saying, 'I'm sorry, I'm just so sorry.'" So it is Emily and Peter who insist on helping the produce specialists—there are two of them—who come to clean up the mess, and when they glance up to check on her, they see our mother has been surrounded by customers and Price Chopper employees, all of them trying to comfort her and assure her that dropping a melon in the floor is nothing to be upset about.

"Here's the weird thing," Peter says later. "She looks grand and startling there with her tears and her wide open eyes and her apologizing face, her cheeks all shiny and wet. I don't think it was just me," he says. "Everybody who sees her came over and tries to make her feel better. She's like this living, breathing work of art. 'Grown-up Deeply Upset Over Trivial Accident' would be the caption that goes with her. She actually looks frail, and you know how vain she's always been about her strength. People stop and stare. None of us can keep our eyes off her."

OLD STANTON FAULKES,

the legendary South Dakota patriarch, had sayings that came down through the generations. "A Faulkes will maybe flinch, but a Faulkes persists" was one of his bromides. "Where others see obstacle, difficulty, and setback, a Faulkes recognizes opportunity" was another. Yet another was "The world loves a pretty sunrise and an eloquent sunset; a Faulkes prefers regular old daylight."

Our father is our source of information about our father's grandfather. At supper, if a quiet moment falls upon us around the table, our father will clear his throat and utter something like, "Old Stanton Faulkes claimed that work had a bad reputation — he said that if he had to choose between a holiday at the South Dakota State Fair or a ten-hour day behind a team of horses plowing a field, he'd choose the horses' rear ends every time." In our father's voice we hear a tone he uses for no other kind of communication, a tone that causes us to go still with listening to him. The patriarch's sayings and anecdotes seem to promise something surprising or shocking, but then our father's utterances almost always end before they're decently begun. There seems to be some kind of lesson in the deliberate disappointment of their conclusions. Our mother has a way of looking at our father when he comes forth with one of these additions to the legend of the patriarch. Her face takes on a smile that seems almost a willed effort to convey thoughtful respect. Because she directs her expression only to our father, not to us children, as we grow older some of us begin to wonder if she isn't secretly amused by our father's passing on the patriarch's wisdom to his children. Or if she might be sharing a private joke with him. A few of us even wonder if our father might be inventing the sayings of Stanton Faulkes.

"Maybe he's making up old Stanton Faulkes himself," suggests Patricia one evening when several of us are out walking the dogs through the neighborhood. The thought of our father bamboozling his own children throws us into a silence that endures for the rest of our outing with the dogs.

Not long after our parents' foray into the Iron Boots New Year's Eve party, our father finds a suppertime moment that's right for a patriarch installment. He clears his throat and begins. "Old Stanton Faulkes was one of the first people in the state of South Dakota to see a moving picture show. He saw *Birth of a Nation* in 1916, when he would have been well into his fifties. When Old Stanton came out onto the street during intermission, somebody asked him what he thought about the show, and he said it made him want to move to a place where he'd never again have to see a spectacle like that."

Our mother clears her throat in a way that definitely echoes our father's throat-clearing. "Old Stanton Faulkes was — " And she looks around the circle at us all, finally settling her gaze on our father at the far end of table. We wait for her to go on — and while we do so, eager as we are to hear what she has to say about the patriarch, we can hardly help scrutinizing our mother's face. Until now, she's never said a single word about him. Later that evening, upstairs in the dormitory, we agree that in that frozen moment we saw something childish about her, a lightening of her complexion, an almost silly and enchanting fluttering of her nostrils. And a slight loosening and puckering of her lips. "Like she was thinking about flirting with somebody who hadn't shown up yet," offers Jane, our oldest girl, who's about to leave the house to go to college and who, we think to ourselves, must be deeply in the throes of thinking about flirting with somebody who hasn't shown up yet.

"Yes?" our father says softly across the table. At first our mother gives no sign she's heard him. Then she waves her fork, actually twirls it in the air above her plate, and says, "That's just how he was. Old Stanton. He was like that."

We're confused. We feel we almost witnessed or heard something important. We were on the verge of revelation. Instead we came up with a meaningless observation and a fork diddling with invisible pasta. Gathered around Emily's bed that evening our mood goes somber. "I'm getting tired of this," says C.J., who being only nine has no justification for being tired of anything. We've been letting C.J. go with us on the evening dog walk only a few months. Then he blurts, "This stupid dying she's doing!" and that shuts us up. Evidently C.J. has more to offer than we've previously given him credit for.

We witness our mother

sitting more than she usually does. Given how the chemo has weakened her, her sitting is not surprising, though the manner of it is notably un-Faulkeslike. She seeks out places in the house or the porch or the lawn where she can be alone. If she wanted solitude, she could go to her room and close the door. In our family, we are respectful of closed doors. Also our mother gives the appearance of posing. Or of being aware of how she looks. Instead of sitting back normally on the sofa or in one of the big living room chairs, she'll be sitting forward and slightly sideways, with her knees very properly together. There'll be a magazine or a book open on her lap, the pages of which she'll turn now and then, but we have a sense that her mind is elsewhere and that the reading material is more a prop than something that holds her attention.

"Her legs are really pretty," Jack says to us one hot afternoon when we've gone wading in the brook across the field from our house.

"I noticed that, too," says Pruney, whose real name is Brunhilde and who's thirteen now. "I'm not sure her legs used to be pretty. Didn't they seem kind of big before? And didn't she have big ankles?"

"Maybe so," Jack says. "It's hard to remember how she was before. I'm not sure about the big ankles. Were they really all that big?"

"I'm not sure her legs are all that pretty now," Tony says. He's fifteen and becoming quite a litigious young fellow. "It's just that when she sits like that, she puts them out there as if she's vain about them. As if we should give them special attention. But they're just legs. Just plain old legs."

"Maybe not Faulkes legs anymore." Isobel is small for her age — twelve — and very shy. She seems to go for days without saying anything more than "Please pass the fig jam," or "Has anyone seen my navy blue socks?" Somehow we've taken to thinking of Isobel as our wise one, our child philosopher. "They're like somebody's legs on TV or in a movie," she says.

"What about her bosom?" asks John Milton. "Has anybody noticed how it's changed? How it gets your attention when you see her sitting out on the glider that way she does? Her shoulders back and her chest out like she's trying to demonstrate good posture? Or maybe it's just she's tucking in her blouses now, and she never used to do that. I don't know. I mean it could be just me."

We tell John Milton that it definitely is just him. We tell him he has his mind in the gutter again. We tell him it's not proper to be thinking about our mother's bosom. We pick on John Milton like this, because he's always so tentative and uncertain — but he likes it when we tease him. It's his own special kind of attention, and sometimes he even gets it from our parents.

"I think she's actually trying to drive us all crazy," Pruney says.

"Should we confront her? Have like some kind of intervention? Ask her what she thinks she's doing?" This is Tony again. If we have any kind of confrontation with our mother, Tony will be the prosecutor. He'll be the one who has the nerve to stand up in front her when she's all dressed up and sitting out on the porch glider. Tony will be the one to stand there and say to her, "We were just wondering what's going on with you, Mother. Why are you so different now? We're not even sure you're our mother anymore." That will be what Tony will say, a very slightly impudent edge to his voice. In our minds we can hear it without his even having to check it out with us.

"I'm sorry, children," our mother will then tell us. This, too, we can play out in our minds. "I'm dying," she will say. And she will look each of us straight in the eye. "I'm still your mother," she will say, "but right now I'm busy."

Even Tony finally admits

it would be a bad idea to trouble our mother with our issues. So we confront our father. He, too, seems distracted nowadays, though it is clear to us that he wants things to go as they always have. Whereas our mother came from another family's blood and was therefore a volunteer Faulkes, one who chose the Faulkes way of life, our father is helpless and instinctive in his steadiness, his tending to his obligations, his day-in-day-out responsible behavior. This is late on a Saturday morning when we find him out in the garage, standing up on the front bumper with his whole upper body under the raised hood of our old school bus, half a dozen tools lined up on a rag on the fender where he can reach them. From up there, he turns to us to listen to what Tony has to ask him. Almost all of us, young and old, are out there waiting for our father to answer.

"A Faulkes's religious life is entirely within himself," he finally tells us. "It doesn't have anything to do with God." Which of course seems like the answer to a different question than the one Tony has asked him on our behalf. Earlier, we had to discuss and negotiate our question, because once we decided it had to be presented to our father, we had trouble finding the words for what we wanted to know. In fact, we couldn't agree on exactly what it was we wanted to know, but we finally settled on the words we thought would require our father to speak to "our issues," as Robert called them. Robert had recently taken a linguistics course at Bard, and he explained to us how the word *issues* was really handy for a situation like this. "The word covers a lot of ground," he told us. "We use it all the time at school. In class and out." We liked the handiness of the word, and we especially appreciated that Robert could bring us a little gift like the word *issues* from his college. This made up for how we'd missed him when he went away from our regular family life.

The words we settled on were *Do you think our mother is properly going about the project of dying? Isn't she sort of off on another track? Is she doing it right?* That's how we decided Tony should put it to our father—three questions, actually, though in our minds they are the parts of a single inquiry originating out of our *issues*.

Our father pauses after his first response and stays quiet long enough to irritate us a bit. He stands atop the school bus bumper with his eyes shut. We know him so well that every single one of us, even the little ones, know he has more to say and just intends to test our patience. Then he opens his eyes and says, "Your mother is fifty-two years old." We refrain from telling him that we know how old she is. "Your mother has chosen to do this by herself. So it's not our death," he says. "We don't have a say in it," he says.

Then he completely surprises us, by hopping down off the old school bus's bumper and saying, ever so cheerfully, "Let's take a walk downtown." This is both normal and abnormal behavior for our father — normal because one of his favorite (and our favorite) customs is to invite one of us to walk downtown with him. This is his way of making an occasion to converse with just one of his children at a time. Today, however, he's evidently asking the whole multitude of us to go with him. We look at him, then we look at each other — a couple of us shrug — and nod. Anyone observing us might think we are a flock of penguins simultaneously bobbing our heads up and down.

As it turns out,

we are such a vision that neighbors, passers-by, and downtown folks turn and gawk and smile and wave and call out to us. "Have to get a license next time we do this," our father shouts to us back over his shoulder. He leads us to the Laney Dates Ice Cream Palace, where he's taken each of us for our one-on-one Faulkes talk. At the counter, he lets us order what we want, though instead of paying with dollars and change, he has to use his credit card. Like any contemporary Faulkes, our father carries a credit card out of necessity, but he uses it with such reluctance that he makes unhappy faces through the whole transaction. Also, there aren't enough available tables or booths for us to sit together, so we head back out onto the mall and gather around a group of benches out there. Once we settle into the situation our mood turns a little silly. Ice cream — and the sugar high that goes with it — must affect almost everyone more or less the same. The older ones of us realize that we aren't often out in public together like this. It's a spring day on the mall where there are also jugglers, folk singers, a magician, a hammered dulcimer player, and a mutated-looking old fellow who plays clarinet solos. Eli and Larry, our brothers who are in the same grade, sort of casually perform a couple of cool little gymnastics tricks they've picked up in middle-school phys ed. So in the spell of the sweet weather, we beg Jennifer to do one of her tap routines even if a Faulkes wouldn't ordinarily display herself in public. "I will if you guys will clap your hands to make some percussion for me," Jennifer says. "That's how we do it at class sometimes." When she demonstrates to us what she wants, we circle around her and clap up a rhythm for her while she does a very brisk tap dance out there on the red bricks of the mall. When she finishes with a twirl, a rattle of double-time taps, and a quick curtsy, we change our clapping to applause. That's when we realize that shoppers and homeless folks and runaway kids and business people out on their break have gathered around the circle of us to watch the show. A few people toss some coins on the bricks near Jennifer, and somebody even throws down a five-dollar bill. At first it's exhilarating — and the little ones get down on the bricks, scrabbling on their hands and knees to gather up the money. But suddenly our mood turns. Pretty much at the same time, this happens to almost every one of us. We can see each other blushing. We are Faulkeses, and we are embarrassed. We are ashamed. And these bad feelings make us really wish our mother were out here with us.

"SOMETHING ELSE I WANT TO SHOW YOU,"

our father says. He waits to make sure we're stirring ourselves, then heads off down the mall in the direction of the south side of town. To follow our father is to be reminded all over again what a solitary fellow he is — and to be reminded of what's in our blood. As old Stanton Faulkes would put it, "A Faulkes may love his family and strive to remain in the company of his family, but a Faulkes understands he is forever on his own." Observing our father's straight back and swinging arms as he turns uphill and strides up Shelton Street, we can feel our destiny in our feet and legs and lungs. Our father never once looks over his shoulder to see if we are behind him. Of course we are, he knows it so absolutely that he doesn't even have to consider the question. His mind is on what lies ahead. Even the fact that he carries our future in his thoughts — and that we have no clue about what his notion is — is pure Faulkes. Another kind of father would be communicating with us as we walk, explaining his plan, his hopes, his worries. Such reasonable behavior would be alien to our father.

He does, however, wait for us all to catch up with him when he stops in front of an unexceptional house on Lake Street. We older children have passed by it a few times — and some of us even have an inkling about the place — but at the moment we can't imagine why our father would be taking us here. The house sits above the sidewalk, with concrete steps rising to wooden steps leading up to the porch, where there are half a dozen chairs and — we see, as our father leads a few of us up the steps — three or four middle-aged people sitting on the porch, two of them smoking. This latter fact sets a disturbance going in our minds. Faulkeses don't smoke. So absolute is this axiom in our family that we've never even discussed it. Even the smell of a cigarette twenty yards away is enough to sicken almost any Faulkes, and here our father is guiding us into the immediate proximity of smokers.

"How do you do?" As he speaks in his loud, sociable voice, our father nods to each of the people on the porch, two men and a woman, weathered-looking citizens, their clothes a little shabby, their faces skewed in ways with which we are not familiar. We worry that they will not discern our father's bemusedly formal tone. The two men do not return his greeting or even move in any way that we notice. The woman — whose yellow-gray hair looks wet or oiled and is combed down straight on either side of her face — takes a drag from her cigarette, looks directly at our father, and exhales her smoke in his direction. "Not so freaking well, big fellow," she says. She wears a sweatshirt and a huge denim skirt. Her expression resembles a smile, but it is anything but friendly. "You here to sell something, or do you have something to give me?" She stands up as she speaks, clutches her buttocks with her hands, and takes a step toward our father. "What you got, big shot?" she asks him in a lower voice.

"I've got my children here with me," our father tells her. We can hear in his voice a guardedness but also a kind of polite request. He has taken the woman's buttocks-clutching as a warning, and he means her to know that he will speak to her respectfully, in return for which he hopes that she, too, will be mannerly. He faces the woman squarely, which makes us understand that he must also be using his school principal's demeanor. "I'd like my children to meet you and your coresidents. I think you folks probably have something to teach these youngsters"—and he sweeps his hand in our direction.

Youngster isn't a term he's ever used for us before, and it makes us feel strange. It also makes us imagine how the woman must be thinking about us. Her eyes seem to follow our father's gesture. When they lock in on us, it's as if we've played some mean trick on her. Her eyes widen and appear to blaze up; the corners of her mouth turn drastically downward. We can hear her harsh breathing through her nose as she looks from one to another of us. She might be trying to memorize the faces of gang members who are about to harm her. She turns abruptly away from us. "Don't you see that sign, Mister?!" she shouts at our father, and she flings her arm out in a gesture similar to the one he made toward us. She directs him to look at the blank clapboard side of the porch. Our father looks, of course — we all do — but there's no sign where she is pointing. It's a white space between the house's front door and a window "Can't you read what it says?!" When she takes a half step toward our father, we all feel how rude it is for her to move in so close to him. We begin to stir and murmur among ourselves. "No children on this porch! No children under any circumstances! Children will be prosecuted to the full extent of the law!" the woman shouts.

Both men stand up from their chairs — though their standing is more a crouching than an upright position — which makes us think they might be about to help the woman assault our father. Instead, they remain silent and shamble into the house. There comes this moment when everyone freezes in place—the woman and our father nose to nose on the porch with a few of us standing on the steps and others down on the ground by the porch. Then the woman commits what comes to be known forevermore in our family as "the ugly gesture." Her mouth opens, though no sound issues from it. There is no adequate way to describe this: She sort of half squats, as sumo wrestlers do in combat, squeezes her eyes tightly shut, and clutches her groin with both hands. The hugeness of her skirt allows her to press its fabric into her crotch while at the same time preventing any exposure of her underwear or genitalia. We shuffle our feet and murmur, because her gesture really disturbs us, though a few of us older ones have seen Michael Jackson grab himself like this in a music video on MTV. What's different is what the woman so clearly can't help conveying — that she is experiencing pain at a cosmic level and that the pain's primary location is in the fork of her body that she clutches with her hands. Her gaping mouth should be bellowing out a monstrosity of sound to match what her body so vividly demonstrates, but it gives forth only silence. We hush and stand still.

The porch door opens. A middle-aged woman in a navy blue pantsuit steps out onto the porch, carrying a regular paper cup in one hand and a small one in the other. She nods at our father and even lets her eyes pass over the crowd of us children. On the side of her chest is a nametag, but of course we can't read it. She steps up beside the porch woman and speaks quietly to her. We think she might be saying, "There, there," as our mother sometimes will say to one of our little ones who's been bee-stung or is having a tantrum. The porch woman nods, closes her mouth, opens her eyes, lets go of her crotch, and extends one hand, palm up. The lady in the pantsuit turns upside down the small cup over the waiting palm, and the porch woman quickly brings that hand to her mouth. The lady in the pantsuit hands her the larger cup, from which the porch lady drinks deeply. Then the pantsuit lady takes both cups in one hand, puts her arm around the porch lady and escorts her back into the house.

Our father stands on the porch with his head bowed for what seems a long time. Then he walks down the steps. We make way for him and follow him down to the sidewalk. When he turns north on Clegg Street, we know he's heading home. Though we all keep quiet as we follow him and though his pace is notably slower than it was earlier, we feel as shattered as we might if we'd witnessed a hanging or a beheading. But this isn't all of it, either. We're so eager to be back in our home that we feel privately—because we don't dare confess it even to each other—a crazy exuberance. We'll soon be back in the company of our mother.

"GOSHEN IS WHERE WE LIVE,"

our father likes to say, "but this town is not beholden to us, nor are we to it." Sometimes we think he's just describing how things are, but other times we wonder if he's not trying to program us to think the way he does — like our family is an independent nation. "We don't need to be loved here; what we do need is exactly what we have — respect." Our father will go on to recite what he calls the relevant facts, which are that we don't really come from here; we don't go to church here; we don't run for political office; aside from our own place, we don't own land, houses, or businesses here; and we don't bury our people here. "We do vote, we do pay our taxes on time, we do support the schools. Your mother and I attend PTA meetings. That's the extent of our allegiance to Goshen." When our father speaks of our relationship with Goshen, he makes the Faulkes way sound reasonable, but among ourselves we agree that it's peculiar. At the same time, we find ourselves aligned with the town and its people in the same distant way as our father. We have friends at school but not close friends. We're not invited to sleepovers. Occasionally one of us will go out with a Goshen boy or girl, but those relationships rarely last longer than a month or two. We observe our neighbors, our classmates, and the townspeople — it's even fair to say that we enjoy and appreciate them. We think they're just fine. But we prefer the company of each other — our brothers and sisters, our parents, even our Aunt Beatrice, who can be difficult, and our Granddaddy and Grandma Elton Faulkes, whom we almost never see. "It's like we don't understand the concept of community," Peter once complained to our mother before she got sick. She merely nodded at him and smiled. Robert, who's nineteen and the only one of us who's lived away from the family for any length of time, says that Faulkeses are genetically standoffish, though he says it in a cheerful voice. He's not ashamed of it. None of us is, really. We can account for ourselves being the way we are more easily than we can account for the fact that the citizens of Goshen appear to like us well enough but nevertheless leave us pretty much to ourselves.

In the living room, our mother sits

in the comfortable chair our father has recently bought for her, her feet up with her ankles crossed on the matching footstool. To her right, our father sits on a dining room chair, his back unnaturally straight. To her left, Dr. Lawson also sits in a dining room chair, wearing a jacket and tie and with a professionally pleasant expression on his face. Some of the little Faulkeses sit on the rug in front of them; the rest of us are gathered into the room, a few sitting on the sofa and several of the older ones standing in the dining room. We're quiet and sad. It seems to us that the only person in that room who's at all comfortable is the oncologist, but we are no longer angry at him.

"Dr. Lawson has provided me with a medication," our mother says in her new whispery voice. "Because I asked him for it." She holds up a small orange plastic container with a white lid. This is the sixth week of her chemo treatment. She won't hear of wearing a wig. Her skin is pale, but with a slightly rosy hue that prevents her from looking completely alien. The weight she has lost in her face has made her nose and brows and cheekbones emerge so that she appears more sharply defined than even her high school pictures show her to have been. And of course instead of her hair, there is the smooth curving expanse of her forehead sweeping back over the top of her skull. It is so pale that whenever she's in a mood to allow us, we children have taken to placing a hand on her forehead as if to check her temperature. When she was well, she'd have told us she was busy and didn't have time to stop what she was doing. Now she is mostly cheerful in allowing us to touch her that way. She will bend her head toward the extended hand. We agree that she feels cool to our palms. On these occasions, we sometimes have quick but intimate exchanges with her.

"Dr. Lawson believes that continuing my life should be my constant choice," our mother says. "He says it is reasonable for me to think about that choice—every day, if I want to." As our mother goes on, we make ourselves especially still so as to be able to hear her. "He also believes that you all — my husband and my children — should be aware of my choosing, and that if you want to, you should be able to speak to me about it. You should be able to tell me what you think."

Our mother casts a glance at Dr. Lawson, and we see that he notes her doing so but that he chooses not to meet her eyes. Instead, he seems to be seeking out the faces of one after another of us. His own face remains neutral. Later, Sarah Jean says, "Maybe he's doing research on us," but she means it more as a joke than a serious thought. Our mother bows her head a moment, then she, too, makes eye contact with each of us in turn, so that—and we later agree among ourselves that we thought exactly the same thing—we understand she's trying to speak as quietly and intimately to the whole room full of us as she would have alone with a single one of her children.

"I think how I die and when I let it happen is my business. Your father doesn't argue with that. But Dr. Lawson begs to differ. In his polite way. He says that the decision is mine, but that you are the inheritors of what I decide. He says my part is easy. He's wrong about that. But he also says that your part is really hard. It lasts a long time, he says. About that I know he's right. So I'm telling you." She raises her chin as she says this. And we can see that feeling is rising in her. "I'm telling you that I'll hear whatever you have to say to me." She waits to gather herself before she goes on. "But you children will have to forgive me — I really don't want to discuss it with you. My death is not up for debate or an argument. I'll listen — believe me, I'll listen. I'll hear you. I might be able to find some things to say to you. But I'm pretty sure I won't be able to talk about it with you."

We might all cry then. Or at least the little ones might. Or she might — our mother. But we don't, because we know she doesn't want us to. We are Faulkeses. Even the littlest ones of us. Not a crybaby among us. She honors that. Even though with every day that passes she seems to be less and less a Faulkes.

On a Saturday afternoon

our father drives us all down to the river in the school bus. He's fixed cushions for our mother on the seat nearest the door. She has found a dress in our attic that she'd worn in eighth grade that once again fits her perfectly. Her mood seems almost festive, and she's strong enough to hold Leopold in her lap for most of the short journey down there.

"When your mother and I were growing up, this whole area was like the town dump," our father tells us when we come to the gravel road beside the river. "Nowadays it's hard to understand why we thought it was okay to treat the place that way. Maybe because companies all up and down the river piped their waste straight into that water. I guess everybody thought the river would filter the chemicals out and the trash would just sink down into the landscape and nature would clean itself up on its own, no matter what we did to it. Anyway, we behaved like pigs. I remember throwing pop bottles out the car window on this road, right over there into the sumac and pigweed and honeysuckle. Faulkeses did it same as everybody else."

Our mother has been listening. She pipes up, "But then Faulkeses were the first ones to pitch in and clean up the mess when the county and state got after us." Her voice has some spirit in it that reminds us of how she was before the cancer and the chemo. "Faulkeses don't try to be holierthan-thou," she says, "but if they know what the right thing is, they never have any trouble doing it."

Our father smiles. He likes hearing our mother talk, especially the way she is today. And he really likes that she continues to appreciate the Faulkeses. The cancer and the chemo might be changing her into somebody else, but at least she hasn't forgotten who she used to be. She's holding onto Leopold with both arms, and both of them are leaning forward to see what's up ahead — a clear view across a wide part of the river to the mountain that rises straight up out of the water on the other side.

When we arrive at the picnic area, our father parks the bus and helps our mother down its steep steps. He'd help her all the way to the table except that she wants to show us how strong she is today. We know it's silly of her to do that, because of course she will never get back her old strength — she'll just keep losing the strength she has. Even so, the smell of the river, like a remembered secret from long ago, refreshes us. And we feel uplifted to see our mother, with our father giving her a hand, actually step up on the seat of the picnic table and settle her butt on top of the table so as to be able see the water passing by a few yards away. Some of the little ones climb up there beside her and huddle in as close as they can get, while the rest of us gather around.

"Roll on, old White River," our father intones. His voice suggests that maybe we are in for yet another Old Stanton Faulkes saying or anecdote. We hope not. We're outdoors, the moving water excites us, and we are unanimous in wanting to be liberated from Old Stanton. "She never was close to being white, but maybe the folks who named her all those years ago were standing beside a waterfall when they did it. They should have called her the Muddy Brown, because that was her color before the towns and factories started befouling her, it stayed the same color all those years, and now that water is still mud brown even though it's not nasty anymore. They say you can take a drink right out of the White River nowadays, and it won't hurt you any worse than a glass of water out of your kitchen faucet." As he speaks our father crosses his hands over his chest and arches his back while he gazes out over the water. Brown as dirt that water surely is, but the river nevertheless has a grandeur about it. There's a wide sweep of water, maybe a quarter of a mile from bank to bank. Over near the middle, the faster current catches the sunlight so that it looks like it might be transporting diamonds downstream. If you stare long enough—which most of us are doing right then—you can almost feel in your body the strength of that steady current. It's relentless.

"Are you going to tell them?" our mother murmurs to our father. Which murmuring of course gets the attention of all of us. *So they had something in mind when they herded us out to that bus and brought us down here.* We give each other the looks that say *Now we know they had a purpose.*

"I was getting to that," our father says. He looks downward and toes the grass in front of him as if it might be hiding a dime he's just now dropped out of his pocket. "When your mother and I were kids, two of her friends drowned out there." He nods out toward the middle of the river.

Our mother puts her arms around herself when he says the word *drowned.* We flinch a little when we see her do it. Our father doesn't speak any more for a minute or so. Then he goes on in a quieter voice. "They were twin girls, both of them in the fifth grade with your mother. Bonnie and Shelby Sutphin. The Hades-bound Sutphins, they used to call that family. You all know them, kind of a beat-down bunch of people nowadays that live on the other side of Goshen. Nobody calls them hell-raising anymore, because after that drowning, they changed their ways. Back then, though, Bonnie and Shelby were right in there with the Sutphins — they were pistols. You had to be careful about daring those girls to do something, because most of the time they would do it no matter how crazy a thing it was. Before they were even ten years old, both of them had had broken bones and cuts that needed stitches and banged-up knees that put them on crutches for weeks at a time. They were wild little girls."

Our mother murmurs something that we can't hear, so we edge closer to the table where she sits.

"Yes, they were dear children," our father says, nodding his head, because as she'd meant for him to do, he'd heard what she said. "And if they were your friends — it was always the two of them together in choosing who they'd be friends with — if they chose you, then they loved you enough to fight for you. That was how it was with those twins and your mother."

"Bonnie was the tall one," our mother says, her voice still low but rising as she goes along. "She was very smart in school, but she was shy and quiet, too. Because she was Shelby's sister, and Shelby was just about the most fun of anybody I ever knew, and they did everything together, people thought they were both wild. It was stupid they said that about them, because if you got to know Bonnie, you understood that wild was the last thing she was. She'd have probably gone to college if she'd lived to be a grown-up. Or if she'd ever been able to separate herself from Shelby. But she followed Shelby, she did what Shelby did." Our mother bows her head then and falls silent.

"What Shelby did that day — ." Our father picks up where our mother left off. "What Shelby did that day was to pester her Uncle Robert and her Uncle Joe to take them out in their fishing boat to check the trot lines the Sutphins always used to run out there." Our father flaps his right hand toward the middle of the river. "They probably caught more catfish out of this river than any other family around here. But of course Robert and Joe Sutphin hardly got out of bed before they started drinking beer, and they definitely thought a certain amount of beer needed to be consumed before a man could take his fishing boat out to check those trot lines."

"Bonnie and Shelby hated drinking," our mother says, keeping her head bowed so her voice is muffled by her skirt and arms around her knees. "Bonnie told me they hated it," she says.

"Whether Bonnie and Shelby would become the first nondrinking Sutphin adults will never be known," our father says. "If they had lived beyond that day in the boat." He settles into a silence that feels as if it might turn into a stopping place.

Our mother lifts her head. "Go on, Delmer," she says, and he nods to her, sighs, and goes on.

"Nobody really saw what happened," our father says. "But afterward people sort of pieced it together from what Robert and Joe told about it. Those young men got along just fine with their nieces, and most people thought Bonnie and Shelby learned a lot of their rowdy ways and saucy manner of talking from their uncles. The uncles and the nieces bickered and teased all the time, but they never fell into meanness. And nobody could feel any worse about what happened than Robert and Joe Sutphin." Again our father pauses and seems ready to stop right there.

"Go on, Delmer," our mother tells him. "I want it all." He nods again.

"So anybody can figure out how it is in one of those little low-to-the-water boats with a two-horsepower motor and four people who are used to having fun with each other. The two so-called adults are not drunk, but they've got a buzz, and the two girls are riled up by the sunshine and the breeze and being so close to the water that there's only about a couple of inches of the side the boat to keep the water from just pouring right over the side and into the boat. They can't resist reaching over for a hand-full of water and seeing how it might be to splash with it. It's Joe up in the bow being the one who'll reach down and fetch up the trotline if they ever get that far out, and it's Robert in the back tending to the motor and steering the boat. And of course it's Bonnie and Shelby in the middle of the boat, which is riding so low that their butts are probably below the water. If you know the people involved, and you picture it, you can hear the voices, the girls starting to splash, shrieking whenever Robert twitches the steering handle just a little bit, and then Bonnie kind of play-rocking the boat side to side, and Joe hollers to her to stop it or he'll throw a catfish in her lap. And of course she has to splash him. If you picture it like that, you can see most of the rest of the story without anybody having to tell it to you."

He stops again, but this time we know he'll go on. We understand now that he's not teasing us and that it's not so easy for him to tell us this. He's having some difficulty keeping going.

"There are two facts that have a lot to do with how things turned out. The first is that Robert and Joe, like most grown men here in Goshen, were wearing work shoes — high-top ones with steel toes. It's still a sign you're a grown man when you start wearing those shoes, even though there's no kind of work around here anymore that calls for wearing steel toes. The other fact is also a common one for people who live here. Neither one of those young men could swim. You'd think people living near a river and especially people who went out in boats to tend trot lines would learn how to swim. Not so. You ask around town, and you'll find out that almost nobody here would claim to be a good swimmer. Now when I say Robert and Joe couldn't swim, what I mean is that they probably had enough experience to splash and dog-paddle their way out of deep water if they had to and if they didn't have clothes and shoes on and if it was just themselves they were trying to save. And of course Bonnie and Shelby had never learned to swim. In Goshen there's no such thing as swimming lessons, and even if there were, no Sutphin would ever have signed up for them. No Sutphin ever had enough money to think that some of it ought to be spent on learning how to do the Australian crawl.

"So when the boat started taking in water faster than they could scoop it out with their hands and they could see they were out too far to get back to shore, we don't know exactly how things went. Robert and Joe somehow made it back to the shallow water, though Joe gave up struggling and Robert had to pull him for the last few yards. They said that's how it was, and nobody doubts them. They also said that they tried their hardest to save those girls and that the girls panicked and pulled them under when they tried to hold them up. Robert even said he dived once and had hold of Shelby's hand down near the bottom, but he couldn't hold onto it and pull her up to surface. Whether we believe that or not doesn't matter. We know how things turned out. Robert and Joe made it out of the water. Bonnie and Shelby made it down to the bottom of the river. And Robert and Joe both went on telling the story to anybody who'd listen to them, crying hard while they told it."

Our father stops there. We all stay quiet and feel the breeze on our faces while we gaze out over the steady-moving water of the White River.

Finally our mother says, "That's not all."

"The rest of it we do know. Or at least your mother and I know, because we were out here, and we saw it. Word spread around town in a matter of an hour. People called each other on the phone to tell what they'd heard. And we heard the rescue squad sirens when they came with their ambulances and trucks. My whole family walked down here, and your mother's family came in their cars. In school I was a grade ahead of your mother, so we knew each other only a little bit back then. Such a crowd of people was here beside the river that your mother and I can't remember if we saw each other that afternoon. Women were crying, people were praying out loud and pacing up and down along the banks — the whole town of Goshen kind of went crazy out here, and there was so much wild confusion that our families could have been standing together, she and I could have been close enough to touch elbows, and neither of us even notice the other. That doesn't matter. We were both here with everybody else, and we saw those girls pulled up out of the water. It's something that once you see it, it doesn't ever go out of your mind."

"Shelby was first," our mother says. It's like she's been waiting for our father to get the story this far so she can take over. "Over the water we could hear the men talking out in their boats while they dragged the hook lines along the bottom. When we heard their voices rising, we knew that the men in this one boat thought they'd found something. They started pulling the ropes, and—oh, Lord, I'll never forget this! — Shelby came almost bursting up out of the water sideways. At first I thought it was some miracle or trick she was pulling, something that would be explained to me later, because her arms and legs moved when she came up. So at first she seemed to have the life still in her. But a second later, I saw how her head was hanging limp and sagging back down toward the water like she was trying to get back down in it. Then I saw how she had the hooks gouged into her side and her hip and how the color of her skin was all wrong, like palest white turning blue even while I looked at it. From the time I first saw her body come up and got this stab of a thought that Shelby was alive, it was maybe two seconds to the next thought that was more like somebody hit me hard with their fist right in my stomach: *That girl is dead*. The word stayed on my tongue for days afterward. It was this awful taste that wouldn't go away." Our mother stopped and took a breath. "Shelby had on that black shirt that had been handed down to her from her brother and her old blue jeans with the knees ripped out. I knew those clothes as well I knew my own. And those rescue men just flopped her over into the boat like some kind of river thing they'd caught — I guess they didn't have any choice about how to do that — then they sped up the boat to get over to the bank where the trucks and the ambulance were parked."

"What I remember then," our father says, "was that the whole crowd of us went quiet, but we also began migrating over toward the truck. Not five minutes later, the other boat found Bonnie and pulled her up, too, and brought her into the bank."

"I couldn't make myself look at Bonnie," our mother says. "I knew they'd found her when I saw them pulling on the ropes, but I didn't want to see her come up out of the water. I turned away. Bonnie's the one I'd been closest to. Whenever they slept over at our house, Bonnie's the one who came into my bed. If I knew Shelby's clothes like they were mine, I knew Bonnie's body, how it smelled and how it felt to press my stomach against her back, put my arm over her shoulder and talk our way down into sleep together. Even our bodies had been friends."

"The other person your mother and I both remember from that day was Mrs. Pettigrew," our father says. Somehow that lady made her way right over into the crowd of scrambling rescue men and Dr. Pope and the trucks and equipment, she got right in there with them while they pressed the water out the girls' chests and did the artificial respiration and CPR on them even though everybody knew by then that Bonnie and Shelby were already long gone. The sheriff and a couple of deputies were in that crowd, and they wouldn't let the uncles get close to the twins. They kept their own kin away, but somehow Mrs. Pettigrew just kneeled right down in the middle of it, as near the girls as she could get, and when Dr. Pope said it was time to stop the CPR, she stood up and wailed out in this voice you could have heard from miles away, 'Dear God,' she yelled, 'Can't you make them live?! Can't you bring them back?!' Mrs. Pettigrew was this prim, white-haired lady whose husband had died years ago, a nice old lady nobody ever much noticed, but when she called out like that, everybody all up and down the river heard her. I guess it was a prayer or a request, but it sounded more like demand or an accusation. It was like her voice came out of us. We felt it — the ones who were close to the trucks and the ones of us who had kept away from that crowd. She called out the words that we were holding inside ourselves. Then she didn't say anything else. But from what she had said, we knew there was no more need to stay there. We needed to go home then."

Our mother isn't making any noise. She's sitting very straight up on that picnic table. Her face is wet with tears that she isn't wiping away.

"What do they think they're doing to us?!"

Pruney rasps out. She's been upset all week. Now she seems to be grinding her teeth.

"They might not be thinking at all," says Jack. "They could just be doing what occurs to them. 'Let's take the kids to the river,' she says to him, and he says, 'Hey, what a great idea.' So they pile us into the bus, and away we go. When we're all down there, that's when it occurs to him to start telling the story."

"No, no," says Tony. "You could see they had a plan. They'd talked it over."

We all knew Tony would disagree, but in this case we think he was right. They'd had a plan.

It's just after dusk, and ostensibly we're playing sardines over at our grandparents' farm. In fact we're sitting out in the hayshed talking. After enough of us went to her with questions, Jane called this meeting of the children. We were pretty spooked by our parents' story of the twins drowning. It was like those twins got inducted into our family, and then they were dead. Jane said maybe we were actually grieving for the loss of our mother's friends. Two of our little ones, Patrick and Jessica, had nightmares that whole week after the river telling. We'd thought maybe our mother or father would talk to us and help us think about that story. We'd thought maybe they had a way they wanted us to understand it, but neither one of them said any more. Also the visit to the porch with the lady who made the ugly gesture didn't sit comfortably with us. And later on our father had not said a word about that, either. Furthermore, it seemed fine with him that that visit went the way it did. As if the ugly-gesture lady did just exactly what he'd thought she would.

William stands off a ways, because he has issues with space and what he calls *group think*. But he calls over, "Part of their plan must have been *not* to talk to us. *Not* to tell us what they have in mind."

"Why would they do that?" Emily says quietly. "They love us. We know they're not out to hurt us." She looked around at us. "Don't we know that?"

"I think her getting sick has made them both crazy," Pruney says. "I don't think we should even bother trying to figure out what they have in mind. We should talk about what we're going to do about what they're doing to us."

"We can say no, can't we?" William calls over. "We can say, 'You taught us not to go for rides with strangers.'"

"Ha ha," says Susan.

"Have we ever said no to them?" Larry asks "Don't you think we ought to try it out, just to see what happens?"

"You're going to say no?" Jane asks. She's very serious. And a little bit mad, too, but it's a different kind of mad with her.

"Maybe," says Larry. "If we agree somebody should say it, then I don't mind being the one."

"Here's the thing," Jane says. "They may not be thinking. They may not have any idea what they're doing to us. But I'm pretty sure they are absolutely certain they're doing what they should be doing. For her, and for us. If it causes us some pain, a little bit of trouble, maybe even a nightmare or two, can't we deal with that? Aren't we Faulkeses?"

"I hate how she's looking more and more healthy the sicker she gets. She looks like a rock star who's recovering from meningitis or something. Her face has this angelic radiance." This is Angela speaking; she's twelve and a half, and she's had a fondness for the word *angelic* for the last two or three years. "She doesn't look like any Faulkes I ever met."

"But when you look at her, don't you feel more like a Faulkes than ever?" calls William. He's still over there, off to the side and acting like he's not paying any attention to us. Maybe he's just got extra good hearing, because he certainly isn't missing any of our conversation.

"She's still a Faulkes," Jane says. "I don't know how I know, but I do. If you stripped away everything that makes a Faulkes look like a Faulkes, you'd have our mother. Does that make any sense?

Nobody answers her. Then Kathryn says that it embarrasses her having a mother who's both pretty and about to die.

"I don't mind," says Tony. Which surprises us — not because he's disagreeing with one of us, but because we think Tony is maybe the angriest of all of us about our mother being so sick. "I actually think it's pretty cool," he says. We stare at him for a while and try to understand how he could think a thing like that.

C.J. CAN'T SLEEP.

This happens more and more often now that our mother's so sick. Along with most of us, he sleeps in the big room upstairs that our parents call "the dormitory." C.J. will turn ten soon. He's been in the dormitory for at least eight years. There are a number of small bedrooms up there and downstairs, too, which the older ones of us can have if we decide we don't want the dormitory anymore. And of course the little ones stay in the nursery downstairs until they get to the point where they can sleep in regular beds. But sometimes we end up rolling a crib into the dormitory just because we all want to sleep with a baby in the same room.

The thing about C.J. is that he's a quiet boy in his waking life. Every now and then he'll say something that surprises us, but mostly he's silent. Sometimes a little sullen and often sort of goofy, but generally he's your basic Faulkes. He does what he's supposed to do, doesn't shirk his chores, doesn't make a fuss, and steps up when our mother or our father asks for one of us to carry out a task. Which is to say that we know he's completely one of us, and we like having him in the dormitory. But when he can't sleep, he talks. It's not talking *in* his sleep that he does. It's more like trying to talk himself down into sleep. When he actually gets to sleep, then he hushes. Before he was five, he gave up his teddy bear, and he doesn't like anybody getting in the bed with him. In that regard he's an independent little cuss. So it's like a conversation he's having with his pillow or maybe even his whole bed. Whatever. For the rest of us, if we're awake, we just expect to hear this soft little voice coming up out of the dark. It's not unpleasant, it won't wake you up if you're already asleep, and one or two of us even claim that C.J.'s talking actually helps them get to sleep if they're having trouble. Anyway, tonight he's having trouble sleeping, so here's more or less what he's saying.

Book about a boy who flies. Doesn't like flying all that much but he can do it. Likes a good thick cloud. Likes the rain. Wants to like the lightning except it scares him. Wishes his teacher could fly. He'd ask her to go with him. Flying with his teacher and nobody else. She'd ask him questions; he'd know the answers. He'd ask her questions, too. Like how come it's so easy to fly when swimming's so hard. In a book, though, maybe swimming could be easy, too. This boy would rather fly. Look down on his house. Stop by each window like a hummingbird. See everybody without them knowing. Makes him feel good to see them. See his mom and his dad in their room. He likes it when he hears them talking, just the two of them, nobody else around. You know what else that boy likes? Grass. Likes to sit in the grass for a long time. Likes birds, too. A lot more than fish, except he likes goldfish and guppies. Likes his sisters, likes how they talk when there aren't boys around. His brothers are okay. He likes to play games with them, likes running with them. This boy's older sister is really, really nice. She talks with him whenever he asks her to. If he's hurt or sick and his mom's not around he goes to his sister. What he'd really, really like would be to fly into one of those big gold clouds and just stay there all day. Like a hummingbird in a big thick cloud. When it got dark he'd come down. He'd go say good night to his mom. Go to bed in the big room with his brothers and sisters. Wait for his dad to come kiss him good night. Stay awake but pretend to be asleep when his dad came to his bed. What else he likes is sunshine coming straight in the bedroom window, first thing in the morning. Before anybody else is up. Awake in the big room, his brothers and his sisters still sleeping. Sunlight coming in the window. Big room full of sunlight.

Our father makes a contraption

for us to carry our mother on when we go for walks. She wants to go, but she gets tired almost before we get started. The contraption — we call it Her Majesty's Traveling Throne — has a leaning-back chair that we fill with cushions. She can sit up straight or lie down almost like a bed. We bring more cushions for when she needs to change her position. Four of us carry her at a time. She says she likes it almost as much as she used to like walking. The throne sways even though we try to keep it steady. Sometimes the big boys put it on their shoulders and carry her up high. She says it scares her to be up so high, but we can see it doesn't. Her smile won't go away. Mostly, though, we carry the contraption low, beside our hips. We take turns. The younger ones have to change with each other pretty often, and when they change, it sways a lot. Our mother holds on tight. It's not so heavy, because she's not heavy anymore. Our father says she probably weighs less than most of us. In her thin face, we can see how much she likes our taking her out on Her Majesty's Traveling Throne. Color comes to her cheeks. She looks happy but not in the old way. Used to be, she'd turn happy when she was doing some kind of chore. Ironing, vacuuming, making beds, folding laundry — those things put her in a good mood, but she was also always really focused on what she was doing. Like if she stopped working, then she'd have to find something else to keep her spirits up. Nowadays when we take her outside and help her settle into her place up on the traveling throne, she's like a third-grader at the last-day-of-school picnic. She's giddy. She laughs because she sees something we don't notice. She teases us. Bosses us in a funny way. Makes us change places at each of the four carrying handles. "Don't you drop me, you little scoundrels," she'll say. Or "Where are you taking me? Are you going to walk me all the way down to Boston? Are we walking to Boston for ice cream?"

And of course when she's like that, then our spirits rise right up there with hers. We tease her back. We tell her we're carrying her to Texas. She used to say she'd rather face a firing squad than go to Texas. "We're walking you all the way to Houston, Mother," Emily will tell her. "We're gonna put you on a horse down there, big silver-trimmed saddle on a palomino. We'll walk right beside that palomino with you sitting up there like a rodeo queen." That's Larry talking — he's the one of us who most likes walking beside our mother when we take her out like this. Larry has told us he wants to take her out on the throne after dark one night. "Maybe around midnight," he says. "A warm night when the moon's out. Walk her down to the pond. Surprise her. She won't expect that. You know how she likes bats and frogs."

She doesn't expect it today when we carry her down to the post office. Nor do the people downtown expect to see anything like this procession of us Faulkeses carrying our mother like slaves transporting Cleopatra into Alexandria.

"Put your mother down, you children!" Mrs. Delby calls out to us as she waddles down her front steps toward the road through town. She's got her bossy smile on her face. "Set that woman down right here underneath this catalpa tree." We glance up to our mother for a signal, and she nods to us, offers a yawn-smile to Mrs. Delby.

"Oh Lordy, my dear, I haven't seen you since you were in high school." Then she steps back a step to scrutinize our mother. "I'd swear you don't look much different." Mrs. Delby's voice lets slip that she's disappointed. We quickly understand that she'd rather our mother looked worn out from being sick and having to be our mother. Mrs. Delby, in her big old flowery dress, would like to say, "Oh Lordy, child, you look like you're gonna be meeting Jesus any day now." That's the kind of thing a lot of people around here like to say. They put Jesus into their sentences. Our mother has never said so, but we know she thinks it's tacky to throw Jesus's name around like that.

"They said you were sick!" Mrs. Delby shouts at our mother. "They said you were on death's doorstep!" She must think our mother is deaf. "I was just about to bring a casserole over to your house. I could do that anyway, but it looks like you won't be needing it. I'll swear to goodness, child, I thought you were twenty-four hours from meeting your savior. But you look like you could go to the prom tonight. I was going to put you in my prayers, but now I think maybe I should bring you a corsage." Then Mrs. Delby laughs one of her big sociable laughs. This is the kind of talk that Faulkeses can't stand. It makes all of us children feel a little nauseated while we're standing there, waiting for our mother to figure out a way to free us from this lady. Other Goshen citizens are beginning to gather and hover around, and we're concerned we might be trapped here all day. In her old self our mother wouldn't have let this conversation with Mrs. Delby go this far. We're worried she hasn't remembered how a Faulkes woman frees herself from a stupid social encounter. We try to catch her eye.

"I don't mind if you pray for me, Mrs. Delby," our mother says brightly. "I feel good enough to go the prom, but I don't think a prayer ever did anybody any harm." And she sits forward on the throne far enough to reach Mrs. Delby's meaty arm and give it a pat. "Thank you, sweet Mrs. Delby," she says. Then she says, "Let's go children. Let's not lollygag."

We smirk at that. We love the word *lollygag*. It's just the ticket to get us out from under Mrs. Delby's bullying pleasantries. We hoist up Her Majesty's Traveling Throne and set ourselves all in motion, maybe a little too vigorously. Our mother has to grasp the handles of her chair to steady herself. The thought comes to some of us that this whole bevy of Faulkes children is a kind of greater contraption, we children the loosely attached accessories to the powerful force of our mother's life.

"Jesus loves you, Mrs. Faulkes," Mrs. Delby calls after us, and our mother doesn't turn her head to smile and reply, though she lifts a waving hand. "I know he does," she says just under her breath. But we hear her. "Jesus loves every living creature," she says. Then she mutters, "Jesus loves cockroaches, scorpions, Republicans, and snapping turtles. Equal love for everything and everybody."

“I kind of want to die with her,”

says Isobel. She’s eleven, so we can’t tell if she says it because she’s not old enough to know better or if she’s just gotten weepy over our mother’s loss of appetite. We’ve all noticed how our mother picks at her food nowadays, spreads it around her plate, but hardly ever takes more than about six bites. “I mean what are we supposed to do after she dies?” Isobel asks us older ones. Her lower lip is trembly.

We’re all up in the big room upstairs. We know we can talk up here without our mother or our father coming up and bothering us. They’re downstairs in the living room, our mother lying down on the couch and our father in his lazy chair in front of the TV. The TV is turned on, but they don’t turn up the sound anymore. They watch CSI and other gruesome programs with the sound muted. Now and then one of them will say something and the other will answer, but we don’t hear them. Or else we only hear the faint sounds of their voices like a very slow song they’re singing. Or a poem they’re making up. Or maybe it’s just a new language they’ve learned for our mother’s dying. Before the chemo, they talked and bickered but kept the TV off. Or gave it over to us children. Now they watch people killing each other and screaming and fighting and driving cars a hundred miles an hour through busy city streets. Meanwhile, as if they’re making their own soundtrack, our parents speak softly to each other. This is very sweet. We don't have to understand what they say, because just the sound of their murmuring comforts us. If our mother dies while we're not with her, at least our father will be there. And he will call to us — we know he'll do that. We trust him to do it.

"I kind of want to die with her, too," Peter says in a voice just above a whisper. He surprises us by agreeing with Isobel, who's five years younger than he is. "But I don't think it's good that I feel this way," he says.

A crooning comes up among us. Because almost all of us feel like this. Like our lives will just stop when our mother dies. We will be the coyote running into a brick wall in the old cartoons that our father likes so much.

"I hate how she's getting so —." This is Tony. We expect him to disagree with us. But he can't finish his sentence. "She can't help it, but she keeps on making us feel more and more sad. Is she trying to drown us in what we feel about her?"

"She didn't used to be dear," Franklin says. "I mean she was fine, but she was on our cases twenty-four seven. She was showing us this, reading us that, writing us notes in our lunchboxes, asking us to read our books aloud to her. Now all she does is — "

"All she does is what?!" Sarah Jean stands up from the desk where she's been doing her homework and walks over right up beside Franklin. "I want you to finish that sentence," she says. We go quiet. It's not like us to get angry with each other. Even though we know Sarah Jean isn't really angry right now. Or she's not angry at Franklin.

"All she does is make us love her more and more," McKenzie says from across the room where she's lying on her bed. "I mean it feels really good to love her the way we do now, but it's scary. How can we keep on doing it? I'm afraid that one day I'm just going to go like empty. No more love in me. And there she'll be, so thin she almost won't even be here, but she'll still be calling that love out of me. I'm afraid I'm going to come up short," McKenzie says.

"I don't think so," William whispers. We don't even think he means for us to hear him, but the room is so quiet that we do hear him. We look at him, and he understands then that he has to tell us what he means. "She'll know when to stop calling it out of us," he says. "She won't ask us for what we can't give her."

"She'll die," McKenzie says. "That's what she'll do." We can't tell from her voice if McKenzie is really angry or just about to cry. She stands up and looks at each of us in turn, but we don't have anything to say to her. McKenzie is eight and a half, and she's plain old Faulkes, head to toe. Nothing pretty about her. A very solid girl. Strong calves and thighs. Her hair in braids tied at the ends with blue ribbons. A profoundly healthy girl and a dependably good one, who in twelve or fourteen years will get married to some okay man who can come into the family and work on becoming a Faulkes, and they'll have Faulkes kids, too, every one of them working hard and struggling all day every day. She's feeling like she has to say this to keep the thought of it from hurting her too bad. "She'll die," McKenzie says. "I'd rather she just kept going," she says. "I'm sorry," she says. "I don't want to go with her," she says. Then she says, "I know that's wrong, you guys. I'm really sorry."

Our mother stops speaking to our Aunt Beatrice.

This is the most un-Faulkeslike act anyone has committed during the lifetimes of any of us children. We try to stay out of it. Aunt Beatrice has hurt our mother's feelings with the cruel words she's said right to her face; i.e., "You'll be the first one in our family to go to her grave looking like a streetwalker." But we can understand how the change in our mother's appearance and her behavior — not to mention her health! — would upset Aunt Beatrice.

Our father has tried to make peace between them. "Beatrice is hysterical," he told our mother. "She's never encountered anyone who's going through what you're going through. It's made her crazy. You can't be angry about the things she's said if she's not in her right mind," he explained to our mother.

"Which one of us is dying?" our mother asked him. She gave him what in our family we've come to call her "steely eye." He didn't try to answer her. Aunt Beatrice is his sister; he had been extremely close to her before he and our mother were married. Our mother says neither he nor Beatrice ever quite adjusted to the marriage. But somehow through the years — maybe because Aunt Beatrice was over at our house so often, which was because she and her husband, Uncle Norbert, never had children and she said she needed to get her regular dose of Faulkes young'uns — she and our mother became almost friends. Or they got used to each other enough so that they could act like friends even if that's not exactly what they were. And after our mother got to be such a complete Faulkes, then she and Aunt Beatrice were like sisters that had always had some "issues" between them. The comment that finally set off our mother came one evening when Aunt Beatrice was having dinner with us — which she usually did at least once a week or so — and she noticed how our mother was not eating. "You're just playing with your food," Aunt Beatrice said in this hard-edged voice that made us all hush up. "You're like a teenager. You *want* to get skinny. You *want* to look like the women on TV and in the magazines. I think you're lying about dying."

Of course we knew immediately that Aunt Beatrice had gone too far. Our mother could put up with all those comments about her looks, but calling her a liar was not okay. The whole table was as still as a photograph. Aunt Beatrice must have known she'd gone too far, too, but she wasn't about to back down. While we looked at her, we could see how it was with her. She was a Faulkes, solid as a Clydesdale. She'd been built to have children and to raise a house full of them. And here she was with nothing to show for her life but Uncle Norbert, who snuck cigarettes out behind their garage and never wanted to come over to our house because he knew we could smell the stink of tobacco on him. And here was our mother who had everything Beatrice had ever wanted in life and now was becoming pretty to boot. At the other end of the table our mother sat in her chair looking sultry and skinny as a junky supermodel, our mother in full possession of everything Aunt Beatrice felt she had been wrongfully denied — house full of kids, fully evolved husband, even a Labrador–Great Dane puppy under the table hoping for scraps. We could feel the heat rising in Aunt Beatrice. She didn't say it, but we could all feel the thought shimmering in her brain — *Is there anything I can do to help you, dear sister-in-law, reach your destination more quickly?*

Our mother was thin and weak, but she still had the iron of a Faulkes inside her. She locked eyes with Aunt Beatrice and didn't flinch. Finally she said — and her voice was soft but not wavering — "Beatrice, I hope you'll come to see us again sometime in the future." By which of course she meant, "Get out of my house. Don't even think about coming back."

Aunt Beatrice stood up and had to grab the back of her chair to keep it from tumbling backward to the floor. "Hold your breath," she said. Mad as she was, she nevertheless thought to grab her purse before she strode out the front door and shut it with unnecessary firmness.

We passed the rest of that evening's meal very quietly. Our father now and then cut his eyes toward our mother, but she ignored him and sat without eating or even pushing her food around on her plate. Her face didn't show it, but we knew she was savoring what had just happened. Later one of us would say she probably thought it might be one small upside of getting cancer, making her sister-in-law storm out of the house that way.

Desiree comes upon her

sitting by herself in the backyard, her Adirondack chair facing away from the house, out toward the meadow. This is early in the morning, dawn just coming when Desi finds her. We theorize that our mother probably hasn't been able to sleep and so she must have gotten up, dressed, and made her way out of the house without waking any of us. Which can't have been easy, especially for someone who needs a cane or else furniture she can hold on to to steady herself.

Desi's still one of our little ones — a curly-haired tow-head who's unusually alert to what's going on in the family. She's usually the first one in the house to wake, and if the weather's friendly, she goes straight out to the porch. She's also really patient — she'll sit off to herself and study a book or a puzzle or a toy for a long time. Usually she has to be called in to breakfast — or if she hears somebody ask, "Where's Desi?" then she'll come in herself.

Desi loves Jane — all the little ones do, especially now that our mother can't really look after them very well — and so first thing this morning when Desi comes in to breakfast, she goes straight to Jane and whispers in her ear. Jane asks Desi a question and Desi shakes her head. Jane asks another question — again Desi shakes her head. By this time we've figured out that something's up, so when she looks away from Desi and stands up, Jane already has our attention. “She says mother is out there.” Jane nods her head toward the door to the porch and the backyard. “She says she’s sitting out in the yard. Desi didn’t check her out. She left her alone. She doesn’t know for sure, but she thinks she’s okay.” Jane’s serious face and low voice let us know she’s concerned but not panicked. We look at Desi, too, somehow figuring that if our mother really weren’t all right, we would see the disturbance registering in the kid’s body or showing in her face, but Desi gives no sign of being upset. “Do you want to show us, Desiree?” Jane asks, and Desi nods.

You might think the herd of us making our way out of the kitchen and onto the porch and then down into the yard would make some noise, but we don’t. It’s not like we’re trying to sneak up on our mother. We just don’t really know why she’s out here. We don’t say so, but of course the thought’s always present in our minds whenever our mother’s out of sight, or even when we’re in the same room with her but not actually looking at the visibly living person — *she could be dead.* In this case it’s more that we’re afraid we might disturb her when she’s deep in thought, having another of what she calls her spiritual reckonings, or maybe even brooding about the trouble between her and Aunt Beatrice.

We know to be quiet, and so we hush when we catch sight of her chair down the lawn a ways, with the top of her dear, bare head above the chair back. The top of her scalp is all we can see of her, with the morning sun on it, not exactly making it shine but heightening the way it looks nowadays, pearl-like, milky, luminescent. Funny, too, is how just that visible sliver of her head, touched by the morning light, informs us that she’s alive and perfectly all right. Her cane is propped against her chair arm, it, too, appearing to testify that she's fine.

Quiet as Mohicans sneaking up to capture a frontier woman, we come up behind her, then gradually move around either side of the chair. She's covered herself with her old Sycamore Lake forest-green camp blanket. Her eyes are closed; she doesn't move; it's hard to tell whether she's breathing or not.

We could be wrong about how alive she is.

With the sun angled straight across her face, it's early enough that its light is soft, almost respectful of our mother's singular loveliness. Her eyelids are dainty miracles of curve and shades of color — lilac, pink, ivory, and plum. Her nose, which once was thick as a peasant's, has narrowed and rounded to become this cutely sculpted focal point of her face, almost a fantastic little decoration for a face moving toward perfection. We're so caught up in the sight of her, so still here in this light and this place, that the question of whether she's dead or alive becomes less and less urgent. She's here, and she's deeply compelling to us. The moment instructs us to understand that our obligation in these last weeks is merely to witness her. To take her into ourselves, absorb her. This is a precarious moment, standing as close as we can without feeling like we're intruding and really not thinking so much about whether she's alive or dead. In our minds our mother has entered some in-between dimension.

Then she opens her eyes, slowly moves them from one to another of us, seems to acknowledge each one with patience and care. As she does so, her face in the early morning light gradually composes itself into this deepening beatific expression. The sudden sight of us gathered all around seems to make her so happy. Standing closest of all but no taller than the level of our mother's shoulder, Desiree is the last child she takes in. Our mother reaches out from under her blanket to pull the girl to her. She pushes Desi's curls aside and whispers into her ear. Desi nods, turns, and quickly makes her way through the circle of us, then takes off at a run back toward the house. While she's gone, we murmur a little among ourselves and wish our mother a good morning. She smiles at us and moves her lips to signal she wishes us a good morning, too. We can't help thinking that the way she seems to be returning from such a distance to her life with us, maybe she wasn't all that far from being dead anyway. She might have been almost entirely over into death before she turned and came back to us. That thought holds us around her chair in a state of reverence.

In a moment, Desi is running down the lawn toward us with our father's camera. It's a small one, one of the new kind that doesn't use film. We've all played with it so much it's more the family toy than something fragile and complicated. Desi carries it straight to our mother. We watch the little girl pushing the button to turn the camera on and showing our mother the other button to push to take a picture. Then our mother lifts her hand — then both her hands — to signal to us what she wants. We're to go to the fence that separates our yard from the meadow. We're to assemble ourselves into a group for a photograph — a Faulkes-children portrait. Desi stays beside our mother to help her with the camera and to make signals to us about how we're to stand, little ones kneeling in front, big boys and tall girls at the back, a couple of rows of middle-sized children. Finally, Desi and our mother are satisfied with how the group of us has composed itself and how the camera must be operated in order to take the picture. Our mother will have to sit up a little. Desi comes trotting down the lawn to us and takes a place kneeling in the front that the other little ones have saved for her.

Our mother holds the camera still. We hear the click it makes. Like a pin dropping on a tile floor.

"We could call it 'Death Yo-Yo,'"

Sarah Jean says. Our parents have gone for a walk. Our mother hasn't taken her cane. Yesterday we thought she might be permanently confined to her bed. Jane had been on the verge of calling hospice to make arrangements for the final weeks. After supper she suddenly seemed to receive an injection of energy and strength. Our father was the only one of us not to appear surprised by her recovery —but we later decided he was hiding his surprise as an act of support for her. When she asked him if he'd go for a walk with her, he told her it was raining. She actually flashed her old mischievous smile at him. "Afraid you might melt?" she asked. "Are you at all acquainted with raincoats?" As they went out he offered her his arm, but she refused it and slipped out the door ahead of him like a completely healthy woman.

"Are we the yo-yo or is she?" C.J. is the one of us who's always on the edge of a tantrum about what he calls her "stupid dying." "I'm ten years old now," he says. "My mother's been dying my whole childhood. Do I have to go through puberty with this?"

"That's not so different from everybody else's childhood," Peter says. He's interested in C.J.'s anger; he says that at least one of us ought to be angry about what we're going through, and C.J. is acting out on behalf of all of us. "It's just that while everybody else is driving dirt roads through the countryside, our mother's taking the expressway."

"You might be learning something," Jane says. C.J. gets on her nerves. "Wrap your mind around it, you might decide you're lucky."

"I can't even remember normal," C.J. says. "It's like I could fly to China tomorrow, and I'd be thinking about my dying mother so much, it'd be like having her sitting in the seat next to me on the airplane. My mind is wrapped around it, believe me."

"Think of it this way," says Emily. "You could be in prison."

C.J. stares at her like a really mean boy, and even though we know that's not really what he is, it bothers us when he does this. Faulkeses eschew hostility if they possibly can.

"I am in prison," he says. Then he makes a show of going upstairs to the big room where he has marked off an area that he claims is all his own and no trespassing is allowed. He persuaded Jane to buy him some bead curtains from the flea market and hung them up with a ladder and thumbtacks. We don't even threaten him with trespassing. Why should we? We can see him through the bead curtain, and he can see us. It's not like he's set up a tent on the meadow. Or run away from home. C.J. is just as much one of us as he ever was. We all know that. Which is of course what he means when he claims he's in prison.

Our mother gets tickets

for all of us to go to the Spring Dance Concert at Waltham College. It's miraculous that there were ever enough tickets available for all of us to go to anything worth seeing. And we're not all sure that modern dance is something we want to witness. We all do think it's a new and unimaginable phase of our mother's illness that makes her want to attend such an event. If a scholar studied the Faulkes family through the generations, he'd predict zero probability that a Faulkes would voluntarily attend a Spring Dance Concert anywhere on the planet. The complete contradiction between who she is (or used to be) and what she wants surprises us so that finally not one of us wants to hold back. Even C.J. says he wouldn't dream of staying home.

We'll all go; it's settled, and mostly because we want to see our mother in all the possible ways the dance concert will show her to us. We can't all sit where we have a view of her face, but we can see the dress she's going to wear when she walks into the auditorium. We'll be able to see how strangers stare at her bald head and stick-thin calves and ankles and arms, and see what they make of how astonishing our mother looks now, even as close to death as she is. She's like some extraordinary work of art, and no one could look at her now and not be moved. We can also see how she'll hold on to our father's arm as they make their way through the crowd. We can be with her there in that theater that will be strange to us. Or we can be near her, because now that she's so shrunken and her voice is so weak, sometimes it feels as if she's miles away even when we're right beside her.

An unspoken disturbance rises up in the days between when she tells us she has the tickets and the date of the concert. We can't make ourselves say what we know perfectly well to be the case: The tickets came from the oncologist. We know our father knows this, too. It's both a troubling of our spirits and an excitement. Even the little ones who can't process through all the mental steps necessary to figure out where all those tickets came from — even those little ones are riled up and wilder than we've ever seen them.

In the big room upstairs, Desiree dances for us, and we applaud softly, so as not to attract attention from our parents. Leopold is not old enough to walk steadily, let alone dance, but when Desi performs at bedtime, he bounces up and down in his drooping diapers to demonstrate solidarity with her. Our mother says Leopold must go to the concert even if he is likely to poop his diapers when he sees the dancers. That's what he does when he gets excited.

It's a rainy evening when we load ourselves up in the school bus for the drive down to Waltham. Our father makes the older boys hold umbrellas for the girls and the little ones so that their good clothes don't get soaked by the rain. We've never before all been dressed up at the same time. When everyone else is seated in the bus, Peter holds an umbrella for our parents, and through the bus windows we watch Peter shielding them while our father carries our mother down from the porch and across the puddled driveway to the open school bus door. She's such a small bundle. Our father has on a jacket and tie, which at least half of us have never seen him wear before. At the bottom of her raincoat, a little edge of our mother's dress is visible to us, the hemmed inch or so of her wide purple skirt. She has a scarf over her head that hides her face, so that when our father settles her into her seat at the front she's motionless and hunkered down and huddled up against the window. She looks more like a package of something or a piece of luggage than she does a person. And she stays that way through the hour-long drive south to Waltham. We're so accustomed to worrying about her that we know to let the anxiety just simmer. If it turns out that she's not conscious when it's time to go into the theater, then our father will simply drive her — and us — to the Waltham Hospital. If the night's going to turn awful, it won't be for a little while.

In the back of the bus, Emily starts up a song she's taught us, something she learned from being in the band at school and riding the band bus to football games. There are several songs they always sing, Emily has told us, but this is the one she likes best, the sweetest of them. *Tell me why the ocean's blue / that's why I love you* is the part of the song where even a bus full of Faulkeses can harmonize enough to sound respectable. Even our father's tone-deaf bass seems to find the right notes for those words. Ordinarily we know our mother would love hearing us sing like this, but tonight in her seat at the front, she doesn't move and she makes no sound. As we ride through the rainy darkness, we come around to understanding how it is: For the journey she's turned herself into cargo. When we arrive, she'll rouse herself back into human mode.

Our father is able to drive the bus

directly in front of the theater, where he lets all of us unload before he and Peter help our mother out of her seat and down the school bus steps to the great glassy theater entrance. In a snazzy black raincoat, with a bright yellow bow tie showing at his collar, Dr. Lawson is there waiting to help—he's holding up an oversized umbrella for her. Our mother is so small and drawn into herself and so completely wrapped up against the rain that though she's moving now, she could be any old lady. We don't even see her face or hear her voice when the oncologist greets her and moves to her side to take her arm. He and Peter help her navigate through the crowd outside into the theater. If our mother were a terrorist with a jacket of explosives wrapped around her underneath the raincoat, right now she'd be able to murder three hundred people. She attracts almost no attention whatsoever. Glittering dance fans glance at her as she enters the lobby, then quickly turn their heads away. The lobby is infested with anorexic teenagers and young women wearing shockingly bright and revealing dresses. They chatter in urgent high voices and gesture extravagantly with their whole arms. Wherever we look, we see thin young men dressed like fashion models, also in conversation and standing as if they're certain a photographer is about to catch them in the moment.

We Faulkes children witness everyone moving out of

our mother's way without even acknowledging that it's a small human being holding onto the arms of the strapping men on either side of her. These people at the lobby entrance don't see our mother — they dissolve her into the artificially chilled air above their heads. The spectacle affects us strangely; we murmur and jostle and direct each other's attention this way and that. What we really want is to shout, "Can't you see! That's our mother?!" Of course we know such shouting would be sheer craziness. We also know it might startle a few people, but it would mostly be ignored by everyone. Because we've been so immersed in the drama of our mother's dying, we've come to feel that our role in the world has been elevated: the gods constantly observe us; the spotlight of the universe shines upon the Faulkes family with a mother who has cancer. And yet right now, in the Waltham College Theater, we feel ourselves relegated back to the daily ignominy in which Faulkeses have carried out their lives for generations.

Then Peter folds the umbrella while Dr. Lawson helps our mother off with her scarf and raincoat. It's a wild moment — a silence spreads outward from where she stands. It's as if a great blue heron had suddenly glided down from the ceiling and landed silently in this crowd. We see it — we had known something like this would occur — but it shocks us, too. The little ones shake their heads as if to clear their minds of some dream. If she came into this public space as a profoundly ill little lady, now she straightens her back, lifts her chin, and takes a deep breath, so that bright light catches her shoulders and arms, her collarbone, exposed to everyone by her tiny-strapped dress. She wears no make up, so her face rises into the light like that of an angel. She's beyond beautiful, maybe more so here than she would be elsewhere. In this place where young females have outdone themselves in aspiring to a conventional kind of allure, here is our mother demonstrating what God must have had in mind in designing the human creature — a body with every bone and muscle and ligament outlined, a face so intricately detailed that it seems to convey the whole spectrum of human feeling.

Our mother smiles faintly. She just means to be polite to these strangers staring at her, but the smile also seems to release them from the silence into which they'd fallen. Now they break into even louder chatter and nervous laughter. As Peter and Dr. Lawson lead her toward the doors to the auditorium, bystanders make way for our mother as if she were a princess from a distant galaxy. We children start to follow her in. Then we see our father entering the lobby after having parked the school bus. He has no umbrella, and so now he's wet from the rain, but no one else notices him. From her purse Jane hands him a little handkerchief, which he uses to wipe his face, looking around for our mother and anxiously smiling at everyone, but we are the only ones who pay him any mind. Jane points him toward the auditorium door.

Our tickets have us sitting

in a block of three rows of seats. The idea amuses all of us, our mother included. When has anything so organized our family that we would arrange ourselves into three parallel lines? Susan hands Leopold to Emily, because he will sometimes let Emily rock him to sleep. We try to settle in, but we can't help shifting seats and generating ripples of chaos among ourselves. Surrounded by hundreds of strangers, we're nevertheless Faulkeses. At the very front and center of our block sits our mother, her gleaming head and shoulder blades commanding the attention of those seated behind her. The littlest ones are directly in back of her, and Desi can't resist standing up and touching her shoulders and arms, whispering to her. Our mother allows this and even seems to take strength and energy from the attention.

We keep an eye on the oncologist sitting between our mother and our father. In his fine jacket, white shirt, and dashing yellow bow tie, the doctor looks more her equal than does our slightly bedraggled father. At this moment Dr. Lawson could easily be mistaken for our mother's husband — though of course no one scrutinizing the band of children in this block of seats would mistake him for our father. With his patrician face and greyhound body, he's Yale or Princeton, whereas even in our best clothes we Faulkeses are Central Vocational School. Now in preparing our parents for the performance they're about to see, the oncologist makes such complex gestures with his doctor hands that he's quite evidently of another species. And because of our mother's death-progress, she looks like exactly the right woman to be seated beside the debonair oncologist. Our father appears to be engrossed in the concert program, but we children can all feel a blood disturbance rising among us, noting how Dr. Lawson's jacket sleeve brushes our mother's bare shoulder when he raises his hand and arm to suggest a leaping dancer up on the stage.

We're calmed by the lights dimming—it's as if a current of cool air has blown across our block of seats. There's a short moment of absolute darkness, then a spotlight suddenly illuminates a black male dancer in black tights, a black tank top, and a black fedora. His stance is jaunty, but he's still as sculpture. Then music jump-starts him into astonishing life. It's James Brown's "I Feel Good," to which James Brown danced in such legendary fashion that he himself said, "No one follows James Brown." This dancer, however, has evidently accepted the challenge—his feet in their invisible slippers do a version of what James Brown's feet did in their gleaming patent-leather shoes, but from the thighs up, this man's body leaps, twirls, and gyrates in ways that suggest the original dance moves but that raise those moves to heights James Brown could not have imagined. It's a two-minute slice of a song that Brown would often allow to go on for ten minutes or more. Almost immediately we Faulkeses entirely forget the oncologist — like everyone else in the audience, we're completely electrified by the driving music and the dancer before us. Suddenly it stops. We're slapped with a truncation of the dance we've just gotten used to, accepted, even begun to love. The song goes silent, the dancer freezes in his circle of light at center stage, then the spotlight shuts off. We hear the curtain being pulled shut. We hear the footsteps of people we can't see. In the stilled and darkened auditorium, Leopold wails — he wants the dancing back! — but Emily manages to shush him.

Very quickly the curtain reopens to six female dancers in tight tops and multicolored flamenco skirts, their hair up in identical buns. When they begin to move we see and hear that they have castanets. Their skirts twirl thrillingly. In a classic flamenco, the dancers perform their synchronized steps with a refinement that we begin to feel as a form of restraint — as if what their bodies would prefer would be lewd and lascivious movement, but the dance forbids the bodies' true wishes. Even the clicking emanating from their hands suggests a cadence deliberately slowed and contained. The first movement ends with the dancers kneeling on the floor, their skirts pooled around them, their heads nearly touching the stage floor. Instantly a brash second movement commences. The dancers spring up from the floor, each one leaving her skirt in a puddle behind her. They're wearing thongs. Flamenco has gone obscene, this section of the dance has become hip-hop, break-dancing, and strip-club pole-dancing. Whereas the dancers have previously moved in unison, now each has her own spotlight, her own moves, her own dancing universe. No one could have imagined even one version of such a coarse dance at a spring college concert, but now the stage presents us with six variations on the theme of female lust. It's short lived — as if a vice president of the college had risen from his seat and run backstage to put a stop to it. But this is probably an intentional effect. The dancers return to their skirts, step into them, pick up their castanets, and the formerly traditional flamenco ensues as if it had never been interrupted. Now, however, because these decorous movements are infused with the raw sexuality we've just witnessed, we have a completely changed understanding of what we're seeing. The restraint contains a simmering history within it.

The flamenco performance is many times longer than the single-dancer execution of "I Feel Good." When the curtain closes, we Faulkeses are not alone in feeling restless. The order and chaos of the flamenco left us with some interior simmering of our own. But soon the curtain opens to a stage with a straight-back chair, a platform with several steps rising to its top, and what appears to be a child's swing. A red-haired woman in a floor-length dress walks to the chair, sits formally, hands atop her held-together knees, and stares with a neutral expression at the audience for more than a minute of silence. Somehow she holds our attention and our silence, but it's almost as if she's turning into a mannequin before our eyes. Just at the point when we might lose our concentration on her and begin murmuring among ourselves, a stirring version of "Woodchopper's Ball" begins. The dancer rises and flings herself into movements that seem more gymnastics than dancing. We now see that there are slits in her skirt that allow her to move freely.

She's very intense, very animated, apparently determined to push her body to its limit. To finish this part of the dance, she executes a tumbling move that lands her, at the end of "Woodchopper's Ball," miraculously standing atop the platform with her hands raised, her face shining with sweat. She takes some moments to catch her breath, then lowers her hands, steps forward, and delivers a monologue, the title of which she announces as "The Moment I Discovered I Was a Girl." It's a narrative about her kindergarten experience — a cute story — and her delivery is that of a high school public-speaking competition. As she finishes up her story, with the audience chuckling over her description of a boy asking if he can come home with her, the red-haired woman very decorously descends the steps of the platform. Her story ends when her foot touches the stage, which is exactly when Aretha Franklin jolts us in our seats by belting out "R-E-S-P-E-C-T" at top volume. After it startles us so severely, the song gets us moving involuntarily in our seats. The red-haired woman in the floor-length dress gives her body to the music in moves that — especially with the slits in her skirt — might be thought sexy if they were not so outlandishly athletic. She actually does a cheerleader's split on the floor, then immediately jumps back into the dance. The assault of her movement, the loud music, the bright lighting makes us blink at the stage as if we might slow things down or somehow minimize the effect on us. Suddenly Aretha shuts down, and everything goes dark — except for a brilliant pale spotlight on the red-haired dancer standing at the front of the stage, with — and this is so disquieting that it's mentally difficult to accept what we see — her hand pulling the front panel of her skirt aside to display the neatly-trimmed triangle of her orange pubic hair. *Is she really doing this?* rings through our minds, *Doesn't she know there are children among us?* The dancer's pugnacious facial expression answers our questions: *You're damn right I'm doing this! Children have genitals, too!* The vision lasts about twenty seconds, though it feels as if time has stopped, at least for us Faulkeses. The spotlight switches off, the stage lights come up, the music switches to Ella Fitzgerald's "A Tisket A Tasket," and very soon the dancer is seated in the swing — swinging very mildly in the swing — with a little-girl-smile pasted on her face.

When the auditorium lights brighten

to signal intermission, as other members of the audience stand and move out to the aisles, we Faulkeses remain sitting, hardly moving. This includes our parents. We all feel stunned. Simultaneously thrilled and bludgeoned by what we've seen. The oncologist stands up, smiling, tapping his rolled-up program into his palm, speaking pleasantly first to our father and then to our mother. They turn their faces up to him, but we can see they hardly know where they are, let alone what they should say to Dr. Lawson. Or to each other. Or certainly to Desiree and Leopold and the other younger ones. Finally we see our father say something to the oncologist, but there's so much noise around us now that we can't make out his words. Then we hear the oncologist say in a voice that's loud enough for us all to hear, "Yes, well, you've been sheltered. But there had to be an end to that." He's still smiling, but there's sharpness in his voice that's new to us. We can't help thinking he means for us all to hear what he's pretending to say just to our father.

"So you think our father was right

to make us leave at the intermission?" Larry asks Jane, who's most at ease in talking about the performance. And that's probably because she's the only one who hasn't really declared herself as being for or against what we saw.

"I do think he was right, but it wasn't just because of the dancer who opened her skirt," Jane says. "It was raining, we had a long drive ahead of us, the little ones were up past their bedtime, and our mother was — " Here Jane has to stop. None of us is really sure how to name the state our mother was in when the lights came up at intermission. Shocked — but then that's what we all were for quite a few minutes. In fact, our being in shock probably explains why our father was able to herd us out of the auditorium and out of the theater without a single one of us questioning him.

"She wasn't tired," Patricia says. She's a quiet fourteen-year-old who always seems on the verge of disappearing into the crowd of us. But she keeps such a sharp eye on our mother that sometimes she notices things about her that all the rest of us miss.

"She was kind of crazy," Eli says. He's a dreamy boy, who will say the first words that come to him. "She wouldn't put on her raincoat. Wouldn't let anybody help her. I think that red-haired girl's dance threw her into a temporary state of insanity." Eli's face shows that whether or not it's correct, he likes what he's said.

"More a woman than a girl," says Pruney.

"Whatever," says Eli. "The one who was too much for our mother."

We shush Eli and tell him he was the one for whom the red-haired dancer was too much. But he just keeps grinning like a pervert.

Peter clears his throat. He knows he has to speak to this point, because he's the one who was right with our mother the whole way from the theater to the bus. "She didn't want to put on her coat, and she didn't want to take my arm — that's right. Also she didn't want me to hold the umbrella over her even though I did it anyway, though not so close over her head that she really noticed. But I don't think she was crazy or anything like it."

We murmur our agreement with him. We like seeing Eli's smile dissolve because he knows better than to dispute Peter. None of us ever does that.

Peter goes on. "She looked to me like she was concentrating. Like she was still seeing not just the red-haired woman with her skirt spread at the very end, but all three dances. Our father would say, 'Her blood was up.' Her face was pink, she was walking strong and steady, her eyes were wide open, but I don't think she was seeing any of those people out in the lobby who were staring at her. Or even seeing any of us. I think she was seeing those dances. Running them through her mind like a movie."

"And?" says Tony. He hasn't put in his two cents yet, which is odd, because it usually doesn't take Tony long to come up with an opinion.

"And — And I don't know," says Peter. "I know I could feel the energy coming off of her when we walked out of that auditorium. It was like walking beside a human-sized nuclear generator."

"I think she liked it," murmurs Cassie.

"If she liked it, why doesn't she say so?" asks John Milton. "She's never been shy about telling us when she's liked anything before."

"*I* didn't like it." These words have just occurred to Eli. Just by looking at him we can tell that. He wants anyone who will say that we did like it to argue with him. He wants a Faulkes free-for-all. "Waste of my time," he says.

"What that red-haired girl did?" John Milton says. "She did that just for you, Eli. So you wouldn't have to go through the rest of your life being ignorant."

We tell John Milton to shut up. But we like what he said to Eli anyway. Even the girls are pleased, though they won't say so. And besides, after a while we understand that our being split the way we are — about whether the dance concert was a good or a bad thing — doesn't much matter to us anyway. What we really like is talking about it. Even the little ones who don't have much to say still like pretending that they have an opinion. Running it through our minds again. Hearing what the various ones of us have to say about it. The dance concert is a topic we'll keep bringing up for discussion for years. Even after our mother is long gone.

Our mother calls us in

to the living room where she's lying on the sofa. Our father has put a dining room chair beside the sofa to be near her if she needs him. He says she has something about herself she wants to tell us all while she still has the breath to tell it. "She's never told me, either, so I guess we'll all be hearing it for the first time." We can tell he's a little anxious. He looks at her, and she returns the look, then turns her eyes to us. "It's more for you children than for your father. It will tell you what kind of person I was when I wasn't yet grown. I've never told this, but I want to, and you're the only ones who might be able to do something with it. I don't know," she says. "Maybe you won't know what to do with it. But I need to tell you anyway." She lifts herself up to raise a glass of iced water from the coffee table and sip. Then she eases herself back down on the sofa, closes her eyes and begins.

"I was fixated," she says. "I wasn't a Faulkes back then, and if I had been, I probably wouldn't have gotten fixated. I didn't even know the word — I'm not even sure they had the word back then. But I went through this phase where I couldn't think about anything but Johnny Crockett. Day and night. Johnny Crockett. He wasn't from around here, so none of you know the family. But he was a nicer boy than anyone in his family, so that's what you need to know about him. He was nice because that's who he was, not because his parents were making him be that way. He and I were both fourteen, both of us loners, and as far as I know, there was nobody quite like either one of us in our school. So we sort of knew each other, but we couldn't ever find a way to talk. I tried, and he did, too, but something or somebody always got in the way.

"Likely Johnny would say that what happened was something I did to him. He wouldn't be wrong. But I meant it as just something only he and I could know and think about. Also probably a test. And maybe he passed, I don't know. Before I did it, I thought he was clueless and I knew all the secrets. Afterward, I decided he and I were about the same. Johnny didn't seem to hurt like so many others of us in high school did. It was like he'd gotten a shot of something that kept pain from getting to him—an inoculation. I'd seen the big boys try to pick on him, heard them call him names. He didn't run or walk away, he just walked over to them and started talking. I know you'll think this was awful, but it wasn't really. First I persuaded Lauren O'Brien to spill her lunch tray all over him, and he laughed about it, told Lauren he noticed her face just when she let go of the tray. Told her she looked like an angel. Told her he knew she wouldn't have done it on purpose. Then he went to the office to call his mom and ask her to bring him a change of clothes. Even another pair of sneakers, because the ones he had on were soggy with chocolate milk. Lauren said she'd never forgive me for getting her to do that. But she did forgive me the very next day. I never asked her to do anything like that again. Kids saw Johnny Crockett the same as I did—a boy who needed to be educated in pain. Then they'd do something to hurt him, which wouldn't work, so they'd change their minds and leave him alone.

Nobody could explain exactly what changed their minds. So I started really wanting to find out what his secret was.

"I'd watch him all through the school day. Didn't plan to, just found it happening. I'd turn or move from where I was to be able to see him. Not so hard since most of the time he and I were in the same classroom. I kept wanting to see his shoulders, his neck, the way his hair was shaved down close at his collar. Just kept wanting to look at that stupid part of him. *Is this a crush?* I asked myself. Scary thought. If it turned out that I had the hots for Johnny Crockett, my life would turn into everlasting dog puke. That's the kind of thing I thought before I became a Faulkes. If I was sweet on that boy, I'd have to make my parents send me to Saint Anne's. This wasn't a crush, though, I was pretty sure of that. I told myself it was a little thing. And not exactly a bad thing, but I knew it had some meanness to it. I can't claim I didn't know better. I wanted to do something to him that he wouldn't forget. Not so much hurt him as shock him. Make him stop walking past me at school with that can't-touch-me look on his face.

"Johnny Crockett got to be like my research project. Took up way too much space in my brain. But I liked keeping track of him and him being oblivious. Plus I needed time to think about what I wanted to do. I knew that on Thursday afternoons he stayed late at school. On Thursdays his dad didn't show up in the parking lot until close to four o'clock. Johnny did his homework in the library until around three-thirty. Mrs. Gingras's room was right next to the library, and she left it open. I could wait for him in there and catch him as he walked down the hall. The library was on the second floor of our school, and almost nobody was up there at this time of day. That Thursday morning I told my mom not to pick me up until after four.

"The lights were out in Mrs. Gingras's room, so when I stepped in there I felt almost invisible. I stayed out of sight just inside the open door until I heard the library door open. I timed it so that I stepped into Mrs. G.'s doorway at exactly the same time Johnny was about to pass by. I saw him startle when he caught sight of me. He stopped and half turned. 'Step in here, please,' I said. I'd known I'd say that to him, practiced this in my mind. Then I told him something about needing help. I used my nice voice. I knew he'd do what I asked. He'd be wary of me but not enough to say no. Especially if I said please. For that boy *please* would do the trick even if you asked him to please step off a cliff.

"He didn't step into the room right away. Instead he stood still and stared over my shoulder. Not unfriendly but like he was thinking it through. As well he should have, as my mother would have said. Then one of his smiles — the one that included eye-contact — came on his face. Lauren O'Brien had told me she thought Johnny Crockett could smile his way through hell and back. I'd thought she was silly to say it, but that was before he'd turned such a smile directly on me. That's when I realized that he was a completely beautiful boy. And that's when I realized that the look of him was what my problem was. The boy was so beautiful it was freakish. I wanted to take that away from him. Or some of it.

"I don't have to tell you that when I was a girl I wasn't beautiful. So that explains a lot of this.

"Johnny stepped toward me into the room. I stepped back, my steps matching his. A short little dance. No music except for the huge drum in my chest.

"I swung the door shut. From here on out, I was making it up. I could see ahead only as far as the next step of what I wanted him to do. The lights were off in there, but there was plenty of daylight coming through the windows. Even so, the shadowiness made the room feel really empty. Except for the two of us.

"'Around here, please.' I pointed to the little alcove beside the door. A blank wall. Johnny lifted his eyebrows at me. I pointed again. 'Here, please,' I said. I patted the wall with my hand. 'Your face right here,' I said. The tile felt cool to my hand. 'Please.' I still used my nice voice. Like this would be something he would enjoy, to put his nose against that wall. No getting around how strange my request was, but I was pretty sure he would do it.

"Johnny's eyes seemed almost to glaze over. I'd taken care with what I'd worn, but that morning I'd had to guess what top and skirt and tights and shoes would work best to make him do what I wanted. Whatever that would be. I went for the least sexy clothes I owned — it made sense that that's what a nice boy would like. But for maybe half a minute I thought he was going to say no, going to turn and walk out of the room and leave me in there by myself.

"Because that's what he should have done. I knew that. I was still thinking I meant to do him no real harm. I hadn't pinned it down, but once I had him standing there, he'd be my prisoner. Then I'd know what to do. I wanted to make him a different boy. Wanted to install the fact of me in him. So he'd have to carry me around in his brain for the rest of his life.

"But right then I felt something in me wanting him to walk away. Wanting Johnny Crockett not to let me change him. Right then I saw through what I thought I wanted into what I really wanted. Crazy, I know.

"I wanted him just to shake his head at me. He wouldn't even have to say the word *no* aloud.

"I had my hand against the wall where I'd told him to put his face. And I looked at him and said in a voice that was so low I didn't even recognize it as mine. 'You don't have to do what I tell you,' I said. 'You can leave this room. You can walk down that hall. And I swear I'll leave you alone.'

"That's when he stepped up. Dropped his backpack to the floor.

"I felt his breath on my hand, so I took my hand away.

"Johnny put his nose against the cinderblock, right where my hand had been.

"I couldn't let go of the breath I'd taken in.

"When I was fourteen, most of the time it just didn't occur to me that I was a kid. My mom says I had way too much confidence, and she was right about that. Confidence is part of what made me capable of becoming a Faulkes. My mom also said one of these days I was going to sink myself into the deep do-do. But I wasn't scared of the deep do-do, I didn't make me who I was, and I didn't have a problem with how I had turned out. If I'd been somebody else, I would not have liked me very much. But kids my age were mostly just waiting for somebody to come along and show them what to do, what to say, what to eat, what to wear, what to think.

"I'm just trying to explain what an extreme moment this was for me. Johnny Crockett, Johnny Uptight Mr. Right, nose against the wall close enough for me to hear him breathing. Nobody around. The two of us alone and me in charge. Angel boy waiting for me to tell him what to do.

"I thought this must be how it is for God all the time.

"I'd thought if I could just get him to stand against that wall, then what came next would come to me. Now he was, and it wasn't. I might as well have had my own face up against those painted cinderblocks — that was the first thought that came to me.

"Another thought came right behind that one. That boy's neck was so close and right there that it could just as well be my neck. His hair, cut and shaved down to invisibility right at his collar. His head, his neck, his shoulders. Now they were as much mine as they were his.

"I took a step and a half. Two inches between us. The smell of him that close was like grass after it's been mowed. Thick in my nostrils.

"'Do you know what I'm going to do to you?' I whispered.

"I could feel him thinking. 'No,' he said. A whisper like mine. Same tone, same volume. Rabbity little whisper.

"So then I knew.

"I closed the space. I pressed right up against him, which took some shifting around. I did the shifting. He didn't move, but he didn't pull away either. My chest on his shoulder blades. My stomach at the small of his back. My pelvis against his butt. My nose against the side of his neck, a little behind his right ear.

"'This,' I said. I didn't put my hands on him, I kept them at my sides. And I kept making little adjustments of my body so that as much of me as possible was touching him. No hands. Just stomach, chest, shoulders, hips.

“That was what I wanted. I didn’t know why. Not skin on skin. I knew it was right we both had our clothes on. All I wanted was the way we were right then.

“He was quiet and perfectly still for what seemed like a long time. It felt like Johnny Crockett and I were growing into each other. Trees planted so close they just give up and become one tree.

“‘Okay,’ he said.

“I didn’t know what he meant.

“A long time passed.

“‘You’re crying,’ he said.

“His voice was so soft it was like he had floated the words from his brain to mine.

“Until he said I was, I didn’t know.

“I shook my head a little. I didn’t want to be crying. If anybody was going to be crying, I wanted it to be him.

“‘I’m pretty sure you are,’ he said. Words floating brain to brain.

“Okay, so I was crying, fine. That didn’t mean I wanted to talk. I just wanted to pay attention to what I was feeling. What my body was trying to tell me. I was pretty sure that pressing against Johnny Crockett wasn’t sexual. Or mostly that’s not what it was. Okay, my pelvis and his butt, there was some energy there, no use lying about that. But this was something else, something childish. Like a baby wish — innocent but powerful as a truck. Like the way you get a crush on a kid at somebody’s birthday party, because of how the sun makes her hair shine while you’re playing musical chairs. I always got crushes on girls when I was little. You love the way she looks so much you run after her and hug her with everything you’ve got. You want to take her home with you. You want to take her to your bedroom and cuddle with her like your big Winnie the Pooh. It's not like that's not sexual, but it's kid desire. It doesn't have a destination. My body. His body. We were where I wanted to be. So I was crying, I could stay right there a hundred years. And I didn't want to talk. We'd kill it if we talked.

"He let enough silence pass that it was okay when he did speak up.

"'I have a clean handkerchief in my pocket if you'd like to borrow it,' he said. This time he used his good manners voice. The way he'd speak to Ms. Wosniak in our classroom if her nose was running.

"Somebody had just swept a flamethrower over me.

"I stepped back and slapped his silly white neck — not as hard as I could, but pretty darned hard. His forehead smacked against the cinderblock, and his neck where I hit it turned scarlet.

"I didn't wait to see what his face looked like when he turned to me. I spun around and walked down the hall. That morning I'd worn flats with hard heels on them, and those heels clicked on the shiny school floor. That was part of what I wanted, too. I clicked them hard as I could."

Another day she almost nods off

right in front of us at the dinner table. She looks and acts exhausted. And this is only a week since she didn't need anybody's help striding out of the Waltham College auditorium. What we've begun to understand is that the more we let our mother sink into herself here in the house, the stronger death takes hold of her. Though we've all left them untended for many months, we do have lives of our own that have nothing to do with her. Even the little ones. Our grades in school have suffered, as have our after-school activities and the part-time jobs of some of our older ones. Of course our father's work can be left untended only so long, and he hasn't hesitated to call on Jane and Peter and others among us to give our mother some of the attention he'd like to give her.

When we talk with him about the need to bring stimulation into our mother's life without having to mount an excursion into the outside world, he comes up with an idea. For years our father has been making mixtapes from his record and CD collection. In high school he was a serious musician and something of a prodigy as a baritone saxophone player. He claims that since he doesn't play an instrument anymore, he's become a passionate listener. And his appetite for music extends into just about every area except mainstream country and New Age. He buys our mother a Walkman with a set of earphones. Then he sets out to make her a collection of mixtapes made up entirely of tunes he knows she'll enjoy hearing.

He surprises her by bringing the little machine to her in the dining room where we've coaxed her to have breakfast this morning. We've set out green tea, dry toast, and fig jam. We've fixed pillows all around her in the chair we call her Upright Softy. She's wearing the pink-and-white-checked cotton housecoat she prefers to everything else she could wear — Emily washed and ironed it for her last night. And just now Patricia has massaged her scalp and her face with jasmine oil. We know our mother wants to rally — we can see that in how the corners of her mouth try to make a smile for us and how her eyelids valiantly struggle to stay open. She looks like a lady who desperately wants her nap but doesn't want to offend company that has come to visit her. Desi has carefully spread a thin coat of fig jam on a piece of her toast, and now she's tempting our mother by gently wafting it near her nose. But by now we're so keyed in to our mother's state of being that we know how it's likely to go if things don't turn in our favor very soon. Our mother's lip will begin to tremble, her eyes will squeeze shut, and tears will come sliding down her cheeks. More and more often we come to this point where we simply can't defeat the despair into which our mother gradually sinks whenever she's awake.

Just then our father brings in the Walkman, places it in her hand, plugs in the featherweight earphones, places them ever so gently over her ears, then starts the little device playing the first tune. It's something slow and soft enough that we can't make it out from the barely audible sound-leaks from the earphones. We do see, however, that our mother's face is slowly changing, a smoothing of wrinkles so faint we hadn't noticed them on her forehead. She raises her index finger and brushes the face of the instrument in her other palm.

Then we hear a rise in the volume, a beat, a tune, a tropical syncopation of saxophone, drums, and guitar, with a song we remember that she loved ten years ago but that now we can't think of by name. "It's that Paul Simon thing she used to play all the time," our father says.

"You Can Call Me Al," Robert tells us. Robert's like the Faulkes family music archivist — if a song has ever been played in this house or in the school bus, Robert remembers. He's utterly neutral in his opinions of music, likes everything pretty well but nothing all that much. Also, he usually knows who every musician was who played in the recording session. Eli accuses him to his face of being autistic, but Robert doesn't care. "Just means I can remember things and you can't," he says to Eli. At the moment, though, nobody's bickering. Our mother is sitting up at the table, very slightly bobbing her head, chewing a bite of toast with fig jam, reaching for her cup to take a sip of green tea.

"You Can Call Me Al" has injected some spirit into her. We're on the verge of applauding, the whole room full of us, but knowing this uplift won't — can't — last very long is like knowing there's a ten-foot shark cruising beneath the little rescue boat that has just saved us from drowning. Jane's face shows both our pleasure and our agony while she stands behind our mother looking down at the frail arms and hands and fingers bringing food to her mouth.

Our father is happier than we can bring ourselves to be, but then he's also likely to sink lower than we will when our mother's spirits start plummeting again. The song ends, and our mother takes off the earphones and smiles up at him — a smile that hurts us so much we can hardly bear it. "You Can Call Me Al," she says, her face shining its light on us. "Thank you!" she says. "Thank you!"

"Have we ever had a suicide watch in this family?"

asks Tony. "Swear to God, I don't think C.J.'s gonna make it." C.J. is five years younger than Tony. One minute the kid's laughing like an idiot, the next minute he's running out to the meadow to weep and bam himself with his fists and scream up at the clouds." He shakes his head. "I'd be doing the same thing except there's no point in both of us doing it. He's doing it for me as much as for himself. But I don't know what I'm supposed to do instead of that. Maybe start cutting on myself. Except I think that's just for girls."

"There's nowhere we can go," Colleen says. "There's nobody who can help us. It's like we're on a spaceship that's headed for the death star. We can't get off, nobody else can get on, we can't change where we're going or what's going to happen, we can't even control how slow or how fast we're going." We all appreciate Colleen, but she's usually got her head in a book and almost never says anything. Which shows you how bad it's gotten.

"We're Faulkeses," says Jack. "Faulkeses put their heads down and move forward," he says.

"I used to think that," Tony says. "Now when I say those words to myself, I just start laughing. It's a joke. Maybe being Faulkeses is just one big joke. Didn't we decide that our father made up Old Stanton Faulkes?"

The days are long now,

and this evening after supper we decide to take our mother on what we used to call a streamside stroll. Along the meadow runs a little brook called Fancy Creek. We don't know where or why it got that name, it seems a plain enough creek to us, but its water is cool and clear. Best of all, it never lacks for minnows, crawdads, tadpoles, frogs, and turtles. Our mother used to claim she was inordinately fond of turtles, and she proved this by never being afraid of them, even the snappers. She'd squat down beside one trudging along on the mud or grass and speak to it as if it were an old friend. If anyone caught a little box turtle, our mother would ask to hold the creature in her hand, then she would hold it up to speak to it and give it a careful examination, turning it over and running a finger down the plates of its underside. "Frogs never appealed to me," she liked to say, "but a turtle can be my pal."

In the summer when it's really dry, Fancy Creek shrinks down to just a trickle but never really stops running or disappears. When there's a hard rain, or several rainy days in a row, the water rises up rough and muddy, and runs hard as if to show us that it can be a serious creek, that it will do some flooding if it ever rains hard enough. Before there were so many of us, our mother often walked us over to Fancy Creek for a whole morning or afternoon of playing, splashing, and pretending to swim. The bottom is muddy in places, rocky in others, sometimes mossy along its edges, but at least there are no pieces of broken glass or rusting tin cans. When we went there in the days before our mother got sick, we almost never saw anyone else, and Fancy Creek felt like it halfway belonged to us. The stream weaves in and out among some trees — two or three of which are willows that make hospitable shady places. A farmer occasionally mows the patches of grass here and there alongside the water. Long ago, we had a legendary picnic here when a fearless groundhog came up to the group of us and would not be shooed away until our father made threatening gestures with the picnic basket at the crazy little animal.

It's been a while since we've taken our mother for an outing in Her Majesty's Traveling Throne. We hadn't remembered how long a haul it is from our house to Fancy Creek. So even though our mother is lighter than ever to carry, we still must change our teams of throne carriers several times before we reach a place where we can set her down. "I can smell it," she says from up on her high place. This the first she's spoken since this morning when we told her we were going to take her to the creek. "It smells like mud and watercress and cedar," she says, sitting up straighter and pulling pillows around her. "It smells like the foot of a turtle," she says.

"Go on," says Franklin. He is intoxicated with her lilting words after a couple of days when she's had almost nothing to say to us.

"It smells like an elephant's footprint, a groundhog's underarm, a muskrat's ear, a heron's wing when it's just stretching to fly."

"A crawdad's pincer," Desi tries, and our mother says, "Yes, exactly, that's it, Desi."

“Tongue of a crow!”

“Yes, Leon. Thank you!” She’s very excited now and stirring around up there on the high seat, as if she might stand up, though surely she won’t do that.

“Top of a duck’s head when it comes up from feeding!”

“Oh, Sarah Jean, yes, love, yes! Set me down here, you brilliant children. I want to put my feet in this grass!”

“Are you sure, mother?” Jane asks. We know Jane is thinking maybe our mother has lost her wits from the smell of the creek wafting over the meadow toward our procession. “Remember, you’re not so strong nowadays,” she says.

“Oh, pooh, Jane,” our mother says. “I’ve lost a little weight. I’m still strong as a just-lit match,” she says as she sets her shrunken foot on the grass while still holding onto the arm of the throne.

We hold our breath while she places her other foot down beside the first one, slowly lets go of the throne, and straightens herself. She’s wearing her old gray pajama pants and a blue sweatshirt that’s frayed at the neck and the wrists, both now so loose on her they almost look like they’re on a coat hanger. She’s tied a raggedy bandana across the top of her head. But her face is bathed in gold by this late afternoon light, and there’s no explaining the force of it. Anyone looking at her would say, “That woman’s on the brink of death,” but someone else would whisper, “Yes, maybe so, but she sure is alive right now.”

“Web of a goose’s foot after it’s stepped in mud.” This is Peter. He’s teary-eyed.

Our mother sees him and moves to speak but can’t for a moment. “Yes, love,” she whispers to him. “Come and give me your arm,” she says.

“Salamander’s belly when you pull it out of the water.”

“Yes, Eli,” she says. “You come here, too. I could walk by myself, but I’ll have a better time if you two boys keep me close beside you.”

“Mud!” calls Leopold with a big gummy smile—at least that’s what we think he’s trying to say. “Mud!”

SOME OF US ARE LAGGING BEHIND AND TALKING.

"You can't call it beauty," says Tony. We know he thinks what we think — our mother is crazy beautiful. But it makes him uneasy, the way she looks. Is a skull beautiful? A skeleton? It makes us all so anxious we don't want to talk about it, but Tony wants us to.

"Dr. Lawson would call it that," Pruney tells him. "Have you seen the way he looked at her that night we went to the dance thing? I thought he was going to get down on one knee and ask her to divorce our father and marry him."

"Dr. Lawson is a pervert," Tony says. "He goes swimming in death every day. He showers with death and uses death for deodorant."

"I think if it weren't for him, she'd have died months ago," Jane says.

She surprises us with that, and we don't like hearing it. "No way," we say, and "That's just wrong," and "She's got cancer, but she hasn't lost her mind," and "That guy is so far away from being a Faulkes."

Jane doesn't put her hands over her ears, but she does close her eyes and stop walking for a moment. When she does that, it's like an invitation to us to study her face. Familiar as her face is to us, we're not used to seeing it with her eyes closed. It spooks us. It's our mother's face before she got sick. Our mother's Faulkes face we won't ever see again. We go quiet.

"Listen to me," Jane says and opens her eyes and stares us down. "I didn't say I liked it. But that's how it is. The jerk is keeping her alive."

We're not about to argue with her, so we hurry to catch up with the others.

Once she stands up on the grass

and takes a couple of steps with Peter and Eli holding her up, she understands that she's too weak to walk. "Put me back up there," she tells us. Her voice is strong enough that we're not worried about her, and her face tells us she's very happy we brought her here. When she's back up on Her Majesty's Traveling Throne, she's in a jolly mood. She tells Desi she wishes she could have her up there to sit on her lap, but she knows Desi weighs too much. True — Desi's our third-littlest one, but she's already starting to get the Faulkes heftiness. "The ballast," our father sometimes calls it. Desi doesn't mind. She likes any attention she gets from our mother. Which of course is what we all like nowadays.

Our mother wants to be close to the water. She keeps directing the carrying team to try the difficult footing an inch or two away from the creek banks. And of course the carriers have to jostle her when they follow her directions. She treats the wobbly throne like a carnival ride, holding on and letting out little shrieks and giggles. If she could, she'd trail her hand in the water as we carry her, but she can't ask the carriers to get down into the stream for her to be able to do that.

Jack walks up ahead of us a yard or two, pretending to be our scout. When he stops and raises his hand to us, we go along with him and stop where we are, a few paces back.

Our mother lifts herself a little and raises her head to try to see what Jack sees.

It's a brown blob, a rock or chunk of a tree limb, in the startlingly green water-soaked grass up ahead. The blob doesn't appear to be moving, and Jack stands only a couple of yards away from it. We think his imagination has taken over, but then we see that the brown blob is actually moving very slightly. So we all shift into sneaking-up mode — we take slow steps toward Jack, setting our feet down softly. Ridiculous, really: a herd of youngsters of all sizes transporting an invalid on an apparatus the size of a library table, trying surreptitiously to get an intimate look at an unknown something-or-other a little smaller than a football. Our mother is perched up there above us, amused by what we're doing but also eager as she can be to find out what Jack has come upon up there. She sees it, too.

We move right up to where Jack stands waiting, then he takes sneaky steps right along with us, no one saying a word, though it's all we can do not to ask out loud, *What is that thing?* We do get very close, less than a yard away. Beaver-shaped but with a snaky tail, the creature has its face down in a low grassy place overrun with water, and the little bit of movement it makes comes from its rooting around down in there, probably finding something good to eat. *Muskrat*, we hear our mother whisper, soft as a breeze over our heads. The muskrat is so caught up in its eating that it doesn't see or hear the audience of Faulkeses that has surrounded it. Our mother whispers, *Hello, sweetheart. Having a tasty snack this afternoon?* She can't help making friendly gestures with her hands and fingers toward it. As if she's trying to sink down into her muskrat self in this moment. *Rooty, chewy stuff, isn't it, darling?* she whispers.

Yum, yum, she says, and her words take us far back to when we were babies nursing at her breast and she crooned to us just like this. *Are you a greedy sweety?* she asks it.

The muskrat raises its head. A huge thought has entered its brain, but it holds as still as a stuffed muskrat while it processes the message it has received. *Many large creatures only five tail-lengths away!* A muskrat is not a graceful or intelligent animal. On the food chain, it probably ranks right down there with bunnies and field mice. It does, however, have one crucial instinct: *If in doubt, make for the water.* It lurches into the creek, its ratty tail snaking behind. It dives as deep as it can go, which is only an inch or two below the water's surface before its paws hit bottom, then it wriggles its muskrat butt downstream, making a slight wake as it goes.

Our mother spontaneously and recklessly stands up on the throne to applaud. If she falls, there are a dozen of us right beside the throne reaching up our arms to catch her. But she doesn't fall, she catches herself, sits quickly back down, and then we join her in cheering the muskrat's performance.

"A baby," announces Desi. Though we're all pretty sure that creature was at least half-grown, we don't correct her. In fact, later when we tell about that afternoon, we call this part of it the legendary episode of the baby muskrat.

THE SUN IS LOW OVER THE MOUNTAINS,

but when we ask our mother if she's ready to go back home, she says, "No way." If she'd said a simple no, we'd understand she didn't mean it—and turn and take her home. But now we keep going. The worst that can happen is what's going to happen anyway, except that it'll happen out here by Fancy Creek. Up on her throne instead of in her bedroom. We don't have to ponder even a second to know which she'd prefer.

We walk slowly and more softly than we would if we weren't here by the water. We speak only occasionally and in low voices. Our mother seems to be humming something up there on her throne, but we can't catch enough of the sound to know what song it is. It might not even be a song. Her mood may have taken her someplace where she just needs to make a little random humming noise down in her throat. Maybe it's a song you make if you're near enough to dying that you just want to check to see if you're still alive — your brain sends the command to hum down to your larynx, then you listen for the noise to come out of yourself. At any rate, we sense that she's content up there, that traveling this way is just what she wants.

We lose track of how far we've gone or how much time has passed. It's late afternoon; the twilight's slight dimming has begun to turn Fancy Creek otherworldly. In particular, the grass here by the water takes on a shocking intensity of green. With the pack of us slowly walking like this together, we feel as if this is the world we were born to live in rather than the one of lawns, picket fences, houses with rooms, doors, staircases, and beds.

Stop!

We don't so much hear the sound as feel the syllable emanating down from Her Majesty's Traveling Throne. We've been moving so slowly it's no trouble to stop. We were already half in a dream state, the whole passel of us, but of course now we've raised our alertness, we're doing everything we can to catch sight of what our mother might have seen. She's the one who has the best view of what's ahead, and of course we trust her not to have sent down that signal if she hadn't seen something of note. No guarantee, though, that what she's seen is real.

Then Jack's arm rises and extends his hand with its pointing finger.

We squint, we widen our eyes, we can't see it. Then Cassie raises her arm, and Peter his. Finally we're all seeing it, or pretending we do—out there at the edge of a mirror-still place in the stream up ahead—but then what is it?

Go slowly!

Again, the words are less audible words than something like musical tones we pick up from the air around us. At this hour, in this place, in her precarious state of health, maybe our mother has tapped into a method of communicating directly from her mind into the minds of her children. We certainly don't question her. We go slowly. A step every five seconds. On her throne our mother floats in the space above our heads. The creature up ahead makes a darting movement. Then a word enters our minds without anyone having to say it.

Heron.

As if our silent naming generates some kind of signal in its heron brain, the two-part gray wings unfold, its neck stretches, and the bird lifts off the water in ghosty silence. If we weren't staring directly with such concentration, we might not even have seen it at all. The color of twilight, that contrivance of a creature rises over the stream, its legs folding straight back under its tail, its extended wings astonishing in their span from one tip to the other. That thing navigates like a spirit along and through a narrow width of streamside trees, rocks, and brush. Our eyes hold onto the sight of it as long as possible.

Then it's gone. As if it has dissolved into the air.

The carriers set down Her Majesty's Traveling Throne. We don't know exactly why — we want our mother among us, maybe because she saw what we saw. Her eyelids are closed now. She's breathing deeply, but her face is serene, exalted. When Desi goes to her, our mother lets the little girl cling to her lap. Susan carries Leopold to her, though he's too big to hold in her lap as he wants her to, so Susan sets him on the ground beside the chair. Our mother puts a skeletal arm around the shoulders of each of these little ones.

It was just a bird is what we think. *It's nothing to hush us up like this, nothing to make us so quiet. A bird that eats fish and tadpoles. A common creature.* But we can't convince ourselves to say anything. A few of us are even shivering.

Eli steps up beside the throne. "Should we keep going until we find a turtle?" he asks.

Our mother opens her eyes, mouths the word turtle, smiles a little at Eli. Then she decides no and shakes her head. Lets herself relax back among the pillows. She's sad now, but we can tell it's not her indoor variety of sadness — this has some wildness in it, a little current of joy like the cool air we feel sliding along the stream now in the direction the heron took. As if it left a benign wake behind.

Something's wrong with Jane now.

More than a week ago we began seeing it. C.J.'s known about it longer — he's the one who keeps an eye on Jane. Now he's the one who goes to talk with her quietly in the big room upstairs. They're so muted and intense in their conversation that the rest of us keep our distance. We pretend we're not aware that something's wrong over there. Then we hear a muffled sobbing. We've noticed Jane doing that in recent days, crying but stifling it, mostly trying to keep us from noticing. But of course we have, and she knows that. A crying Faulkes is an occasion of alarm for the rest of us, even if it's one of our little ones. For one of our oldest to be doing this — and not for the first time in the last several days — causes every one of us to make our way over to the sitting area where they've been talking. Jane's head is down, her face in her hands. C.J. stares at us coldly.

"She ate nothing at supper this evening. Pushed her food around on her plate like You-Know-Who. Hasn't washed her hair for three days. I'm pretty sure she didn't even brush her teeth this morning. Just came downstairs and went straight out onto the porch." He speaks to us as if he's a prosecutor laying out a case against a perpetrator. Peter sits down beside Jane and puts an arm around her shoulder. She allows it, though we can see she doesn't really want to be comforted.

We can't think of what to say. Most of us know what's wrong, but we know no clinical name for it, and we don't really want to describe it aloud.

Jane is becoming our mother. What's killing our mother isn't contagious, of course. But now we see that it might as well be. As our mother has grown weaker and less and less able to function as our mother, Jane has taken her place, more and more. For a while none of us thought about it. Even Jane didn't seem to be noticing how she was the one who did the last cleanup in the kitchen at night after everyone went to bed, the one who made sure everybody got up in time to go to school or music lesson or softball practice, the one who made a shopping list for our father, the one who felt the foreheads of the little ones to see if they were running a temperature.

"Everybody pitches in" is how we explain it to outsiders, and that is the truth — we've all taken on responsibilities that we wouldn't have if our mother had been healthy. But it has all come to rest on Jane. She has become the center pole of the big tent that shields us from the storm and holds us together as a family. The day-in-day-out has gotten the best of her. She's nineteen and doesn't know what to do. We don't either. We stand around, looking at our shoes, glancing at our crying big sister out of the corner of our eyes. Emily pats Jane's hand. Jennifer strokes her hair and tells her she'll help her wash it tonight.

"I'm so sorry!" Jane wails. Now she's so loud it's as if she means for our parents to hear her downstairs. And maybe, without realizing it, that's what she does want. Asking them to take back the heavy burden of all of us that she's been carrying these last months.

"I know I've been awful" she blubbers. She's having a

breakdown, but she's also having a tantrum, and she's acting out for all of us. "I'm putting a stop to it right now," she says too loudly. "I'm going downstairs to get something to eat. I'm going to eat something!" she shouts. Tears wetting her cheeks, she breaks through the crowd of us and clatters downstairs.

Now we don't know what to do. We look at each other. We end up looking at Peter. At first his face shows some panic — he's next oldest, maybe he'll be the next one of us to fall to pieces. Then he stands up. "Come on," he says. "We might as well watch her. What else is there to do around here? Homework? TV?" He heads downstairs, and we follow him.

When we reach the kitchen, we find Jane kneeling in front of the open refrigerator. The light's shining on her face, but her eyes are closed. She's definitely not looking for something to eat. We're quiet going in to help her, and she doesn't move on her own. Then Colleen comes up beside her, puts a hand on Jane's shoulder, and reaches into the refrigerator with her other hand. "Come on, Jane," she coaxes, helping Jane stand up. "Strawberry yogurt. It's that Greek yogurt you like. I'll help you." Colleen and Jane sit down side by side. We stand around the table watching. Jane lets Colleen feed her spoonful after spoonful of the thick pink yogurt.

After we tell our father about Jane,

and after he comes home from talking over the situation with the oncologist, and after he has discussed the idea with our mother, they call us downstairs to tell us what they've decided.

"We're taking a Farewell Tour," our father announces. Our mother is lying on the couch, and he's sitting beside her. "We're going first class," he says and grins at us. Then he explains that Dr. Lawson has funding for such excursions. The oncologist and his department at the hospital are conducting research in a program they call the Special Operations for the Dying Project. "For a couple of years now, they've been trying to find a large family who'd let them underwrite a special mission for their end-of-life person. They have extra funding for such a family."

Our father grins at us again. Just bringing up the topic of a large family never fails to amuse us. At school we children constantly take kidding about the size of our family. Whenever we're out in public together, somebody will inevitably come up and ask, "Are they all yours?" Our father will sometimes say, "No, we rent a few of them." Of course everybody assumes we're Catholic, and even when we tell them otherwise, they think we're probably lying because we're ashamed of how the Catholic Church has behaved in recent times. The true explanation — according to our parents — is that our mother and father kept on really liking every kid that came along, so they saw no reason to stop having more. "Also Faulkeses are generally born easy," our mother told us. "Not a one of you gave me any trouble. It got to be easier having one of you than it was to go in for my yearly physical exam."

We've never entirely believed our parents' stories about why they had so many babies, but we give them credit for telling an approximate version of the truth. "They don't know, but in their subconscious minds, they think there ought to be more Faulkeses in the world," says Creighton. Creighton is not even eleven, and he says he's going to be a shrink when he grows up. He loves the whole idea of the subconscious. "People know what they're doing, but they don't know that they know," he likes to tell us. "Or else they don't know what they're doing, but they do, actually," he says.

"We know," we tell Creighton, as we nod at him vigorously. "We know."

"So tell us about the tour," we beg our father. "Give us the details." We like it that he's in a good mood this afternoon. He never broods or complains or gets depressed, but he hasn't been himself as our mother has become more and more visibly ill. Whereas all of us children and almost every stranger we meet can't keep from gazing at her, our father misses the way she used to look. It's not easy for a Faulkes man to find a wife who fits the genetic profile. He fell in love with a Faulkes girl who wasn't yet a legal Faulkes. He misses her wholesome plainness. He misses the honest heft of her old self.

"We get a big new bus. Like the ones the rock stars use when they go on tour." Our father grins. "It's going to be customized just for your mother and us. And I get to drive.

I have to take a training session to learn about it. But we'll travel as a family the way we always have, me driving and your mother in the right hand front seat as usual, except everything fixed up fancy. You kids are gonna start complaining because those seats will be too soft for you. You'll all go to sleep because those seats will be so comfortable, and they'll rock like a cradle when the bus is moving."

"What's the hitch?" Tony asks. C.J. is standing right beside him nodding. "What do we have to do for the funding?"

"It's not bad," our father says. But the way he says this, we know it's not good either. Or at least we know it's not sitting nearly as well with him as does driving the big new bus.

"The details?" C.J. asks. C.J., the ten-year-old stickler.

Our father clears his throat. "Dr. Lawson and a couple of other people will be going with us."

A disapproving silence descends upon us. We can't help scowling at our father. He studies his knees.

Then our mother tells him something.

"We can't hear her," Isobel says from the back of the room.

"Separate bus for them," our father says. "Or not really a bus — more of a van. It'll be fixed up with computers and communication equipment. It'll follow along behind us."

Being followed by Dr. Lawson and his team is far from ideal, but it won't be as awful as having them ride in the same bus with us.

"Will we have to talk to them?" asks Peter. His voice is polite, and his tone conveys to our father what we all feel, that as much as we don't like this part of the arrangement, we'll probably go along with it.

"Mostly they'll talk to your mother and me," our father says. "And maybe Jane. But, yes, occasionally they will ask you questions. But you can always say you don't feel like talking."

"Who are the other people besides Dr. Lawson?" Tony asks.

"Dr. Prendergast, his colleague. And Ms. Anderson."

We try to think who Ms. Anderson might be and why she'd be going with us. But we don't ask out loud. Our father knows what we're wondering about.

"She's the hospice worker," he tells us in this very low voice.

We don't say anything.

"You'll like her," he tells us and smiles when he says it. "I've met her. I've checked her out. I promise you you'll like her."

We believe our father. All the way down to our little ones, we know what the word *hospice* means and what Ms. Anderson's coming on the trip with us means. And it's not as if we haven't been talking aloud every day about our mother's coming death. We don't do so in front of her, but we could — she wouldn't mind. We know, we absolutely know, that now our mother is officially in what they call end-of-life care. It's not shocking to us. It really isn't. Nevertheless, the word changes everything. We murmur a little among ourselves.

Our mother whispers something to our father, and he passes her question on to us. "Don't you want to know where we're going?"

Actually we hadn't thought about where we were going. We thought a long trip in a fancy bus was what people did on a Farewell Tour. But of course there has to be something or somebody or someplace to say farewell to. Athletes and musicians are the ones who take such tours, and they go to different cities around the country. But our parents haven't ever had much to do with any cities. We wouldn't need a big fancy bus to go to just about every place we've ever been. The state fair over in the central part of the state. Grandaddy and Grandma Elton Faulkes's farm up in the northern part of the state. Tuperville, the little town over on the other side of the lake, where we sometimes take the ferry for a Sunday afternoon excursion.

"Tell us, tell us," we say. We try to sound enthusiastic in our asking, because surely we're going somewhere that our parents think we might like. At least they seemed to think the news of it would cheer us up.

"First, we're going to the beach at Cape May," our father says. "Your mother and her family went there for a week three summers when she was a teenager."

"The beach," we say and smile. "We haven't been there before," we say.

"Then we're going to the National Gallery in Washington, D.C. Just before she met me, your mother saw a painting there she wants to visit again."

"The National Museum," we say. "Washington, D.C.," we say. We know we sound silly just repeating what he's told us, but what else are we to do?

"Then we're going to Hollywood's Restaurant in Hamlin, Pennsylvania." Our father gives us a big smile, but we see right through him. The only reason he's smiling is that he thinks it's hilariously strange that our mother wants to have a last visit to a restaurant in Hamlin, Pennsylvania. We don't share his bemused view of our mother's third destination, but we can't find a thing to say to him. We make an effort not to let sour expressions make their way onto our faces.

Finally Jessica asks, very quietly, "Which picture. What's the painting she wants to see?"

Our father turns to our mother, and she tells him the answer to our question. "The Girl in the Red Hat," he conveys to us with a nod.

We've never seen it, of course. The only real paintings we've seen are of landscapes and former governors in the state capital, and the ones on sale at the Goshen Craft Shop that are painted by local people.

"The Girl in the Red Hat," our father says again. "Sounds pretty exciting, doesn't it?"

We can't quite bring ourselves to answer him out loud, but we do manage to nod at him. Then we go quietly upstairs to the big room to look up "The Girl in the Red Hat" in the encyclopedia.

A FEW DAYS BEFORE WE ARE TO LEAVE

for the Farewell Tour, Jessica knocks on the door of our parents' room, listens a moment, then slips in to talk with our mother. We've stopped asking Jane to do all that she was doing, and she seems grateful. And we didn't ask Jessica to speak with our mother. Jessica's only fifteen, and though she's maybe the smartest Faulkes of us all, she enjoys the company of the middle children and the little ones. She's been very slow even to act like what she will be soon — an older child. But she volunteered to have this talk with our mother, about whether or not our mother truly wants to take such a long journey and what she thinks she'll get out of it and what she wants us to take from it. After all, this is Dr. Lawson's grand idea, as our father has explained to us, and we just want to be sure this is what our mother wants. If not, we've agreed we'll speak to our father and make a stand against it. Jessica said she'd be willing to check it out with our mother. She said it felt to her almost like Dr. Lawson and our father were kidnapping her mother, pulling her away from us children. So she thought she'd be a good one to ask our mother those questions and have a long, slow conversation with her about everything, and not just the tour. But of course mainly the tour. We agreed, because Jessica's middle-child manners might make our mother speak more frankly to her than she would to Jane or Peter.

In fact, Jessica is in there talking with our mother from ten in the morning until lunchtime. Then she comes out to fix our mother's small plate of tofu and fruit. She shakes her head with a very serious expression on her face. She says she can't talk to us until she and our mother are finished with their conversation. She carries in the lunch for our mother, along with her own peanut butter and banana sandwich and chocolate milk. She closes the door behind her and doesn't emerge until after two.

"She took two naps while we were talking," she tells us when she sits down with us at the picnic tables. There's an old willow tree here that has presided over our outside meals for as long as any of us remember, and that tree makes us miss our mother because our mother loves it so much. She once told us that if she hadn't married our father, she'd have wanted to marry this tree. Jessica explains that two naps and the lunch and our mother's general weakness and low spirits were what caused her to have to take so long finding out what we all want to know.

"The short answer is that yes, she wants to take the tour. I'm certain that's really what she wants. And the short answer about what she wants us to take from it is that this will be up to each one of us individually but that she can't bear to be away from us. 'If I die and you children aren't there, I will be so sad it will be like dying eighteen times all at once instead of just the one time it will be if I can do it with you all there,' she said."

Jessica's words sort of fade away quickly when they're spoken outside, which makes it all the harder for us to bear what our mother told her. It's as if we want to hold onto each one of those words, but the breeze floats the whole sentence away like so many dandelion seeds down toward the meadow. This is a hard time for us right here under this tree. Feeling wells up in us so much that if we were alone, we wouldn't hesitate to let our tears come. But since we're all together, we hold them back. All that is saving most of us from coming apart is being Faulkeses. The breeze sways the willow branches very slightly, while the sun slips in and out of the clouds, casting shadows that coast across the lawn away from us.

"What else did she say?" asks Sarah Jean. Sarah Jean is the one of us who knows when it's time to ask a question, and we're grateful that she's spoken up to break this silence. We want to know anything about our mother that Jessica can tell us, but mostly we're glad to be free of the too-sad news that our mother wants us with her when she dies.

Jessica goes on. "She said if it were up to her body, she'd stay at home in the room. She said her body has gotten to be really difficult for her to deal with. 'Like a bad child,' she told me. She said she knows her body must be scary to us because there's so little of it left. But she doesn't see it that way. Her body doesn't scare her. She's used to it. She says as you live in your body over time, it makes sense to you. You know why it got strong or weak, fat or thin, saggy or tight. Other people look at it and wish it looked some other way than it does. But if it's your body, you get along with it. Even pain, she says — if it's yours you don't really argue with it. Even if it makes you scream, the pain is yours, and you understand it."

She stops and looks around at the circle of our faces. We're not sure we understand what our mother was telling her. Jessica sees this in our faces, and she shakes her head and grimaces. "This all made more sense while she was explaining it to me," she says.

"Go on," we tell her. She does, after a moment — and after she takes a deep breath.

"She says she can see how we are when we look at her. It worries us to see her getting so thin. So she's glad there's something about her that makes us still want to see her. Still want to look at her. She said she knows she can't expect us to understand what her body is doing, but *she* understands it. And she said we shouldn't worry."

We study Jessica. She's a good girl, there's no question of that. She put her heart into the mission of talking to our mother and then telling us what our mother said — even though what she's just told us doesn't entirely make sense, and maybe she hasn't told it quite right. But it's approximately right, and we're grateful for the words. Anything our mother says — we're glad to have it.

THE BUS IS A WONDER!

Painted in a pattern of trees in the rain, the bus makes almost no noise whatsoever, and its exhaust is invisible and odorless. The inside smells like moss and cedar. It has an upstairs and a downstairs, huge side windows on both levels, and on the upper level there are tinted overhead windows that make it seem like you're flying when you lean back in your seat and look up at the sky. Our father is so proud of this bus that if we didn't know better we might have thought he'd invented it. Of course when we come home from the tour, we'll have to give it back to Dr. Lawson and the hospital.

Our mother's seat can be raised from the lower level — where she sits up front, just behind and across from our father at the wheel — to the upper level, where she can have a pilot's view out the front and overhead and all around. Her seat has its own set of controls in a console she can swing around in front of her like a panel in a space ship. With those controls, she can not only raise and lower herself between the levels, she can also make a hundred and twenty-two adjustments in her seat, including height and angle, temperature, massage, vibrate, and back-and-forth rocking-chair rock or side-to-side cradle sway. She can command that the seat strap her in and stand her almost straight up. She can plug her Walkman into the seat and play her songs from a dozen different speakers embedded all around her. "I can tell this thing to sing to my feet if I want it to," she says.

We can see that our mother feels weirdly empowered and proud of herself. It's probably not the way she's worked it through in her mind, but what it comes down to is that now her death is officially the most important event we've ever had in our branch of the greater Faulkes family.

The morning of our departure Aunt Beatrice stops by the house to see us off, but our mother still won't speak to her, and not even our father — her own brother — will suggest to Aunt Beatrice that she have a look inside the bus where our mother sits in her extraordinary chair. For all we know, the chair may be equipped with a stun gun for unwanted visitors. From our windows, however, we can see by the way she talks with our father that Aunt Beatrice really wants to go along with us on the tour and maybe even hopes our mother will relent and invite her at the last minute. We hear Isobel whisper from the back, "I'll bet she's got a suitcase packed and waiting in the car in case we ask her." We see our mother glancing out her window at Aunt Beatrice, too. We also see something we've never seen before, a vengeful little smirk making its way onto our mother's face.

Dr. Lawson's van is a miniature of our bus, same color and design, so that anyone seeing the two vehicles together would understand them to be traveling as a pair. Just before we leave, Dr. Lawson escorts his associates, Dr. Prendergast and Ms. Sally Anderson, onto our bus. The two men and the woman make their way down the aisle, so the associates can meet us Faulkes children and generate a little small talk. Dr. Prendergast has a shaved head and a mischievous face, and he makes notes on a clipboard as each of us talks with Ms. Anderson, who has a slight limp and who insists that we call her Sally. We're charmed by her, mostly because she manages to ask us good questions about ourselves, not just how old we are but also what we like to do and what kinds of books and music and food and movies we like. She doesn't take notes on us, but because she listens so carefully to what we tell her, we're pretty sure she'll remember our names. She's a light-skinned black woman who is built like a Faulkes — Eli later says she's a Faulkes of color. Our father hears what Eli says and smiles and tells us she's an RN with a PhD, who has written two books on the politics of hospice work. He says he doubts Ms. Anderson wants to be a Faulkes, but if she ever does want that, he will support her application.

The two doctors are in the van behind us while we make our way to the interstate, but Ms. Anderson is standing up and bracing herself against the back of our father's seat so she can converse with our mother. Their voices, first one then the other, make a comforting sound. Even if we miss most of what they say, we can tell that our mother likes Ms. Anderson. When the buses stop at the first rest area, Ms. Anderson tells our mother she has to go back to the other bus. Our mother reaches for her hand and thanks her for coming on the trip. Just before she steps down through the door to leave, Ms. Anderson looks back, sweeps her eyes over all of us, and raises her voice. "Sally," she says. "Remember, please. I want you to call me Sally. Little ones, big ones, every one of you. Call me Sally, okay?" And we tell her okay, we say the name out loud, because her voice made us understand that she wasn't kidding. "Okay, Sally," we say.

"Old Stanton was a liar,"

mutters Delmer Junior. He's sitting by himself in the way-back of the bus's upper level, and he's probably bored because we've been on the road for more than three hours. Delmer Junior is the one of us who is most inclined to dark moods.

Pruney hears him and immediately stands up and heads back there. "Scoot over and say that again, please," she says, pushing Delmer Junior's knees over to make room. Pruney has an ear for disturbance. Also she thinks that Delmer Junior is the most interesting of our brothers and that the rest of us don't really understand him.

Delmer Junior smirks and doesn't slide over all that far, but we can tell he's pleased that he's got enough of Pruney's attention that she wants to sit with him. "Old Stanton lied about who his parents were, where he got his money from, and how much education he had," he tells her. He claimed he went to the University of South Dakota for two years, but he actually never finished high school."

He's not muttering now, so all of us on this level of the bus can hear him. We're not sure what he's up to, but we like thinking about Old Stanton as a big liar. Pruney is staring at him with her nostrils twitching. "Where did you get this from?" she asks.

"Research." Delmer Junior closes his eyes and smiles at her. We know he won't tell her where he got it. "Also, instead of chopping off the heads of chickens," he intones solemnly, "Old Stanton liked to bite them off. Liked to use his teeth. Liked to spit out the blood."

We stay quiet while we wait to hear what Pruney will say. Or what else Delmer Junior might tell us. Pruney's face is flushed, and she's jiggling her foot.

"And didn't he rip a coloring book right out of his little daughter's hands?" she asks in this shaky voice.

"Yes, yes! He did that!" Delmer Junior says, sitting up straight. "And when she asked him why he did that, Old Stanton told her it was because she wasn't staying inside the lines."

"He refused to wear underwear," says William just loud enough to be heard but not looking away from the book he's reading.

"They say instead of deodorant he used to rub cow patties under his arms," Susan says. "And he went to church only because he wanted to sit down beside the nice families and make them move away because of the stink."

"Murdered frogs," says C.J. "Shot robins and chickadees for target practice. Kicked cats whenever he could."

"Snuck up on old ladies sitting by their windows at night and scared them with his devil face." Colleen has never said anything like this, but it's clear she's enjoying herself.

"Pushed over outhouses while his neighbors were in them," announces Creighton. "Spat on people's shoes."

"Told his wife he'd fallen in love with a sheep." Robert surprises us — we thought he might too old for this.

"Threw rocks at kids on their way to piano lessons." Jessica's bouncing in her seat.

"Took his pants off in Sunday School." This is Franklin,

who when he was little used to think it was funny to spontaneously take his pants off in the grocery store.

"Smooshed grasshoppers with his boots whenever he could. Tried to swat butterflies with a tennis racquet." McKenzie is giggling so much she can hardly name these crimes of Old Stanton's.

"Farted in the dentist's chair." Eli is inclined to talk about farting when grown-ups aren't around.

"Ate his own boogers."

"Drank his own snot."

"Peed out his bedroom window."

We're giddy with naming the despicable acts our research has shown Old Stanton Faulkes to have committed, but then we go quiet when the bus pulls over into a rest area. Our good feeling quickly goes bad. Sure enough, in about a minute our father comes up the steps and faces us. Desi is tagging along behind him, and she's pretty evidently been crying. Our father looks at each of us long enough to make us blush. Then he gives Desi a hug and tells her to go back to her seat.

"I think they'll change the subject, Desiree," he tells her quietly. "I know they didn't mean to make their little sister cry," he says.

Then he glances at us once more before going back down the steps and leaving us in silence. In another couple of minutes, the bus pulls out onto the road again. Only after a long while can any of us think of anything to say aloud.

"I THINK DR. LAWSON AND DR. PRENDERGAST

are a couple," Sarah Jean says, using the same voice she might use for *I think that cloud up there looks like a cow*, or *I'll bet we'll see dolphins at the beach*. We've made it as far south on the Garden State Parkway as the Philadelphia Exit. We're settling down now — for a while we were all too wound up to be quiet and stop fidgeting. For miles and miles, we were all over that bus. Now, on the lower level, we're still chattering, but at least we've claimed our seats and started getting used to them.

Suddenly our mother's chair starts rising. We'd forgotten about this trick the bus can perform for her, and this is the first time we've seen it. The ceiling above her slides open, and the whole apparatus elevates to the upper level. We hear our mother laughing as she goes up, but then the ceiling panels slide closed, so that her voice, along with the sight of her, is snatched away from those of us on the lower level. We're stunned into silence for several miles. Then we hear C.J. in the back say, "That's probably how it'll be when she goes to heaven. Except maybe a little quieter."

"I suggested that she try it out," our father says from the driver's seat. He's very proud of himself, and it cheers us up to see him feeling good again. We're reminded of how long it's been since he's been anything like his old self. "I wish I could see your mother's face now," he says.

"Hope she didn't have a heart attack," Kathryn tells him. She's thirteen, very critical of grown-ups in general, and thinks that our father goes too far all the time and that we should stop letting him get by with it.

"Nah, that ain't gonna be how she goes," he says. "Your mother has shrunk down to the size of a hummingbird, but her ticker's strong," he tells us. "I can sometimes hear it after she goes to sleep." He's obviously full of himself from being behind the big steering wheel of this bus. Just the sight of him must get on Kathryn's nerves.

"I want to talk about Dr. Lawson and Dr. Prendergast," Sarah Jean says, turning to peer around the side of her seat. "I said something interesting! Why are you all ignoring me?"

Exuberance breaks out among the little ones when they see the expanse of wide open water as we cross the bridge near Ocean City. That same sight seems to turn our mother pensive as she stares out the window. She's brought her chair back down to the lower level to be near our father, and they've been speaking back and forth, pointing out things they see that interest them. But now, with the voices of the little ones rising in excitement, our mother stops her side of the conversation and simply looks ahead. And it's the same with us older ones — we stare out our windows. The bay we're crossing is a dazzling blue in the sunlight, and we seem to have been driving in a straight line for mile after mile. We're eager to see this place so new to our eyes, and we're not afraid or unhappy, but our mood is tentative, a little unsure.

"How you doing, love?" our father asks, casting a sidelong glance back at our mother. We know, of course, that he asks the question because she's gone so quiet.

"I'm just fine," she tells him with a smile. "To see this again makes me go back to ten years old. I'm like those little ones back there. I want to put a toe in the water."

"Won't be long now," our father says. "Won't be long at all."

The Inn at Cape May is hugely white,

a one-hundred-year-old hotel that's been kept up in spite of the building's ongoing inclination toward decay and collapse. It's been tarted up with purple awnings all around the front side. In full sunlight, however, its whiteness is almost blinding to us when our buses pull up. "They must need fifty carpenters and a hundred plumbers to keep this place going," our father says as he steps down from the bus. He asks us to wait until he and Peter lift our mother down. The hotel has a wheelchair waiting for her, but she rashly waves it away. She's been riding the bus so long that her body isn't ready to move on its own, and so our father and Peter, with Dr. Lawson helping as best he can, carry her like an injured basketball player into the hotel lobby. As she always does, she draws the attention of some folks who can't stop gawking at her—hotel employees and guests—but almost immediately the rest of us fill the lobby and distract the gawkers with Faulkes confusion, chattering, and horsing around. Our father would probably put a stop to it, but he sees our mother observing all of us, especially the little ones, savoring the spectacle of her children in this very fancy hotel lobby. She smiles at us as if we are her work of art. Her face is flushed—and nowadays when we see that color, we know it's in part a low fever that runs through her. That light shade of pink in her cheeks almost always appears in a time when she feels some energy lifting her spirit.

When our father and Dr. Lawson stand at the main desk registering us, C.J. steps up beside them, his head at the height of their elbows. He manages to catch the attention of the especially haughty fellow in a suit who stands behind the other two clerks. "What is your policy on running through the hallways?" C.J. asks.

Since we don't quite know how serious C.J. is in asking the question, we're not surprised that the officious person widens his eyes, squints down at our brother, grimaces, steps forward to examine the paperwork and the computer screen related to our reservation. He twitches his nose and rubs it with his finger before looking back at C.J. and bending forward to speak to him. "Your party has booked the entire North Wing of our hotel," he says. Then he actually winks—who would have thought him capable of winking?! —and says, "Therefore, our policy on hallway running is that you should stop only when you have run to your heart's content."

"What's your story, Dr. Prendergast?"

asks Sarah Jean. We know Sarah Jean has been itching to get him started talking, and now she's trying not to appear to be a brazen smart aleck. This is at lunch at Alethea's, in the Inn of Cape May, where they've given us a separate dining room.

Dr. Prendergast is startled by her question. His shaved head turns pink, along with his boyish face. He's probably always looked younger than he really is. He looks at her slightly wide-eyed, then glances across the table at Dr. Lawson, who shrugs as if to say he can't help him. Then he looks back at Sarah Jean. The two of them stare at each other while he seems to think a moment before he begins to speak.

"My story? Okay, I probably do know what you mean, Sarah Jean. In a couple of ways mine is the opposite of yours — I had no siblings, and I grew up in the city — West 73rd Street in New York. My parents worked for Columbia. They were scientists who had their own lab and who were extremely dedicated to their work. I don't think they realized how hard they were working, because they came and went as they pleased. But I grew up thinking that parents were people you didn't see very often.

"I didn't mind that so much. A shy Ethiopian woman named Candace Dawitt lived in the apartment with us, and from my earliest memory, she was the grown-up who came when I cried — who fed me, bathed me, dressed me, put me to bed, helped me learn my first words, and said my prayers with me at night, all of that. Candace was the one who knew what I needed or wanted, she was always available, and she was so kind to me that I loved her more than I did either of my parents. I probably still do, though I know it's inappropriate. My parents were very sweet people, they knew they didn't understand me as well as Candace did, and I'm sure they were aware of my devotion to her. Maybe this troubled them a little, but since Candace was also extremely considerate of them and since I seemed to be turning out to be a good boy, I think they decided things were as they should be.

"I don't mean to say that my mother and father didn't care about me. They certainly did that — and they often came home to join Candace and me for our evening meal. I have pleasant memories of those dinners, and it's only when I look back on them that I understand how strange they were. As if Candace and I were 'the family' and my mother and father were a devoted aunt and uncle who sometimes dropped by to visit. They usually brought me a toy, a book, or a special sweet for dessert. All three of the grown-ups asked me questions, they all seemed very interested in my answers, and they often laughed at what I said. At first I didn't understand why they laughed, but I liked it when they did. After a while I began trying to say things that would make them laugh. On those occasions it was like I was the star of a movie that was all about me. I think their laughter must have given me an inflated idea of my place in the universe."

When Dr. Prendergast pauses a moment, smiling down

at his empty salad plate, Robert clears his throat and asks, "Did Candace take days off? Do you think your parents took advantage of her?"

Some of us squirm in our chairs because Robert's questions sound rude to our ears. But he's the one of us who's most familiar with city life, and now that he's asked, we're eager to hear how Dr. Prendergast will answer him.

"I've wondered about that, Robert," he says. "Candace did take days off — I'm pretty sure she got them whenever she asked for them, and then my mother or my father would look after me. Since they made their own work schedules, it was easy for them to make adjustments on short notice. Which of course meant that they were choosing to spend a great deal more time in their lab than they were with me, but that's something I realized only after I'd gone away to college. As I remember, Candace rarely asked for time away from the apartment, and she never revealed the slightest evidence of discontent. This could be because my parents paid her well — they probably did — or because Candace's life before she came to our family was harsh. I don't think it was. She was educated, her English was impeccable, and when she spoke of her home life in Addis Ababa she always called up happy memories and spoke wistfully of her sister, her cousins, and her parents."

Dr. Prendergast looked around the room at us, a dining room full of Faulkeses. "I think Candace came from a family of many cousins," he said. Then he said, as if he'd just thought of it, "Her life with just the three of us on 73rd Street must have seemed peculiar to her. But my impression is that she liked it. That she liked it a lot. She cooked the evening meal for us, but another lady came to do our cleaning and our laundry. Candace shopped and ran errands for us, but she never appeared to be other than cheerful about her duties."

"Did she have an accent?" asks Tony. "What about her clothes?" Tony is being fresh as usual, but at least his tone is friendly.

Dr. Prendergast smiles as if he'd been hoping one of us would ask him that question. "Tony, she had an accent, yes, but since I'd heard her speaking from the earliest months of my life, it wasn't an accent — it was my 'first language.' In fact, her voice was so soft and comforting that I loved hearing it — and in this regard Candace and I were perfectly suited for each other. Because she spoke so softly, my parents often had to ask her to repeat what she said, but I never had any trouble hearing her. It's my opinion that she most enjoyed talking when I was her only audience.

"As for her clothes, yes, they were more brightly colored than my parents' clothes or those of people I saw in our building or our neighborhood, but since I saw more of Candace than I did of anyone else, her clothes were just right in my eyes. There was a particular shade of blue — just slightly bolder than what we call royal blue — that she favored for blouses and scarves that I rarely see and that always calls Candace to mind whenever I do see it."

"Did she have a boyfriend?" Pruney asks. This is an obvious question, but we're glad Pruney has asked it. As Dr. Prendergast has been talking about her, Candace has become more and more real to us, so much so that we don't mind now that he's talking more about her than about himself.

"She used to say that *I* was her boyfriend." Dr. Prendergast says these words softly and shyly. Then he laughs, though his laugh has a tinny sound. When he closes his eyes, we suddenly understand that he's talked himself into a place where old feelings are arising in him.

"She wore glasses, and she was the thinnest grown woman I've every known," he says. "She was so thin that it made her seem taller than she actually was. Her teeth were white, her skin was very dark, her hair was long, and she wore it in dreadlocks tied together by a scarf at the back of her head. This was long before dreads became fashionable. She used a particular kind of wax for her dreads that surrounded with her a lime-ginger fragrance. Also — I noticed this about her when I was no older than nine or ten — she seemed to take it as her duty to lift the spirits of all three of us. She did this naturally — and usually in a specifically personal way. Candace knew so many little facts about our family that she had an exact sense of what she might say if one of us seemed pensive or tired. 'That peach cake?' she might ask my father. 'Should I fix it tomorrow?' Then my father would be visibly cheered by his anticipation of a special dessert tomorrow evening. I know that this makes her out to be selfless and subservient, but it never seemed that way. Candace had a talent for aligning herself with us in a deeply friendly way. I've never known anyone else like her."

We don't all sigh, but the mood in the dining room right then is that of a communal sigh. Dr. Prendergast has fallen into a smiling silence. He must have conjured up Candace Dawitt so vividly in his mind that now he's having a little visit with her. Our forks and spoons make little clinks and tinks on our plates. "It's true," he says softly, and his smile disappears. He goes on murmuring as if he's forgotten we're there in the dining room with him. "It's true that I don't like to think of her as a servant. I mean it's possible that she kept her true feelings hidden, that she actually detested us for using her the way we did, that she was just clever in the way she could put us in a good humor, that she…" He shakes his head, evidently trying to clear away thoughts he doesn't like.

Then Isobel speaks up in this squeaky little voice, as if she, too, has been having a visit with Candace Dawitt and has become somewhat troubled. "Something happened to her, didn't it, Dr. Prendergast?"

He stares at Isobel. Again there's that wide-eyed look of his. Finally he says in a voice that matches Isobel's in its softness, "I don't know."

He doesn't say anything else. Our father's teasing ways have taught us to be patient. But this isn't teasing, and his silence goes on too long — we're all uncomfortable, most of us have stopped eating, and even Sally Anderson and Dr. Lawson stare at him with their faces encouraging him to say more.

"Leo."

When Dr. Lawson says his name, Dr. Prendergast meets his eyes and begins to speak directly to him. "I'd just started high school. I was fourteen. One afternoon I came back to our apartment from school to find my mother waiting for me sitting in our living room. Always Candace had been waiting at school to walk me home, or when I got older, she'd be waiting for me at home — there had never before been a surprise like this. I was happy enough to see my mother, but of course I immediately asked her where Candace was. My mother's face told me I wasn't going to like what she had to tell me.

"'She had to go home,' my mother said. 'Her father is very ill.'

"I kept waiting for my mother to tell me when Candace would come back. My mother didn't say anything more but just kept looking at me with that sad expression. Suddenly I understood what her face and her body were telling me that she didn't want to say aloud: Candace wasn't coming back.

"I actually shouted at my mother — 'No!' I was shocked to hear my voice sounding so loud and high but also angry, as if my mother had sent Candace away. My mother blinked and sat back in her chair. Then she shook her head as if she'd understood my thought; she shook her head to tell me that I was wrong to think she was responsible. But she said nothing.

"I turned away from her and ran down the hallway to Candace's room. The door was open. The bed was made. The curtains and the blinds were open, so that the whole room was filled with light. Everything was tidy — and Candace was a very tidy person. But there was nothing that belonged to her left in that room. I stood just inside the door and felt my eyes sting.

"I'd been in there only a few times, but I'd remembered it as filled with knick-knacks, photographs, and souvenirs Candace kept on her desk and dresser and book shelf to remind her of home. The room was spacious enough, it had its own bathroom, and even her hallway was in the opposite end of the apartment from where my parents and I had our rooms. We had come to understand that her room was the one place Candace could go to get away from us. My parents and I almost always left her alone when she was in there. Even so, when I was younger she'd occasionally invited me in to sit with her before my bedtime. I'd come to imagine in some detail how Candace spent her hours in there. There was a chair where I knew she sat in the evenings to listen to jazz on her radio, to hum softly to herself with her eyes closed and absentmindedly put the wax on her dreads.

"This particular afternoon there was that scent that I knew as Candace's and no one else's. My whole body knew that waxy fragrance from sitting so close to her while we read or played games together. Or even from as far back as my sitting in a high chair while she spooned baby food into my mouth. Now her complete physical absence spoke for her: *I am not coming back*. But in her room all around me was the way Candace smelled. The space she'd lived in was holding on to the only trace that Candace had ever been here. The scent of her both hurt and comforted me.

"I sat down on the bed, facing the open doorway. My mother stood out in the hallway, watching me, as I'd thought she would. 'Poor Leo,' she murmured. I knew she meant well, but those words infuriated me. Probably any words she'd have spoken then would have angered me.

"'I'll be all right, Mother.' Those were the words that came out of my mouth. And I give my mother credit—she nodded at me and left me alone. She must have known as clearly as I did that what I'd said was the opposite of what I felt. I was very glad she didn't question me.

When Dr. Prendergast looks around now, his eyes widen again, as if he's startled to see us and to realize that we've been listening to him. "I'd forgotten what a bad time that was," he tells us, shaking his head. "And that was just the beginning. I fell into a pit of sadness, and it took me a long time to climb out. I knew that mothers and fathers sometimes died and the death of a parent is an awful experience for a child. And both my mother and father were just fine. I also knew that — ”

“Dr. Prendergast,” Jane says, “what happened to Candace?” Her voice is calm, but it’s very definite.

We’re shocked to hear Jane speak up like this. The minute she does, we realize that she’s probably the only one of us who would press Dr. Prendergast this way. And he doesn’t seem to be bothered by the interruption.

“Here’s what I know, Jane. A little after noon that day my mother had received a call from Candace from our apartment. Candace told her that there had been an emergency at home, that her father was ill, and that she’d been able to book a flight leaving La Guardia in just a few hours. She wanted to be sure that my mother would be able to be at the apartment when I came home from school. She said she’d be in touch with my mother to let her know how her father was and when we might expect her to return.”

He looked around at us. “So far, so good,” he said. “But when my mother came home, she knew something had changed. She walked slowly through the empty apartment, then she walked down the hallway to Candace’s room. That’s when she realized that Candace had removed every trace of herself from the place she’d lived for fourteen years.”

“So your mother knew,” Jane said.

“That’s right — my mother knew Candace was very likely gone for good.”

“There wasn’t a note?” Sarah Jean asks. “Wouldn’t she have left a note?” Some of us nod at Sarah Jean’s question.

“No note,” Dr. Prendergast says.

“Did you and your parents talk about it?” This is C.J.

"We did. In the days and weeks that followed, we talked about it at some length, because talking about it with each other helped us feel a little less hurt and lost. My parents were having to change their lives more than I was changing mine. They worked out a schedule so that one or the other of them met me after school. And in our talking, we came up with several ideas, including the most awful of all, that Candace might have been killed or severely injured and her family would not have thought to let us know what had happened. But all our theories began with the facts that were most troublesome — Candace must have been planning her exit for at least a week or more, and she must have wanted us to have to figure out for ourselves that she wouldn't be coming back. She knew us so well that we thought she must have taken into account how much it would hurt us to grapple with the way she'd left.

"Why would she want to hurt you?" Isobel asks. She sounds upset. Sometimes we think Isobel feels pain more than any of us.

Dr. Prendergast bows his head and says, "I'm sorry I've made you sad with my story, Isobel. If it's any help to you, I can say that when I started telling you about Candace, I did it because my memory of her was a happy one. She came to live with us in the first month of my life, and she was twenty-five then. Hers was the first human face I remember seeing and examining at great length, while she held me in her arms. I remember my baby fingers touching her face and her smiling at me with such bemusement and pleasure that I will never forget. So she gave me fourteen years of her life — when she left us, she was a couple of months away from turning forty. In all those years, Candace was kind to me in every possible way. And that's usually how

I think of her. I had the great luck to have this gifted and affectionate young woman as my companion-mother for fourteen years. Even now that name, whenever I read it or hear it, makes me smile."

"You said that when she left you went through a very bad time." John Milton leans forward when he says this. We know that he really wants Dr. Prendergast to explain the contradiction.

"Yes, I did say that, and I did go through a bad time. That's right, John Milton. And I don't have to tell you that even if you have the very best family around you it's not easy being fourteen and fifteen and sixteen. For most of us those years have a lot of pain in them. At fourteen I'd reached the age when I was really fed up with how relentlessly my classmates had been teasing me — for a long time — about my name.

"Of course I'd never thought of it as being funny, or being anything at all except just the word that was my family's name. But once they get started, you can imagine how much fun kids can have with Pennygrass. And Fender bass. And Blender ass. And Spender fast. And on and on and on. I went to the Dalton School, where every child was a prodigy of some kind. So *Prendergast* was a word game for any kid who had a little bit of language sophistication. Bender mass. Gender class. And on out into the ridiculous. Wiener Blast. Hinder Puss. Slender Brass. Even Pederast! But finally they settled on Pretentious Ass, which they sensed was the one that hurt me most of all. Please don't ask me how they got that far. Bright kids in a group at recess are like a wolf pack, except instead of teeth, they use their brains to chew you up.

"You see, I'd just had a talk with Candace about that

teasing. Candace always took me seriously when I talked with her about a problem. She'd ask me questions until she thought she'd understood me. This time she had me say aloud the names they called me, and I could tell that hearing those names made her angry. When she gave me her advice, she looked me straight in the eyes. I could see that she was forcing herself to smile at me. 'Just don't pay attention to them, Leo. Once they see they can't bother you that way, they'll stop it.'

"So I believed Candace, though I should probably have known better. I tried ignoring the teasing for several weeks, but of course it didn't stop. I told Candace it was still going on. I asked her, 'Why do you think ignoring them will make them stop?' I thought maybe she knew some secret about how kids behave. This time she didn't look me straight in the face, and her voice sounded flat and tired. She told me just to give it more time and eventually the kids would get tired of such silliness. From that conversation, I decided that Candace had no idea what kids were like at the Dalton School.

"All right, here is my theory." Dr. Prendergast raises his voice now and lifts both hands as if he's surrendering to someone. "Candace was nearly forty years old. She'd given fourteen of those years to me, and — I hope this is true — they had been rewarding years for her. I'd needed her, she and I had gotten along probably better than if I'd been her own son. And I was a good and happy kid. She would have known that mostly because of her I was a good and happy kid. The discussions she and I had about the teasing might have marked the turning point in both our lives. Before those talks I don't think I'd ever doubted Candace's wisdom about the world. And Candace must have been realizing

— probably for at least a year — that my need of her was diminishing and that she was going to be of less and less use to me in the years to come."

He looks around the room at us. We're quiet because we understand what he's telling us.

"But you went though a bad time, and she wasn't there to help you," John Milton says quietly.

"Yes. But I was probably going to have to go through that anyway. The teasing didn't let up, though I got a little better at acting like it didn't bother me. But I had no talent for making friends. At school I felt like a freak. At home my parents and I didn't know how to talk to each other. Without Candace, I was completely on my own."

"How long did it last?" It's almost as if John Milton and Dr. Prendergast are having this conversation to themselves.

"Until I went to college." Dr. Prendergast pauses, and his face takes on a perplexed expression. He shakes his head slightly. "I was so lonely it felt like an illness — like a flu that gives you a low-grade fever and makes you feel achy and tired. That feeling just settled in me and wouldn't go away. I got used to it enough that I stopped thinking about it very much. When I did think of it, I'd tell myself, *It's because of Candace. It's because I can't stop missing Candace.* I actually started thinking of my schoolmates' teasing me as being just a symptom of how much I missed Candace. *They haven't stopped yet, Candace,* I would whisper to her in my mind.

"You went to college," Sarah Jean says. She's impatient now, and we all are.

"Yes," he says, nodding. "That's what I did." Then something changes in his face, and he just sits there grinning. He's suddenly acting just like our father, holding out on us.

"AND THEN WHAT HAPPENED?!" The whole room of us yells at him.

He waves to shush us. When we are sufficiently quiet, he says, "Two things happened to me. Number one — I went to college. Where no one knew me from The Dalton School. My life suddenly belonged to me in a way that it never had before. Number two — I met Ted Lawson." He nods over at Dr. Lawson, and Dr. Lawson nods back.

"I met Ted Lawson at a fraternity rush party at the University of Maryland Deke house. It was our freshman year. The two of us were drinking keg beer and trying to chat up the brothers of this ridiculous fraternity, and the brothers were playing very hard to impress. They were being jerks, except to a couple of young men they must have already decided they wanted as brothers. So Ted Lawson and I — Leo Prendergast, formerly known as 'Pretentious Ass' — struck up a conversation. The somewhat reckless conversation of two people who understand they are being snubbed at a party.

"Within ten minutes Ted and I both experienced this revelation that came to us like daylight dawning on people who'd lived their whole lives in caves. For years, on opposite sides of the continent, we'd both had this sense of desperately wanting to connect with somebody and miserably being unable to make that connection. Ted and I left the frat house almost immediately, and we walked all over the campus. It was a clear September evening with the weather just turning from summer into fall. We walked downtown and back again. We even went to the football stadium and climbed over a fence and trotted out onto the football field and ran around like idiots, and then finally lay down, side by side, right out there on the fifty yard line and looked up at the stars and talked and talked and talked. When the sun came up that morning we were still lying on the grass out there talking."

Dr. Prendergast glances over at Dr. Lawson — whose face is red now — and he stops talking right there. He's still looking around and grinning at us, but he doesn't have to say anything else for us to understand him: he's come to the end of what he had to tell us.

Once we start applauding, we realize what we really want to do. We give him a standing ovation.

IT'S LATE AFTERNOON.

Once we've checked out our rooms, we're eager to get closer to the water. Most of us have ocean views from our windows, but we're hungry for the ocean itself. We're so close we'd probably break through police barriers if they were between us and that water. Faulkeses are genetically disposed to distrust elevators. So out in the hallways we find staircases and clatter down them — some of us in shorts and sandals, others in flip-flops and bathing suits and carrying towels — to assemble where our father said we should wait for him. Soon he appears, also in shorts and carrying a small box of beach tags, which he distributes among us. He tells us to go ahead while he waits for our mother. We troop out into the sunlight, fidget and pace until the crosswalk's light turns green, scurry like lemmings across Beach Avenue, make our way up to the boardwalk, where we can hear the surf, then file through the entranceway, and finally scatter out across the sand, most of us running or trotting toward the water. Isobel goes flying out ahead of everyone, then makes a dead stop at the water's edge, looks back at us, flings an arm up to point to the ocean horizon, and shouts "Come on!"

It's a rare Faulkes who's a good swimmer — the majority of us are nonswimmers, which is just how we are in our family. We're landlubbers. That fact had remained far back in our minds as we made the long journey from home down to Cape May, and it came forward in our thoughts only slightly as we changed into beach clothes in the hotel and crossed the street and trotted across the sand. At the water's edge, however, with our toes and ankles shocked by the cool temperature and the breakers rolling toward us, we suddenly remember — probably all of us in unison — what lousy swimmers we are. Some of us step back from the water to gaze out over its moving surface with mixed feelings, while others venture forward. Only Desi has the courage simply to lift her arms, point them, curve her body, and dive forward into the face of a breaker. She comes up and begins thrashing her arms and legs in a swim-like fashion, but soon she finds her feet can touch bottom, so she stands up, spews water and snot from her mouth and nose, wipes her face, and laughs back at us. If not for that child, we might all have taken the cowardly option. We've seen that we have it in us to become beach potatoes. But because Desi is out there — and clearly enjoying herself — C.J. and Emily and McKenzie and William and Peter and Isobel and Sarah Jean all wade in and head out beyond the breakers. Though they don't actually swim a great deal, it isn't necessary. They hunker down and bob up and down with the waves, they giggle and splash and demonstrate that Faulkeses do have it in them to enjoy the beach.

Jane remains the last of our shore-standers, a little off to herself. A breeze blows back her hair. She has on a new navy-blue one-piece. The afternoon isn't cold, but Jane holds her arms crossed in front of her. We keep glancing back at her, because though no one has said so, we understand that this is a crucial moment for her. After all, without meaning to, Jane instigated the Farewell Tour with her emotional collapse from shouldering too many burdens. She's started eating again, though not with her old appetite, and she's still skinny by Faulkes standards. Her face appears to us washed with feelings that change as she stands there. At first her mouth is tight and her brow wrinkled, but over the course of several minutes, with the breeze and the vast moving sea out there, the gulls, the sand, and the shouts and laughter on all sides of her, the lines of Jane's face smooth out. Though she never actually smiles, an expression of serenity settles in and stays. When she raises her arm to wave at Desi and Isobel and William, they yell to her. "Come in, Jane! Come in!" Their voices are faint, but their words are clear.

We see Jane raise both hands to her mouth to shout back at them, but then she shakes her head and simply begins walking forward. The breakers splash her and stop her and knock her back, but Jane continues walking straight out through the surf to the ones who called to her. The four of them put their arms around each other's shoulders and bounce up and down and around in a circle. Then others of us out there notice them, move toward them, and insist on joining the circle. The circle becomes ridiculously huge when all of us try to join it. We can't do it with so many non-Faulkeses in the water among us, but it doesn't matter — we have constructed an occasion of family exuberance in the hospitably shallow water alongside the New Jersey Shore.

From out in the water, we see them coming —

our father on one side of our mother, Dr. Lawson on the other, with Dr. Prendergast and Sally Anderson following along. They move slowly; people make way, then stare at them as they pass. These spectators must wonder who they're seeing — a celebrity, an invalid, or one of those wealthy widows like Mrs. Astor, someone whose wealth and fame requires that she be accompanied by an entourage. We're certain that not a one of those people knows or can imagine that it's just Mr. and Mrs. Faulkes from the little village of Goshen far to the north, a middle-aged couple notable for being the parents of an unusually large number of children. Our mother wears a wide-brimmed straw hat, sunglasses, and a wide-sleeved, bright yellow beach dress long enough to touch the tops of her feet.

"Incognito," C.J. says with a sly grin. "The latest in beach wear." We give him a look. Our little ones don't know what he's talking about, but the older ones get it and wonder how long it will take C.J. to figure out that his mind is not truly that of a Faulkes.

The sight of our mother settling into the beach chair our father opens for her draws us out of the water and directly to her. We want her to see us, want her to acknowledge our pluck in getting ourselves out beyond the breakers, want her to know that we are children brave enough to swim in the Atlantic Ocean — even though none of us actually swam more than a stroke or two. We stand around her, dripping salt water, toweling off, chattering our descriptions of what the water's like, touching her sleeves, her hat brim, her shoulders. Sally stands with us, almost as close to her as we are. Our mother's hands are pulled up into her sleeves, and her sunglasses hide most of her face. Without even being able to see very much of her actual person, we can tell she's exhausted from the journey and intimidated by the rolling waves in front of her and struggling against the confusion of her children surrounding her and speaking to her all at once. But we can also feel that she wants us here with her, and so we stand as close as we can to her without being weird about it. We realize that she's not so much speaking to us as making faint crooning noises, clicks of her tongue, an *ooo* and an *ahhh* every now and then. She's speaking to us in Aquatic Mammal or Crustacean.

"Excuse me, please," Dr. Prendergast says, needing some of us to move away from our mother's immediate vicinity. He's pushed a post into the sand behind her chair, and now he's raising an umbrella over her. Dr. Lawson explains that because of her medication, sunlight won't be good for our mother but that since it's late in the day and she's covered up, he thinks it won't be a problem. He admonishes us to keep an eye on her, though, and to help her stay covered. We've gotten used to Dr. Lawson, and even though he still seems pretty smitten with our mother, we now understand it's not anything we should worry about. After all, he's never made a move on her, at least not one that any of us has noticed. And our father seems fine with him. All that being said, there's a peculiar neutrality about him. It's as if his interest in us Faulkeses is professional, but also personal. The disturbance we used to feel around him has vanished. Even so, though we've never said it aloud, most of us think there's something about him that we're not getting.

"Hey, hey!" we hear. "Patricia Faulkes! Colleen Faulkes." We turn to see who's calling from so far away. "Delmer Faulkes Junior. Patrick Faulkes." Without our noticing what he was doing, our father has gone out into the water, and when we finally pick him out among the swimmers, we see that he's farther out than we were, he's up to his shoulders in the water, and he's bobbing up and down waving to us. "Jane Faulkes. Desiree Faulkes," he calls. At first, the sight of him so far away troubles us a little, but as we stare at him, we realize that he's just full of himself. And that he's actually not out over his head — his feet are touching bottom. "Peter Faulkes. Emily Faulkes!" he calls. *Joyful* isn't a word we'd ever think of using for our father, but it's hard for us not to see him waving like this and hear his voice without suspecting him of joy in that moment. "William Faulkes! Kathryn Faulkes! Tony Faulkes!" We know he's not going to stop until he's called out every one of our names. We look around as he does it. The face of whichever son or daughter whose name he calls brightens. One or two step forward when they hear the name — as if they mean to make their way out through the surf to where our father stands, shouting and waving his arms. "C.J. Faulkes! Sarah Jean Faulkes! Larry Faulkes!" he calls.

"I think he's gone back to being twelve years old," our mother says.

Dinner is at Henry's By The Sea.

At the center of the menu is Henry's Famous Fried Fish Sandwich with Curly Fries. Our father persuades us all to have the same meal, then he asks the manager for a discount. The manager agrees, and we cheer. We're at tables under the awning with only a flimsy wooden wall between us and the sand leading down to the water. A sumptuous breeze blows in on us. A few of the boys order seconds on the fish sandwich, while a few of the girls don't finish theirs and say next time we eat out they hope they can order what they want. On the way down here we packed food on the bus to eat. The only times we've ever eaten out as a family, we've just had a bunch of different kinds of pizza and split them up according to who likes what. We wonder how we're going to manage while we're here and when we get to Washington, D.C., and when we go, God Forbid, to Hamlin, Pennsylvania, where probably they've never seen a family like ours before. This question gives us something to talk about, and we are darned happy doing it with a sea breeze blowing in our faces and some of us still chewing the last few fries, and ice cream coming to us for dessert. Even our mother's spirits have lifted. We watch her snake a bone-thin arm across the tabletop to our father's paper plate to nab one his fries and sneak it back to her mouth and grin at him while she chews the pillaged piece of potato. He pretends not to see her until the fry is entirely in her mouth. Then he pretends to be shocked. She grins. "Yum," she says, smiling flirtatiously. They're putting on this little pageant for us, and we know our mother is pretending she's not almost dead. She looks happy.

There's no good explanation for this.

Or maybe there is an explanation, and it's just too obvious. We're in more luxurious rooms and softer beds than we've ever dreamed of sleeping in. But all up and down our block of rooms, we can't sleep. We're moved by some kind of instinctive herd migration — one by one, we get up in the dark, put on enough clothes to be respectable, and make our way down to the lobby. With the first few of us, we laugh at the coincidence of meeting each other at this time of night. As more join us, we feel sort of awestruck. We wonder what this prophesies for our future. Will we be forever slipping out of beds and leaving our sleeping spouses behind in the middle of the night as we climb into cars and drive many miles to join our brothers and sisters back at the old home place?

Our father joins us. He's wearing a big white terrycloth bathrobe from the closet in his room. He has the same groggy look we all do, the look of a person who wants to sleep but can't. Some of us scoot over to make room for him on the huge couch that has become the center of our gathering. He sits down heavily, then looks silly and dear, arranging his bathrobe around his legs. It's a weird and corny occasion when your father joins you in a hotel lobby at two in the morning. The night-shift desk clerk gives us a look and a polite smile, then disappears back into the office behind the desk.

We're all feeling woozy and sentimental, but then it's awkward, too, because before our father arrived we were fine talking among ourselves without him, but now that he's here — and this big public room is unlike any room in our home — we don't know what to talk about. Our father is yawning like he could probably go to sleep right on the couch with Carlton sitting on one side of him and Jessica on the other. So we know he's not going to take charge.

"You know what, Dad," says Colleen, and he answers a muffled *what?* with his hand over his mouth stifling a yawn. "You never have told us any stories from before you and our mother got married. She's told us a few little things, but we don't have any stories from you."

"Oh criminy, Colleen!" He says it like it's an impossible request. Like he wasn't even alive back in those days before he married our mother. Like he's about to tell us it's too late to get into all that. Or maybe he'll just tell her it's out of the question, he's too tired.

"We've got a lot of Old Stanton Faulkes stories to tell our children," Carlton says almost in a whisper because he's a small boy and he's sitting right up against our father. We see him trying hold back a sly smile. "Guess we could pass some of those on to our own kids," he says, kind of muttering down into his chest.

Our father sits up straight. Evidently what Carlton said about the Old Stanton Faulkes legends has struck a nerve. It makes us all the more suspicious that our father was making up Old Stanton Faulkes. The idea of a pack of his lies being passed down to his grandchildren seems to have perked him right up. He's quiet now, and his eyes are hooded, but his posture is upright. We know he's going to tell us something, and he ought to know that we'll wait him out.

"Your mother and I once played together when we were children," he announces. "It was the first time we ever saw each other. I think maybe I was eleven, and she was ten." He looks around at all of us. "A very impressionable time in a person's life," he says. We nod at him.

"I can't remember exactly what made it happen — a church picnic or some kind of family reunion. There were Faulkeses from all over, but there were other people, too. Whatever it was, there weren't ever again any other events like that that I can remember. A one-time occasion is what it was. Nobody even thought to introduce us — she and I just sort of ended up being in each other's vicinity — in a group of kids and youngsters who understood that we were all supposed to go off on our own and leave the adults alone. Later on when your mother and I met each other for real — when we were in our late teens — we both agreed that we remembered each other clearly from that first meeting and that we'd each thought about the other a lot over the years.

"Across a dirt road from the picnic area was a big hillside that a farmer kept mowed, and this will tell you how young most of us kids were. Great fun for us was to run up to the top of that hill, then lie flat on the ground and start ourselves rolling down to the bottom. Then we'd get right up and run to the top again. It was fun, but I almost get out of breath right now, thinking about it. I don't remember your mother and me paying much attention to each other while everybody was rolling down the hill, but after a couple of trips I took a look around the top of the hill. There was a wonderful view for miles around, on three sides of that hill, but then there was also a brick wall around a graveyard. I'd turned in that direction and was just about to walk over there when your mother came up beside me. A regular-looking girl in blue jeans and a red T-shirt. Short and very straight black hair but shiny in the sunlight. Maybe a little more cheerful in the face than the others. She glanced up at me. And these were the first words I remember her speaking to me: 'I wonder if it's locked.'"

"So you might not make much out of words like that. At the time I didn't think it was an unusual thing for anybody to say. Since I was pondering that exact same question, it made sense to me that anybody else standing beside me, looking at the iron gate at the front of that wall, would have the same thought. It was some time later — let's say a week or two — that it came to me that it was like your mother had plucked those exact words right out of my brain. My point is that your mother and I were 'of similar minds' in the first minute of our meeting each other.

"I wasn't surprised or shocked, but I was kind of pleased. I hadn't had much to do with any of the other kids there that day — I don't remember that I even knew any of them — so I'd have probably been pleased if anybody had spoken to me. But at the moment, I just said the next logical thing to say: 'Let's go see.'

"And there you have it," our father says. He leans back into the sofa, acting like that's the whole story. He even closes his eyes, as if now that he has obliged us with what we've asked for, the time has come for him to take a rest. This is our father: nothing makes him half so happy as to have his children panting for more of a story he hasn't finished telling. None of us knows why he's such a tease in this way. He doesn't do it to other people, not even our mother, which makes us think this game he plays is exclusively for us.

The truth is that, frustrating though it may be, we love the game, too. The moment just hangs there — we want him to go on, and he wants to go on, too, but meanwhile there's this family ritual to be carried out.

We wait in silence.

Our father lets his head tilt back even further, lets his mouth open and audibly slows his breath. He might start fake-snoring any second now.

What we know is that his patience is greater than ours. There will always be one of us — almost always one of the littlest of us — who can bear the silence no longer. A few of our oldest ones would keep quiet until he really does go to sleep — we'd do that just to show him that our stubbornness had grown sturdy enough to match his stubbornness. But we also know that he's capable of just letting the rest of story remain untold. He wouldn't do that out of meanness, he'd just do it because we hadn't followed through with our part of the ritual. If we complained, he'd say something like, "Oh, I thought I'd bored you with that old story I was telling. I thought you'd lost interest."

So eventually even the strongest of us would give in and beg him to tell us the rest. Years later one of us will say, "Remember that thing he did when he got us completely hooked on something he was telling?" And the rest of us will hoot and hiss and holler about how awful he was and how he drove us crazy and how it was cruel of him to enjoy our frustration so much. C.J. — who by then will have become a professor of political science at Hampshire College — will raise his voice: "You know there are some therapists who would say that our father was committing child abuse when he did that." Then of course all the rest of us will begin shouting down C.J. and saying how out of touch those therapists are and how they don't know anything about big families. If he could hear this, the whole conversation would please our father enormously, because it would be an ongoing continuation—an affirmation, really—of what he calls the Faulkes dynamic. "Once a Faulkes, always a Faulkes," he often proclaims, as if he has a direct connection with Old Stanton Faulkes and the two of them have much to be proud of.

"Don't stop, Daddy," Carlton whispers up to him. Carlton has an angelic look on his face, but when our father actually releases a snore in response to Carlton's directive, Carlton gives him a firm elbow-nudge to the rib cage. Our father sits up, looking all around as if he's just been pulled out of a sound sleep. "What?" he says, faking confusion and disorientation.

"Keep going, please." Carlton's face is still angelic when our father glances down at him.

"Oh yeah. Where was I?" our father says.

"Let's go see!" About half of us shout out his cue.

"Oh, yeah. 'Let's go see.' Okay, I got it. 'Let's go see,' I told your mother, and the two of us walked over to the closed gate. When she put a hand on it and tugged very lightly, that gate came open like it had just been waiting for her to come along and give it the old magic touch.

She and I were both surprised and maybe a little spooked, but of course we stepped in. Softly, like we'd seen a do-not-disturb sign posted on the gate. It was that kind of a graveyard, actually—it made you go quiet just to step into it. It was about the size of a baseball infield—sort of cozy, but at the same time, sort of spacious. The brick wall set it off from the big field, then there were these hundred-year-old cedar trees towering over the grass and the rows of stones. In each corner of the cemetery there were boxwood bushes that must have been planted when they put in the cedar trees. Then right in the center there was a huge boxwood. Maybe twenty or thirty yards away on the other side of the wall, the kids were still shouting and laughing and rolling down the hill, but we could barely hear them.

"Your mother and I stood there quietly for a minute or so, then we started having a look at some of the gravestones. That's what there is to do when you go into a graveyard — start getting acquainted with the residents. There were maybe seventy-five or eighty graves, some of them only ten or fifteen years old, but most of them had been there fifty or sixty years. A few went back to the 1850s. And there were regular stones, about a dozen sizable rectangular concrete lockers, and a few ornately carved stones. Nothing really huge or commanding, the way you see in some cemeteries. We separated off from each other, following our own inclinations from one grave to another.

"'Little Charley,' your mother called out. 'Safe in the arms of Jesus,' she said. I couldn't tell if she was cheerful or sad with what she'd found. Maybe she didn't know either. I went over there, and we both stood at Little Charley's feet. His dates were May 23, 1917, to January 12, 1920. It was strange the way the information on the stone — and even the carved roses on either side of his name, or rather nickname — made you start seeing this kid in your mind. Like falling under a spell. When we finally did move away from Little Charley, I remember shaking my head and wondering why we had stood there so long.

"Not far from there was Betty, with nothing else but just her dates. But you knew she'd died when she was only two. 'Wonder why no family name,' I said out loud. Your mother just shook her head. You'd think she and I would have had much more to say to each other than we did, because we really had fallen into a kind of partnership in our exploring. I don't think either of us had anything like a love-interest then — and we both knew plenty of kids our age who got crushes on other kids. So it wasn't like we didn't know anything about 'young love,' we just hadn't yet thought of it applying to us. Or maybe neither one of us had yet grown into the person the other one would get a crush on. But from the moment we'd stepped over to that gate, we'd become instant pals. Pals for the moment, maybe, or pals for the occasion, because I'm pretty sure neither of us had been thinking any further ahead than stepping inside that brick wall, staying a while and then coming out and probably rolling down the hill some more.

"She and I separated off from each other again. We'd become extremely involved in reading what the writing on the gravestones had to tell us, and that's an activity that automatically sends you off on your own. It's funny how one stone sends you to the one beside it, because you'll see that that one was the wife and the next one is the husband, and in the next row down, it's a son or a daughter. I got very caught up in reading the inscriptions on the stones, most of them verses from the Bible, but a few of them poems or maybe even just words the family decided to put on the stone. Each one was a little speech the dead person made to you while you stood there.

"The sunlight gradually changed from mid-day to mid-afternoon, a kind of deepening that turned the grass a little more golden and softened the newer stones just half a shade of gray. The day was settling into itself — I felt that happening without giving it any thought, first with my body and then maybe a little while later with my mind. I was staring at the inscription on some old guy's stone — *My strength has the strength of ten because my heart is pure*—and I remember wondering how you could know if your heart was pure, because I wanted to believe that mine was pure—remember, I was eleven then, so to me the thought of a pure heart wasn't out of the question—but I could think of lots of reasons why mine might not be pure. I wasn't so deep in my thoughts that I didn't hear your mother call out something to me from a little ways off. But her voice didn't sound urgent, and so I didn't immediately turn and start walking straight to her, I just lingered there beside the grave of this guy, because I was wondering if the dead guy was the one who had picked out those words for his stone or if it was his family who'd wanted visitors to believe their old man had had a pure heart. But then I turned to see what my new pal had found that'd made her call out.

"And your mother was gone. Or she was invisible. Or I'd just imagined her and she'd never been there in the first place. It was the strangest moment I'd had in my life up to that time. I turned in a circle where I stood. Then I started searching anywhere that looked like a hiding place. I'd have called out her name, but I didn't know it yet—this was when I realized that we hadn't even exchanged names with each other! I did call out, 'Hey! Hey!' But I didn't do it very loudly. I could hear the other kids calling out from beyond the wall, and they seemed far away. I don't know why, but I felt certain your mother wouldn't have gone back out there without letting me know. The thought that she'd just evaporated made me feel like I'd wandered into somebody's dream. I got this desire to sit down on the grass and put my face in my hands.

"Then I heard the boxwood bush in the middle of the graveyard start laughing at me. To my credit I quickly figured out that she was inside it. That bush was as big as a medium-size dinosaur, I'd noticed that, but I hadn't thought of a boxwood as having an inside. Now I saw an opening that made me have to stoop down to get a look inside. Your mother was in there, on her hands and knees, a grin on her face, very pleased with herself. She had an empty plastic Dr Pepper bottle in her hand, which she waved at me. 'I looked in here because I saw the sun making this bottle sparkle, and from out there I couldn't tell what it was,' she told me. 'Then when I saw what it was, I came in to get it, because just leaving it would have been wrong. Some idiot threw it in here. But look at this place,' she said, and I heard the excitement in her voice. 'Isn't it like a secret room?'"

"Well, I saw what she meant — that big boxwood had this inner chamber that you'd never know about unless you deliberately walked up and stuck your head in the opening. There was room in there for your mother and another two or three kids her size. The sunlight slanted in through small openings in the top and sides, so that the interior glowed with this yellow-green light. The floor was dirt, of course, but since she and I had recently been rolling down the hillside, neither one of us was much concerned about messing up our clothes. 'Come in here,' she told me. 'There's something you have to see.'

"Before she finished inviting me in, I was down on my hands and knees. I still believe this was a kid thing — that I wasn't scrambling in there because she was a girl and I was a boy. A) I wanted just to get into that space to see what it felt like to be inside the boxwood, and B) I wanted to see what she'd found. Of course I probably did feel a little excitement about going in there with her. But cozying up with her certainly wasn't my main thought right then.

"Once I was inside, I felt how much cooler it was, and the smell of boxwood and slightly damp earth was thick all around us. Your mother backed away a little bit to give me room to see what she wanted me to see. Until that moment I hadn't noticed. 'It's a gravestone,' she said. 'This bush just swallowed it up. Take a look.'

"About the size of a person's head, the stone was darkened and damp from being always in the shade. I had to scootch myself up close to see what she was showing me. 'See the writing on it?' she asked. Her low voice made me aware of how close we were to each other. 'It's a name, isn't it?' she asked. I put my fingers on the stone's surface to try to get a sense of what the name was. I could tell that most of the engraved front of the stone had been chipped or cracked and fallen away. But she was right, there was a smooth surface still left with a single name on the lower right hand side — there'd probably been a first name, too, but that writing was long gone.

"'Davis.' My fingers helped me make it out, and I said the name aloud. Then I felt some other writing farther down on the stone. I scootched even closer. The writing was tantalizing — it was just visible enough for me to see that there were dates, but I couldn't make them out. I rubbed on that place with my fingers and squinted. 'March 18,' I said. Then, '1901.'

"Your mother repeated what I'd said, as if she might have been writing my words down — though I knew she wasn't. It took me a long time to figure out the other date. It was only about an inch above the dirt. I scratched at the engraving with my fingernail and still couldn't make it out. Just when I was about to give up, I heard myself say, 'August 2, 1912.' The whole date came across my tongue as if it had gone straight from the stone to my fingertips to my brain and out my mouth in a single instant.

"She and I said nothing, and we hardly moved for what felt like several minutes. Long enough for me to notice how close we were to each other. I could hear her breathing, and she must have heard me, too. Then your mother said, very quietly, 'He was eleven.' That, too, was a thought that had been sitting in my brain. *He's our age.* And that was maybe the second strangest moment of my life up to that point. Six feet below where your mother and I were hunkered down beside each other inside the secret space of that huge boxwood bush were Davis's — *remains*, I guess you'd have to say was what was down there. If there was anything at all. You could say there were three of us kids in there right then.

"After a while I asked your mother, 'How do you know Davis was a he?'

"'I don't know,' she said. 'But I know he was.'

"We said no more while we were in there. Finally your mother made a little outward-waving gesture with her hand, from which I gathered it was time to leave. I scooted out, and she came right behind me. We stood up right beside the boxwood, blinking and looking around as if that bush had been a spaceship that had just let us out back on own planet. It felt like we'd been gone a long time.

"Then your mother started for the gate with me right behind her. We were surprised to see that outside the brick wall, there wasn't a single kid around. The hillside was huge and bare. It was quiet, too, but we could hear the crowd of people down in the picnic area over on the other side of the road, and so we knew they must be starting to serve up the food. When she and I started down the hill,

I remembered to ask her name. She turned and told me what it was and stuck out her hand. So we actually paused for a moment there on the grass-flattened hillside to have a handshake. I told her my name then and said, 'Pleased to meet you,' which made her laugh and say, 'Pleased to meet you, too.' For some reason, we both felt like we had to act like grown-ups."

Many of us are asleep —

including our father — there in the lobby. The clock over the registration desk shows the time to be approaching three a.m. The few of us still awake have our eyes closed, and we are in the mode of exchanging goofy observations in low murmurs. We should go upstairs to our rooms and our beds, because we're right on the verge of sleep. And certainly no one is alert. Which accounts for only Desi and Peter noticing when our mother emerges from the elevator in search of her family. She's evidently gathered enough strength to make her way down here, and she has on a T-shirt that once fit her normally but now is so baggy it looks like a big gray sack. Also blue jeans from when she was in seventh grade, rescued from an old bag of clothes in the back of her closet. The dimmed-down lights of the hotel lobby make her skin — and especially that of her bare head — look gray and papery. When those of us who are awake first notice her, she has lurched her way to the big sofa in the center of which our father snores softly with his head back and Carlton and Jessica, on either side of him, pillowing their heads against his sides. Our mother sits up straight on the sofa arm, looking around at the scene of her family bivouacked like an army platoon in among the chairs, sofas, and rugs of the Cape May Inn. Her eyes are huge. The dimmed lights have dilated her pupils, and her expression is expectant.

Cassie has cuddled up with Susan, the two of them asleep in a big easy chair directly across from where our mother has stationed herself. Cassie later says she woke from a deep sleep in which she'd dreamed that our mother was looking at her, and when she woke up, there was our mother looking at her. "Which freaked me out a little bit," Cassie said. Now she disentangles herself from Susan and goes to our mother and puts her arms around her. More and more we all do this, put our arms around our mother, because her very emaciated state seems to be a request for physical comforting. She perhaps appreciates our hugs, but for the one who embraces her, the experience is mildly distressing. "Until you put your arms around her, you don't realize how little of her there is," says Cassie later that morning. At the moment of the embrace, however, Cassie just murmurs, "What's up, Mom?"

"I want to go out there," our mother says. She isn't keeping her voice down. It's not like her to be so inconsiderate of us, but then nowadays she's less and less her old self.

Some of us stir and make soft grunts or smacking noises with our mouths. As if he's heard an alarm go off, our father sits straight up on the sofa and looks directly at her. He, too, might have been dreaming about her, so that with waking now he's known exactly where to look. "Where's that, sweetheart?" he asks.

Our mother flaps her hand toward the main entranceway of the hotel. "Where else?" she says. "There's only one place I want to be," she says. "And that's out there."

Our father asks her if she realizes what time it is, and she assures him that she does. "All the more reason," she says.

We stir and stretch and stand up and set ourselves in

motion. The older boys take on the task of gathering and assembling the components of Her Majesty's Traveling Throne, which are still tied to the back of the small bus. The older girls help our little ones find and put on sweaters and flip-flops. Most of us need no jostling or having our names called — as if we'd gone to sleep knowing we'd be called to action before daylight. We aren't grumpy as we go about getting ready for the excursion across the street and out to the beach, but neither are we anything like as excited as we'd been the previous afternoon. This is a task to be accomplished — taking our mother out for a nighttime view of the sea — and a task to a Faulkes is something to be carried out with an even temper, even when it may not be to one's liking.

Outside there's a warm wind blowing in from across Beach Avenue into our faces. When Creighton raises his arm to point it out to us, we see an almost full moon silvering up the sky to the north of us. Cassie has fetched a sweater for our mother, and William and Patrick have brought pillows for her. Evidently the air from the sea has given her some strength. It's cheering to see her mount the traveling throne and settle herself in. She's still regal and still very peculiarly appealing in her proximity to death. Dr. Lawson, Dr. Prendergast, and Sally Anderson mysteriously appear in the crowd of us readying ourselves for this night safari. We have no idea what has alerted the doctors and the hospice worker to our plan, but it's fine with us to have them along. They're certainly not Faulkeses, but they might as well be now. Somewhere during our journey down the Garden State Parkway, they became our fellow travelers.

When our designated carriers hoist up the throne with

our mother seated among Her Majesty's pillows, the two doctors station themselves along one side of her, and Sally Anderson walks on the other side. We must look like some kind of bizarre wedding party making our way across the deserted avenue, up onto the boardwalk, then out through the beach entrance. But we see no one anywhere. So far as we know our caravan makes its journey entirely without witnesses.

Down ahead of us lies a long field of dull gray sand, then a band of bright silver catching the moonlight at the water's edge. Out there the deep black ribbon of water rises into whitened breakers rolling toward us, then back away from us. Out on the ocean's surface, white scallops of froth appear and disappear over the wide horizon of blackness. A deep and constant thrumming sounds louder and louder as we approach. Silly though it may be of us, that earth-deep rumbling conjures up a vision in our minds of a tsunami. Were any one of us out here alone, the grand spectacle and that huge sound that accompanies it would very likely intimidate that Faulkes child and send him or her scampering back up to the boardwalk to view the sea from a safe distance. So it is a comfort to be among others — and to us children, a special comfort to be led across the sand and toward the dark water by our father. In the face of the great planetary forces, our father is as puny and feeble as a sand crab — we recognize that. But he's shepherded us through our lives up to this point, he's fed us, clothed us, and given us a safe place to sleep. Now with our mother so ill, above every other person and everything else we know in life, our father is the one we trust, the one who'll do everything in his power to protect us to the end.

From atop Her Majesty's Traveling Throne, our mother shouts and points. In the windy darkness, she's Queen Death herself above our heads, flinging out her bone of an arm. "I want to be over there!" Her voice surprises us with its power, since we know her to weigh no more than eighty pounds. She's bracing herself to stand up behind the chair, so as to be able to see farther ahead. She's greedy to take in everything.

A white-painted lifeguard tower is where she wants us to transport her, enough of a distance up the beach that we have to set the throne down and switch to a second team of carriers. When they lower her to our level, her eyes are widened, her face animated. Sally Anderson steadies her as she steps down to the sand to look from one to the other of us, the wind catching our hair and blowing it. "You're my angel escort!" she shouts at us, reaching out and touching C.J.'s and Emily's and Carlton's faces. "My angel offspring," she says softly to those ones near her then. Then she mounts Her Majesty's Throne again, the new team of carriers hoists her up, and we turn parallel to the water, plodding into the wind as we head toward the white tower in the distance.

Flimsy clouds pass over the face of the moon, so that one minute we're washed with pale light and the next we're darkened by shadows passing over us. The distance to the lifeguard tower seems to remain exactly the same for a long while, though we've plodded and leaned into this wind for many footsteps. Our carriers ask for yet another shifting of the task, and this time the four grown-ups do the hoisting of our mother and the hard plodding through the sand. When we look up at her in her high place, our mother sits forward in her chair, her bare moon-pale head catching the light, so that it appears too big for the body below. The wind blows her T-shirt against her chest, making it all the more evident how little of her there is left. And yet, when her face beams down to one or another of us, her eyes glitter and we can almost feel on our skin the force of her gaze.

"Hold on, love!" our father calls to her when we arrive at the lifeguard tower. "We're going to lift the throne so you can just step over into the chair." It sounds like a wild idea, but the four grown-ups lift that contraption above their heads, and smooth as a circus trick our mother steps across to the tower.

"I didn't realize how strong I was," says Sally Anderson, breathing hard, when she and the three men set down Her Majesty's Traveling Throne.

"The real trick will be to get her down from there," says Dr. Prendergast.

Our mother is up there,

and so are the other grown-ups. It's crowded, but that's how our mother wants it. Our father sits on one side of her, Sally Anderson on the other. The oncologist and Dr. Prendergast perch on the far edges of the platform. The five of them are squeezed in very tight — though our mother hardly counts as a full adult body. We children, old and young and in between, sit on the sand beneath the tower. We, too, huddle in near each other, though we're not cold. The wind is damp, but it's warm. Even so, in the moonlit darkness and just ten yards from the edge of the Atlantic Ocean, we're uneasy enough to want to be close to our brothers and sisters. We stay quiet so as to be able to hear the conversation above our heads. Or maybe, since we can't really make out more than a word or two, we just want to hear the noise their voices make. They don't say much, and we hear nothing from our mother. She's perhaps listening as intently from her place in the middle of the line of them up on the lifeguard's bench as we are from our place below the tower. Dr. Prendergast grunts or hums occasionally, but the conversation is mostly the voices of our father and Dr. Lawson, baritone and tenor, with the contralto of Sally Anderson now and then sounding a question or just filling in the silence. Time passes, time stands still — to those of us hunkered down on the sand, it's all the same.

"YOU WHAT?!" SHOUTS OUR FATHER.

The tower shakes as if he's stood up too fast. Immediately other voices up there respond in tones we recognize as conciliatory. Dr. Lawson speaks in what we remember from our first encounter with him in the hospital is his professional voice, a voice that explains and teaches. We're stirring among ourselves — the few of us who have nodded off to sleep are suddenly wide awake. It's hard for us to make out everything he says, though we pick up some phrases: "It was either that or... We can never be certain ... I assure you..." The tower shakes again. We hear a sound we know to be our mother's voice, then Sally Anderson saying very clearly, "Let's be calm. We can talk about this. We can talk it through." Then Dr. Prendergast speaks up in what is very nearly a shriek, "You don't understand! Just listen to what he has to say!"

The tower shakes again, so violently this time that we move out away from it, trying to see what's going on up there. "YOU MONSTER!" our father shouts. A two-person shadow jumps or falls thudding down onto the sand where we'd been sitting only seconds ago. A cloud slides away from the face of the moon quickly enough for us to see that it's our father and Dr. Lawson rolling around wrestling with each other in the sand. Dr. Prendergast starts climbing down but then jumps and tries to separate them, but in a few seconds he's pulled down with them so that the three men writhe in the sand, grunting and panting, and our father shouts again, "YOU MEDICAL THUG! YOU HEARTLESS GOON!"

Confused and frightened as we are, we know we have to stop this fighting. Peter and Jane and Emily and Tony and C.J. scramble around them and try to take hold of one of the men — we can't even see who's taken hold of which of the fighters — but our brothers and sisters are not strong or determined enough to have much effect on the turmoil taking place on the sand. The grunting and wheezing of the men makes the rest of us want to shrink away from their desperate commotion. Desi's crying. Colleen and Patrick are whimpering.

Sally Anderson climbs down carefully — all the way down to the sand — not especially hurrying but definitely moving with purpose. Creighton and Delmer Junior reach up to help her. She steps over to the struggling figures. Once down on the sand, she walks straight into the fray, bends, takes hold of Dr. Prendergast, and amazingly pulls him up away from the other two and flings him back into the crowd of us as if he were a child rather than a grown man. When he starts back toward the other two fighters, John Milton and Pruney and Robert place themselves in front of him and push him back.

Now Sally has hold of our father, who has used a wrestling hold to pin the oncologist facedown in the sand and who is not so easily separated from Dr. Lawson. Sally is not to be deterred, though — she kneels down on the sand, stretches an arm around our father's neck, her elbow under his chin, then leans back with our father flailing his arms in the air. "Stop it!" she shouts directly into his ear so loudly that she stuns our father into ceasing his flailing and writhing.

Dr. Lawson rolls away from where Sally holds our father against herself. Instead of standing up, the oncologist stays facedown on the sand wheezing and moaning. We children also breathe hard, as if we, too, have been wrestling with the men. Then our father rasps, "Okay, okay." Sally slightly loosens her hold around his neck and speaks into his ear. "Will you stop now?" Our father nods, and Sally lets him go.

The whole pack of us whimpers softly as if we've all been punished for something. The ocean's thrumming continues with no regard for any human disturbance, but now our hearing is so acute we can make out the little swishing noises the tide makes as it washes onto the shore, the shrill gull cries heard from far away. Sally stands up, brushes herself off. Our father stays on the sand, lying flat on his back, still breathing hard, but now gazing skyward. We all stay quiet for some time, everyone listening for something, maybe the sound of a police or ambulance siren. It seems beyond belief to us that such an outburst of violence could have occurred here without the rest of the world taking some notice.

Finally Sally says in a normal voice, "I think you gentlemen should do some talking. These children will need some help understanding the show you've just put on for them."

Peter and Carlton and Delmer Junior go to help our father to his feet — they even take it upon themselves to brush sand off his back and arms and chest. Dr. Prendergast steps over to help up his friend, the oncologist. All three men have stopped breathing quite so heavily. Dr. Lawson swipes at his nose with the back of his hand and examines it carefully for blood. Our father seems to have hurt his hand or his wrist.

"So what do you have to say to us?" Sally asks them. Her voice is not angry, but she folds her arms in front of her, and looks from one to the other of the men.

Finally Dr. Lawson shrugs. "I told him," he says. His voice is so low the wind carries the words away before we can take them in.

"I heard you," Dr. Prendergast says. "I knew that was what you were telling him. Why on earth did you do it?"

We're still straining to understand what's made our father so furious, but from Dr. Prendergast's voice, we suddenly understand that he and Dr. Lawson have been keeping something from us.

"You were up there! You know how it felt! Like we were all in this together!" The oncologist's voice conveys such deep remorse that we can't help feeling some sympathy for him, no matter what he told our father. "And anyway it had to come out eventually. You know it did."

All three men stay quiet for a while. We're aware that our father is kind of snorting now, as if his anger is taking hold of him again.

Dr. Lawson extends his hands, palms up, toward Dr. Prendergast. "Like we all felt about her the same way — so there was nothing to hide!" Dr. Lawson sobs and swipes at his nose with his fist again.

We don't know how we could have done this after she's dominated our thoughts for so many weeks and months, but we'd momentarily forgotten about our mother. Peter is the first of us to lift his head in her direction. When we see him staring up there, the rest of us almost in unison turn our heads up toward the bench atop the lifeguard tower. She's there — or the silhouette of her is — sitting forward, to see us standing in little groups below her. Her face is shadowed so that we can't make out her expression. She says nothing, but seeing her above us now, we can feel how intently she's witnessing what's transpiring down here on the sand.

Jane steps directly in front of Dr. Lawson. "What did you tell our father?" she asks him. Her voice has no threat or anger in it. Wind sweeps her hair in every direction. When he doesn't answer her, she lowers her voice and speaks very slowly to him as if the two of them are alone. "You know we all need to know. No matter what it is. We've all come this far with her."

The oncologist looks around at all of us. His eyes settle on our father's face for a moment. He swipes at his nose again, then turns back to face Jane. He's panting. "I've been treating — your mother — with an experimentally — enhanced Ipilimumab," he says. His voice stops and starts, squeaks and rasps, but he repeats the word for us. "Ipilimumab."

"Explain that, please," Jane asks him softly.

Our father can't restrain himself, though he's not screaming the way he was. "It means she can't die!" His voice is breaking as he speaks. "It means she has to keep going on and on until every cell in her body rots into nothingness!" He turns his back to us and puts his hands over his face. But after a moment our father turns slightly and takes one of his hands away from his wet face to gesture toward Dr. Lawson. "Ask him!" he shouts. "He'll tell you! He's been experimenting on your mother!"

As if to be sure that our father has finished what he was going to say, Dr. Lawson bows his head and waits in the silence. When he speaks this time, he has switched over to his professional voice. We're shocked to hear how calm he's become. "That's not quite right, but it's close enough. I was trying to explain to your father that because we couldn't operate on your mother, we can't understand her tumor with any precision. And this drug is only beginning to be used for other forms of cancer than melanoma. So we couldn't really know how it would play out with your mother. We took a chance. And now she's already stayed with us about seven weeks beyond the time we were certain would be her limit if we didn't do something. So we're pretty sure the drug is sustaining her in a way we'd have to describe as abnormal or at least unusual. But there wasn't time for testing — "

"Your mother *is* the test!" shouts our father, his voice muffled by his hands.

"Your mother is not a test," says the oncologist, raising his voice and shaking his head. "Your mother is my dear friend," he says. He looks up at her when he says it. "*My dear friend*," he repeats with emphasis on each word. Then he hushes for a long while as he looks at her. "I knew this treatment was problematic. I discussed the issues with Leo here." He nods toward Dr. Prendergast. "And he told me that calling it problematic was an understatement. He advised me not to do it. And I went ahead anyway. I did it because — " He catches his breath. Then he blurts, "I did it for personal reasons!"

Dr. Prendergast puts his arm around Dr. Lawson's shoulder. The two of them stand there blinking at us, as if they expect us to start heaving stones at them any minute.

"We're at your mercy," Dr. Lawson says, and Dr. Prendergast nods.

The wind blows steadily over us, the deep thrumming from far out in the sea keeps sounding, and the little waves break and wash up on the sand. The moon has angled down toward the northern horizon, and the sky out to the east may be lightening. We can't grasp what we think or what we feel, but the world keeps reminding us how present it is, how it is here with us right now, and will be here tomorrow and the day after that.

Sally Anderson breaks the silence. "I didn't hear what you said, Dr. Lawson," she says. Her voice makes it clear she's speaking to all of us. "I didn't hear a word of it. Because it doesn't make the slightest bit of difference. We're here, and she's here." Sally gestures up toward the tower where our mother still sits leaning toward us as if she intends to dive forward into our arms.

Now it's our mother who speaks into the silence. "What Dr. Lawson didn't tell your father, I'm going to tell you." Our mother is tired now — we know that voice of hers. It's the way she sounds when she really needs to go bed and get some sleep. "I begged him to give that drug to me. I knew they only thought it *might* work. I knew they didn't know what else it might do to me. I didn't care about that. I wanted more time. Even if it was just thirty seconds. I wanted it. And look what it has given me!" She flings up that bony arm again and waves it over our heads, as if she's just now been handed the deed to the whole planet along with the ocean out there and this crowd of children below her.

"I wanted — " For a suspended instant our mother struggles to stand upright on the tower as if her passionate desire right now is to rise up through the moonlit darkness into the blackness around the stars. "I wanted — " she says again. Her voice has gone hoarse. When we see her begin to waver up there, trying to keep her balance, our hands all lift toward her. "You all — "

She doesn't finish. She really does fall — or topple — forward. And it's all of us pressed tightly together at the base of the lifeguard tower — Dr. Lawson, Dr. Prendergast, Sally Anderson, and our father, too — every one of us there with our arms lifted up, waiting to catch our mother.

"She can't die?"

This is Desi asking the question. But of course it's the question that's deviled all of us ever since we dragged ourselves back from the lifeguard tower. It's late morning now, it's raining, and most of us have found our way to a circular arrangement of tables and chairs at one corner of the Inn's massive porch. The ones who got here first claimed the available rockers; others of us lean against the porch railing. Desi herself sits cross-legged on a woven hemp mat at the center of the conversation area. She's leaning forward, and her head is bowed as if she's meditating or thinking hard. She's too little to have to take up such a question as this one, but we're all in solidarity with her. The question itself hurts us to think about.

Jennifer raises her hand as she would in a class at school. But she starts speaking almost immediately. "Don't we want her to live? I thought this was what we were doing all along. Wanting her to live as long as she can."

"Taking this trip with her to keep her spirits up. Keep her going," says Carlton. He's a middle kid with a good sense of humor, but he's not being funny now. If he weren't a Faulkes, we'd think he was on the verge of tears as he looks into our faces.

We older ones know what's wrong, but we don't want to say. So we all stay silent and listen to the rain and watch people running along Beach Avenue with umbrellas tilted into the wind.

"Yeah," says C.J., finally. "That's what we've all been thinking. Her, too, I guess. Get every last drop of life before you have to check out." Then he sighs and looks around at us. "But it's getting weird," he says. "You have to admit. She's like a mummy. She looks deader than most dead people."

"She's hiding herself," Jane says softly. We don't mind if she sheds a tear or two. She's still in breakdown mode. She can shed some tears for those of us who have kept on being stiff-lipped Faulkeses. "She can barely get down a sip of water," she says in a near whisper.

Our father steps out onto the porch, sees us, and walks over. "Wondered where you were," he says. He leans down and picks up Desi and holds her against his chest with one arm. He's not trying to demonstrate it, but we like seeing him as strong as ever. "I wanted to apologize to you all for behaving the way I did last night," he tells us, though he's pretty much looking at Desi the whole time he's speaking. We murmur *That's all right* and *No problem* and even — this from Tony — *You were about to take him, Dad,* but he raises his free hand to quiet us. He tells us he was all wrong, not only to start calling names and to start a fight. "I was wrong about Ted Lawson, too," he says. "He and I just had a long talk, and I've come around to understanding why he did what he did. He's a good man. He cares as much about your mother as any of us do." He looks around at us, his face sad, but grinning, too. "He didn't have to tell us — and we'd have never known the difference. But he wanted to be one of us. And even after what I did to him last night, he still wants to be one of us." Now it's our father who's about to choke up. We watch him closely, because if he does, it's going to mean something to us, even if we don't yet know what that would be. "It's not just because of your mother," he says. "Here's what he said: 'It's because of that whole crazy contraption of your family.' And I guess it was your mother who taught him that. If he cared about her, then he had to care about us, too."

Again, we make murmuring sounds, though what we're saying isn't nearly so clear this time. But what it comes down to is that if our father wants to take Dr. Lawson into the family, then we do, too. And it goes without anybody saying it out loud that we get Dr. Prendergast and Sally Anderson as part of the deal.

When Peter asks our father

to tell us what Ted Lawson told him, our father rubs his chin and looks at the floor. We're still out on the extravagant porch of the Inn at Cape May. It's not like Peter to ask this of our father — this is more the kind of request one of the younger kids would make. We can see our father weighing in his mind whether or not it's okay to tell us what he found out from Dr. Lawson. "We need to know what you know about him," Peter coaxes him quietly. "After what happened last night — "

Our father lifts his hand. "All right. I'll tell you." He seems brusque at first, but then he settles down. "He'd probably tell you, too, if you asked him the way you're asking me. Right to know, and so on. Maybe better I tell you. Save him having to go through it again. It wasn't so easy for him last night.

"Dancing. He said it all had to do with dancing." Our father shakes his head. "I know it sounds ridiculous," he says, but you'll see that it's not, really. Ted's parents were swing dancers from back in the forties and fifties, the big band days, Count Basie, Benny Goodman, those bands. The Lawsons were fancy people and a handsome couple, still young and light on their feet even after they had kids, and unusually good dancers. All over the country, swing dancing was catching on — the Lindy, the jitterbug, the shag. Ted's parents were among the first people in Los Angeles to start going to the clubs to do that dancing. Ted said he grew up thinking that if they ever had to choose between him and his sister and the jitterbug, they would be out the door while he and his sister would be sitting at home with their grandma. He said he wasn't old enough to question it, but now he understands that his parents felt guilty. He said they felt the most guilt the morning after they'd been out late at the clubs. 'As the day went on the guilt wore off,' he said. So it was not unusual for them to be out three or four nights a week. He said his grandma gave them a lot of grief about it, but they weren't about to give it up. And the grandma never refused when they asked her to look after the kids.

"The way his parents tried to make it up to Ted and his sister was to teach them how to do the dances — starting when they were five and six. They'd teach the kids in the hours between the end of dinnertime and their bedtime. Almost every night. Ted said he and his sister both loved it. It started out for them as just a kind of playing around that their parents wanted to do with them. So that made it exciting from the get-go. When the parents started teaching them the steps, the twirls, the flips, and the tricks, it got even more exciting. Then the better Ted and his sister could do the dancing, the longer they'd get to stay up past their bedtime. Because they were kids, their bodies were naturally suited to the athletic demands of jitterbugging. So before long the kids were as addicted to swing dancing as the parents.

"In a couple of years Ted and his sister were better dancers than their parents, and the parents didn't have anything left to teach them. Meanwhile, the parents' lives got busier and more complicated, so they stopped going to the clubs quite as often. I guess you could say the parents did a little growing up of their own. Ted and his sister started school, and when they were home, they'd go down to the basement to practice their dancing just about every day. They'd invent new steps, new tricks. Or they'd just dance for fun. Ted said he and his sister were completely like-minded — it didn't occur to them that there was anything unusual about what they were doing. They were so close to each other that they didn't even think about that either. When they first started school, none of their classmates had even heard of the jitterbug, let alone tried to do it. But when they reached fourth and fifth grades kids started seeing it on American Bandstand, and some of them were taking dance classes. 'Laurie and I could feel it coming,' Ted said. And they knew that before long there'd come a time when they'd get to show everybody what they could do.

"When Laurie was in eighth grade and Ted was in seventh, they got invited to a classmate's birthday party. 'Classic middle school thing,' Ted called it. He said there was a punchbowl surrounded by little cups, bowls of nuts, and a cake with sticky frosting, chairs around the room, and different-colored paper streamers strung in loops from the ceiling. The parents kept turning the lights up, and the kids kept turning them down, and none of the kids even thought of dancing. The music was turned down pretty low, so you could barely hear it, and it was mostly slow tunes anyway. Even if they'd taken lessons, these kids were still young enough to be self-conscious about walking across the floor to ask somebody to dance. Then Ted said — because the song was new and somebody at the party liked it — they turned up the volume and put on 'Boogie Woogie Bugle Boy.'"

"The Andrews Sisters," pipes up Robert. Our brother's voice startles us and breaks the spell of our father's talking. We look back at Robert and let our faces tell him that we don't like it. He just shrugs. He knows we know he can't help himself when it comes to trivia about music. If Robert knows a fact about a song, he's got to say it out loud.

Our father is amused. And here, too, we know he savors occasions when the Faulkes family dynamic breaks out into the open like this. "Yes, the Andrews Sisters," he says and clears his throat to signal that he's going on with the story.

"'Changed my life,' Ted told me. 'Laurie's, too.' When that song came on, his sister was at one end of the room with some girls, and Ted was at the other end with the boys around the punch bowl. Neither of them hesitated. They met in the middle of the dance floor. In their basement at home, they'd danced to "Boogie Woogie Bugle Boy" maybe fifty or sixty times — it's a great jitterbug tune — and they'd even worked out a showy sequence of steps and twirls and razzmatazz that ended with Ted kneeling and Laurie sitting on his knee at the exact moment the song ended. So you can imagine how people at the party responded to that. 'Do it again! Do it again!' they kept shouting. And Laurie and Ted, they were just blown away by how their schoolmates clapped and yelled and gave Laurie hugs and Ted handshakes. So they were ready to do it again, and they did it even better the second time.'"

Our father paused in his telling a moment before he went on. "Ted said in retrospect he understood that this party — when he was twelve and his sister was thirteen — was far and away the most exciting fifteen minutes or so of his whole life. He and his sister became instant celebrities in their school. 'But we had no idea how it was going to play out from that night on,' Ted told me. Evidently the jitterbug as it was practiced by the people who really knew how it was done had this very specific 'element,' I guess we would call it. It wasn't what you'd see on American Bandstand, but it was how their parents had learned the dance at the clubs. And it was how they'd taught Ted and Laurie. You were supposed to sway, forwards and backwards, with a controlled hip movement, while your shoulders stayed level and your feet glided along the floor. Your right hand was supposed to be held low on the girl's back, while you kept your left hand down at your side, enclosing the girl's hand. If you were really good, you made that backward and forward swaying movement with such grace that it looked easy. Ted and his sister had been dancing that way since they were just little kids — so by the time of this party, they didn't think about it. And of course their classmates loved the swaying, in some part because it was so smooth and precise and understated — but also because it was 'suggestive,' as the parents later said. 'It looked sexual,' Ted told me. He said they learned the dance way before they learned the meaning of the word.

"Ted said the fallout from that birthday party was gradual and strange. Ted's popularity kept rising, and girls paid a lot of attention to him, because he was happy to teach them the jitterbug. Girls would even ask him to show them something in the hallway or the cafeteria, and Ted would oblige them. But almost from the day after the party, Laurie's classmates treated her coolly. Girls who had been her friends started snubbing her and being mean. One afternoon a girl Ted was teaching how to dance inadvertently explained to him what had happened. With this girl, he'd gone to her house after school, and they were in the kitchen because the floor was better for dancing. Ted had gotten to the point of showing her how to do the forward and backward swaying, when she stopped him and said, 'I can't do the dirty part.' Ted looked at her funny and said, 'Dirty?' She told him that that was why everybody at school was saying his sister was a slut. Ted said he wasn't even sure what that word meant, but he wasn't about to ask this girl, and he got out of her house as quick as he could and went home.

"When he went to Laurie's room to tell her what he'd found out, she was just sitting at her desk, looking out her window. Without turning around to face him, she said, 'I was wondering when you'd catch on.' When he thought about it, Ted realized that his sister had been really sad since the night of the party. Also she'd turned him down the two or three times he'd suggested they go downstairs and dance. He asked her to turn around and face him in her room that afternoon. She managed to turn halfway around in her chair, and he could see she was trying to, but she couldn't meet his eyes. She told him she'd gotten the cold shoulder from several parents at the party, and she'd had a pretty good idea what the problem was from that night on. 'I don't have any friends anymore,' Laurie told him. 'I don't think you or anybody else can help me.'

"Ted said sitting there with her in her room, he felt like all the joy he and Laurie had had with their years of dancing had just suddenly been converted into a ton of sadness. He felt like their lives had collapsed, and it was his fault. He said they kept sitting there for maybe an hour, with neither of them able to think of anything else to say.

"In the days that followed he tried to help her, but whenever kids at school saw them together — even just walking down the hallway and chatting — it reminded them of the party. 'It was like the mere sight of the two of us together unleashed this demonic energy among our schoolmates,' he told me. So instead of being able to help her, Ted said he and his sister had to go out of their way not to be seen together at school. With the result being that Laurie was completely isolated."

Our father looked around at us. "I know you kids know what that's all about," he said. "You've probably seen it happen with kids you go to school with. For whatever reason, one kid gets designated as 'it' — the scapegoat, the untouchable, the loser, the one to be picked on. Ted said Laurie was never able to fight her way back from being that one. The victim. He said it wasn't like they completely destroyed her, because she took refuge in reading and her schoolwork. So even though she didn't have any public dignity, she made herself a kind of private dignity. She avoided any occasion where she thought she might get her feelings hurt. All through high school, she was never really a happy person — which she would have been if they'd never done that dance at the birthday party. But she coped. She willed herself to accept having no social life, to spending a lot of time at home, hanging out with her mother.

"Ted said the painful part of the story for him was that from the night of the dance all the way up into his adult life, he had more success and popularity than any one person ever ought to have heaped upon him. Ted said that while his sister went to Otterbein College and almost starved herself to death and got involved with a fundamentalist youth group, he was Phi Beta Kappa at Maryland, first in his class at UVA Medical School, got his pick of internships and residencies. Plus he met Leo Prendergast at the exact point in his life when he needed somebody to be close to. He told me that nowadays his sister lives with seven cats in Hibbing, Minnesota, and barely makes a living as the administrative secretary of her church. He says every couple of weeks they try to talk with each other on the phone, but neither of them can bear it. He says he and Laurie are lucky if they can keep a phone conversation going for as long as ten minutes. 'She's just not the same person,' Ted told me. 'The woman whose only topic of conversation is her prayer group cannot be the girl who had so much energy and fun in her that she could have jitterbugged for two whole days without stopping.'"

Our father stops there. Ah, but we know him. And he knows we know him. Still, he won't tell us any more unless we nudge him forward. It's Emily who does it. She's always more impatient with him than the rest of us.

"And?" she says.

Still, our father waits too long. But finally he tells us. "Ted said when your mother walked into his office, it was like the woman his sister would have been had come to ask him if he could tell her why she hadn't been feeling so great lately."

We're quiet a long moment. Then Emily says it again — "And?"

"Your mother looked him straight in the face, and said, 'Can you help me?'"

Sally's riding with us now.

She's in the seat right behind our father, catty-corner across the aisle from our mother. She makes us all take turns coming up and sitting beside her and telling her something interesting about ourselves. She's tough about the *interesting* part. It can't be just any old thing you'd tell your teacher on the first day of school. "Got to be better than ordinary," she says. Emily tells her she wanted a goat for three birthdays in a row. Peter tells her that he snuck and read some of our father's letters to our mother from before they were married. Desi tells her that she stole a little stuffed kitty from a friend of hers at nursery school. "Did you return it?" Sally asks. Desi looks at her all wide-eyed and says, "I tried to make myself give it back to her but I couldn't." Sally gives her a hug and says she knows what it's like to want something so bad you can't give it up. Jane tells her she's scared of dreaming, and when Sally asks what's in her dreams that scares her, Jane asks if she can be excused from telling that. Sally says okay.

Franklin tells her that he acts stupid in class so he won't get picked on for being a brainiac. Susan tells her some days she wears two pair of underpants just to be sure. Carlton tells her the girl he likes at school informed him she thought he was arrogant, and he told her he thought she was right, but there wasn't anything he could do about that. Sally laughs about it, but then apologizes when she realizes she might have hurt his feelings. Jane comes up to ask if she can have another turn. When Sally says okay, Jane sits down and says she thinks she can tell her about her worst dream — in this dream, Jane says, she does things to hurt people she loves. "Like what?" Sally asks her, and Jane takes a deep breath and tells her like tying them up and burning them with matches. "Oh, child," Sally says, "you won't ever do that. Believe me, you won't ever do that." Sally gives her a hug, and Jane cries on her shoulder, and we're all quiet around them until Jane stops.

Jennifer tells Sally she'd let a boy copy off her history quiz and then told on him. Robert tells her he thinks about committing suicide just about every day. Sally takes his hand and holds it for a while. Peter returns to tell her he wants to be a priest — a Catholic priest, he says, because he'd really liked the two Catholic priests that he met last year. Emily also comes back to tell Sally that when she was in seventh grade, she'd deliberately let a boy look up her skirt and then felt so ashamed of herself she'd faked having the flu and stayed home from school three days in a row. Then Emily shuts her eyes and tells Sally that it looks like her choices are either to be fat or to take up bulimia because she loves eating way too much. Patricia tells her that a boy she liked took her for a ride in his cousin's car at lunchtime one day at school, that he took her out on the Interstate and tried to scare her by driving as fast as he could, but that she hadn't been scared at all. "I'd do it again," Patricia says, "but he's stayed away from me ever since then." "He probably scared himself," Sally says, and Patricia says that's what she thought, too.

C.J. tells her that he wants to go on *Jeopardy!*, because his English teacher, Mr. Temple, went on *Jeopardy!* and won a lot of money for the school. C.J. says he'd like to be the youngest person ever to be a Grand Champion at *Jeopardy!*. Pruney tells her she knows she has too many clothes, she's embarrassed about this, especially since there isn't enough room for even her sweaters in the space she has, so she's ended up keeping a lot of her things folded up in boxes under the beds in the dormitory. John Milton tells her he smells bad — he doesn't think other people notice, or maybe they're just not saying anything about it. He tells her he showers every day, slathers on deodorant and aftershave (even though he's just started shaving), and even after doing all that, he can smell that smell that he knows is just himself. "Is it going to be this way my whole my life?" he asks Sally. He's very sincere. She studies his face a while, then tells him she doesn't think so. Tony tells her he doesn't have anything to tell, he's just a kid and what's interesting about that? Sally studies him a while, then she asks Tony what he thinks of black people. Tony looks startled. "People of color," she says. "Like me." Tony fidgets and can't keep looking her in the face. He stares down at his lap and says, "I like them." Sally pats his arm and says, "There you go, Tony. You've got a little something interesting going for you."

Kathryn tells her the happiest she's ever felt was at her sixth birthday party, when our mother had made angel food cake with pink icing for her and had written on it *Happy Birthday, Kathryn!* and all her friends had come over, and everybody had sung the birthday song to her, and she'd leaned forward over the table and blown out all six candles in one breath, and everybody clapped and cheered for her. "I'll never be happier than that, will I, Sally?" she asks, sadness in her voice, and Sally grins at her and says maybe not but at least she's got that one perfect memory locked up to hold in her heart. Jennifer makes a quick run up to Sally's seat to tell her that she loves the smell of new school books. Robert takes another turn to tell her that his recent week-long study of cats has made him believe in reincarnation. Teary-eyed, Patricia comes back to tell her she's worried that she has cancer like our mother but until now she's been afraid to tell anybody. "I'll take care of you, sweetheart," Sally tells her. "We'll get you signed up for a check-up. That way if you have it, at least you'll know you do, and you can start worrying about something real."

Susan whispers to Sally that she feels like there's been some kind of mistake with how she came out, she knows she's a girl, but she doesn't feel like a girl, she feels like a boy! Sally tells her there's hope, and there are other people like her out there. "And you're not a mistake, my dear child," she whispers back. Tony comes back, looking serious this time. He sits down and tells her he likes shooting birds with his air rifle. He doesn't tell her any more than that. Sally tells him that if he's still shooting birds in a few years, maybe he ought to think about going into the Army or the Marines. Kathryn comes back to tell Sally very softly that she really loves church, especially the singing and the prayers, but she says nobody wants to talk to her about it. Angela tells Sally she doesn't have anything interesting to tell her but would she mind if she just sat with her for a few minutes. Isobel tells her she's been in touch with people in Greenpeace, and as soon as she's old enough, she wants to protest the killing of baby seals. McKenzie tells her she'd prefer not to live to be old, and so she thinks she might volunteer for some kind of experiment where they freeze you and then thaw you out fifty years later to see if you're still alive. Eli says he'd like to be a high school Physics teacher. John Milton comes back with a sly look on his face and tells her he wants to live in Paris and write poetry. "Maybe dirty poetry," he says with his bad-boy grin. Sally asks him if he's going to write in French or English, and John Milton tells her he'll get back to her on that. William asks Sally if she knows what a creeper is. When she shakes her head he tells her that what he really, really likes is lying down on his back on a creeper and sliding underneath a car and working upside down on the underside of the car. He says he helped a friend's dad change his oil one time, and this was like the best experience of his life. Larry sits down, looks straight into Sally's eyes and says, "Veterinarian. Large animals. Dream job would be taking care of elephants." Sally grins at him, shakes his hand, and thanks him for talking to her.

One thing about Faulkeses is that we can figure out how to manage taking turns with Sally, not lingering to chat but getting right up and letting the next Faulkes have a turn. Our father says that this is one of the unsung benefits of growing up in a big family, that you always know how to function in large groups. There's an eavesdropping component that has to be factored into the process, and it's true that some of us do pick up some brand-new information about our brothers and sisters. But somehow it doesn't matter; we're excited that she wants to hear something from us, and she's not a school teacher or anybody who has a professional reason to find out about us. A few of us speak to Sally in low tones, and some of us — boys mostly — speak right out loud. Sally doesn't tell us how we should or should not talk to her. When we sit down with her, she looks glad to see us, makes certain she's remembered our name correctly, and when we get up to leave, she gives us the impression that she's going to think about what we've just revealed to her. When we leave her seat after our conversation, we think she will hold us in mind.

Colleen wants to write children's books and says she wants to learn to be a better artist so she can illustrate them. C.J. is suddenly back to tell her he likes math. He's sort of panting. Sally looks at him and waits for him to say more. "A lot," he says. She nods and thanks him, and he gets up and heads back to his seat. Jack tells her he saw a documentary about crows and how smart they are and that program gave him a purpose in life. He says he wants to do documentary films about animals. "Even like maggots," he says. And Sally says, "Ugh — but thank you." Jennifer changes Leopold's diaper, then carries him up and sits him down in the seat beside Sally. The two of them stare at each other for few minutes. Then Jennifer comes to fetch Leopold and take him back to the seat where Sarah Jean and the other younger girls are looking after him.

Creighton tells Sally he likes teeth. She gives him a big smile. He asks her if he can look at hers, and she obliges him by opening her mouth. Creighton gets right up close to her face and looks at her teeth from several angles. "You've got great teeth, Sally," he says, and she thanks him. Kathryn is back again, this time to tell Sally she's all set, she knows what she wants to do, she likes doing it, and she has some talent at it. Sally raises her eyebrows. Kathryn says, "Baking. I'm lucky. I'll get to spend maybe fifty years making bread, cookies, and cakes. Every day I'll get to make people happy." Sally tells her she hopes that in the years to come she has a chance to sample some of Kathryn's baking. Jessica tells Sally she has a problem with sadness. She says sadness just comes down on her, and she has to wait it out. Sally nods and asks Jessica if she's sad right now, because if she is, she can offer a hug. Jessica tells her she's okay for now, but if she needs a hug she knows where to come to get one. Sarah Jean tells Sally she knows she wants to adopt babies from all over the world. Carlton stops by to say that he's tired of his sisters telling him he needs to pay more attention to his hygiene. Patricia comes back to ask Sally if she has any advice for somebody who just likes to hang out with her friends. Sally tells her she doesn't think somebody like that would need her advice, because her friends would probably be giving her all the advice she can use.

We don't know how much of these conversations our mother is picking up, or even paying attention to. She's in the seat catty-corner to Sally, her ears only about a yard away from where we do the telling, and she's had her eyes closed all the way through New Jersey and across the Delaware Bridge. Our mother could be hearing every word each one of us has said to Sally. Or she could be hearing nothing. We don't know. But just before we go down into the Baltimore Tunnel, Sarah Jean comes up for her turn with Sally, sits down, and says, "We used to tell our mother lots of things. We used to really like it if she got excited about what we told her. I think we told her things that worried her or got her upset, and we even liked that because she was always nice about whatever we told her. Is that why you're doing this, Sally? You know we need to tell some private information to somebody who'll listen to us the way our mother did?" When Sally gives her a quizzical look, Sarah Jean raises her voice and tells her she's bored with everybody coming up to talk to Sally, she thinks the whole thing is stupid, and Sally shouldn't be trying to take our mother's place anyway. But by the time she's finished saying all that, her voice has become quavery. Sally actually bows her head then — it's the first time she's turned her face away from any of us. And she says in this very low and soft voice, "Oh, honey, you can't be mad at your mother for what's happened to her. I mean you can be mad, I know you can't help that, but you have to try to forgive her, too." Sarah Jean doesn't say anything, she just gets up and goes back to her seat.

Peter drops by to tell her he really likes the way stuff gets when it's used a lot. "Like when it's just about to wear out," he says. "Like what?" Sally asks him, and Peter says, "Shoes. Baseball gloves. My dad's old work-shirt he gave me." "Oh yeah," Sally says. "I like that stuff, too. I've got an old wooden tennis racquet I can't make myself throw away." Emily is back. She keeps thinking of things she wants to tell Sally. This time she says she has figured out the exact kind of music she wants to do, but she doesn't know if it'll work out. She likes duets — of all kinds: bluegrass, opera, jazz. "The thing about it is," Emily says, "I've never had a real singing partner. The only person I've ever sung with is my teacher." "And how was that?" Sally asks her. "I nearly fainted I loved it so much," Emily answers. Cassie tells Sally that she and her girlfriend at school sometimes practice kissing. Patrick tells her he wants to try being an organic farmer. He says he's gotten really interested in "the ethics of eating." He tells her that's the first time he's said that phrase aloud to anybody. Cassie is immediately back for another turn — she forgot to tell Sally she wants to study Buddhism, and she's just signed up for a retreat in West Topsham.

Delmer Junior is the last of us to sit down with Sally.

He's seventeen and quiet and very serious-looking. He tells her that he's been thinking about it, and he's figured out that he hasn't ever felt like he's had a life of his own. "The only thing I know is this family," he says. "And all this family has done for this whole year is try to help our mother die." Sally looks away from him and out her window. "I'm not even sure there's a me in here," he says, patting his chest. "So I don't know how I'm supposed to tell you anything interesting." Sally turns back to him. "Tell you what, Delmer," she says. "People feel different ways about whatever's going on in their lives. Tomorrow you probably won't feel exactly the same way you do right now. But I don't blame you for being mad. That's fine. Mad is sometimes just how you have to be to get through something hard. But just don't feel like you have to stay stuck on mad. A time will come when you can let it go. There might even come a morning when you're lying in your bed trying to count your blessings before you get up and face the day, and a realization will come to you like a clap of thunder — you've had one great big blessing while you were growing up, which was this family here." Delmer Junior meets her eyes and presses his lips together until they're thin as shoestrings. He sits with her for a couple of minutes longer. Then he says, "I don't think so." And he gets up and goes back to his seat.

We pester Sally until she finally agrees

to tell us something about herself. Those of us on the upper level come down and share seats with the ones on the lower level, and Sally stands up in the aisle, braces herself against a seat, and faces us with a very serious expression on her face.

"All right, you want me to tell you something interesting about me. I can do that, but it will take me a while. My problem is that the person I used to be was a little too interesting. My father died when I was five, so I have to start with my mother. She was a big woman. She must not have been big all her life, but my earliest memory of her is of a very generous-sized person. And the way I want you to see her is when she's about sixty years old, in the winter, outdoors, with leggings on under her skirt and a couple of sweaters on underneath her big coat, a big wool scarf around her neck, and a hat. A knitted hat she can pull down over her ears if the wind coming in from the bay is really cold. All of those clothes are in dark colors, because she doesn't wear bright colors anymore unless she's going to the big gospel choir contest they have every year in San Francisco. That's where I grew up. That's where my mother has lived all her life.

"What else you need to know about my mother is that she is slightly like this person and slightly like that person, but she has always been about ninety-eight percent herself. She lives life her own way, she thinks her own thoughts, she never seeks anybody's opinions or help or guidance. 'I follow my heart,' she will say, and I am here to testify that that's exactly what she does. It's okay to call her a colored woman or a Negro. It's not okay to call her black, not okay to call her a person of color, and certainly not okay to call her that word that's never okay to call anybody anywhere any time. She doesn't mind if you call her a Christian — 'I try to live that way,' she'll say — but she never calls herself that. And I know that even though she attends almost every Sunday, she has her quarrels with the church. Even more now than she used to. She never was much for praying — 'I'm too big and old to be getting down on my knees,' she's said more than once, and she certainly isn't somebody who talks that Christian talk, praising Jesus and saying Amen every other sentence. She's somebody who will drink a glass of wine or two and whose tongue will be slightly loosened by the alcohol. She has even been known to utter a cuss word now and then — which almost always makes her laugh, as if that cuss word has just sneaked out of her mouth.

"I want you to see my mother, sixty years old, dressed up in her winter clothes, climbing those San Francisco hills on Noe Street, because we lived in that neighborhood, which was mostly white. She always walks from Clipper up to Elizabeth, crosses over at the light, and then back down Clipper to Elizabeth. She still does that at least once a day. And she always has her old walking stick, a big ugly thing somebody gave her so long ago she forgot who it was. Nowadays she has to stop on the uphills about every dozen or so steps. When she was younger, she took that walk twice a day, didn't need a stick, and could do it in under an hour. But at the time I'm asking you to see her in your mind, she has to lean hard on the stick, and it takes her about two and a half hours. Cars will stop and people will offer her a ride; men and women will come upon her stopped on the sidewalk, breathing hard, and they'll ask her if they can give her a hand. One or two people will even ask her if they can call a cab for her. My mother enjoys these occasions, because she will laugh, then thank the would-be Samaritan and inform the person that she's been taking this walk since she was a little girl and she intends to keep taking it until they put her in the grave.

"My mother graduated high school with a pretty good record, but neither she nor her parents ever considered her going to college. She went straight to work for the Cable Car Rail of San Francisco, started as a ticket puncher, and worked her way up through being a driver for ten years, to a job in the personnel office before they renamed it Human Resources. She was good with figures, she was rock-solid responsible, and though she lacked anything resembling charm, people liked her. With just a high school education she made a career for herself at the same time she raised my sisters and me. I like to say that my mother is a completely ordinary person who is highly respected by everybody who knows her.

"I go on this way about my mother, because you need to understand that about the time I turned thirteen, I made it my project to become exactly what she was not.

"My sisters were not troubled by the way my mother was —they were younger, and she seemed fine to them. She *was* fine to all three of us, but when I got to the age where you start being critical of your parents, that woman was just too much for me—she was like twenty-five mothers all at once, every one of them taking that walk up and down the hills, doing her job, wearing the same clothes every day of her life, just being who she was, level-headed Lucy Anderson of the Cable Car Rail. It wasn't like she was on my case or filling my ear with advice and wisdom or trying to control what I did or did not do — none of that. But the example she set with every breath she took set me on fire. Maybe what got to me the worst was that setting an example was the last thing she thought she was doing. If you'd asked my mother what she thought she was doing, she'd have said, 'Why, I'm living my life! Should I be doing something else?' The second worst part was that nothing I did ever really upset her very much. Well, I shouldn't say *nothing*, because there certainly was one thing, and I'll get to that.

"But of course you want to know *my* list, and here it is. Starting not long after my thirteenth birthday, I drank beer, wine, whiskey, gin, whatever was available. I smoked cigarettes and dope, I dropped acid, I took prescription drugs that I didn't even know the names of. I stayed out all night. I skipped school, I didn't do my homework, I talked back to my teachers, I got expelled for cheating, I ran away to Seattle and lived on the street for almost a month before I had to come running back home to San Francisco. To say that I hung out with a bad crowd would be an understatement. All by myself I was a one-girl bad crowd. Through that whole time, my mother talked to me, tried to understand me, tried to love me, sometimes shook her head at me, cried about me once or twice — but I never felt like anything I ever did really got to her. What I wanted was for her to lose her temper, scream at me, throw me out of the house. Maybe I even wanted her to hit me — maybe that would have satisfied me. I wanted to see her so out of control that she would no longer be who she was, and of course I couldn't make that happen.

"And you wonder how the person you know, the one you see standing here and talking to you right now, could have survived such crazy behavior. Well, maybe this is what kept me going. Always inside my crazy mind of those days resided my mother, walking up those hills on Noe Street, going to work, coming home, cooking, washing, living her life the way she did. Because she was always there, even when I was doing my best to put her out of my mind and above everything else, not to BE her. I couldn't do it! If I drank, I never did it to the point of passing out. If I drugged, I did it when there'd be people around who'd take care of me. If I talked back to a teacher, I didn't call her names, and I never came even close to smacking her. And when I lived on the street in Seattle, I did it in the company of a boy who was nice enough, sensible enough, and big enough to look after me.

"Randolph Pendleton went up to Seattle with me. He was like me, trying to get out from under from the black middle-class folks who loved him. Everybody at our high school thought he and I were just the wildest kids ever. But in Seattle, Randolph and I learned we didn't have it in us to be truly wild. The kids who got out that far were kids who didn't have a mother like mine living in their minds. Those were the kids who OD'd, got shot, got sent to prison, got raped, got beat senseless, or who just disappeared off the face of the planet.

"So you want to know how that Sally Anderson got to be this Sally Anderson. I will tell you, but I warn you now, it's not a pretty story.

"In Seattle I did finally, as the phrase has it, start hanging out with a bad crowd. That's what I wanted to do — and up there at first I really had to try hard to make it happen. The truly bad crowd really didn't want much to do with a kid like me. They couldn't see my mother or understand how she'd taken up residence in my head, but they could sense her presence in me. Even when I'd be smoking a joint and drinking a beer in the parking lot with them and doing my best imitation of an angry screwed-up girl. It took a while for me to get in with the band of homeless kids we found in Seattle. And it was Randolph Pendleton who got me in. He was big enough to be intimidating, and if you didn't know him, you'd probably think he was a mean kid. He wasn't, but he was good at acting like he was capable of doing anything. Those kids took him in, and they accepted me as part of the package.

"Randolph crossed a young man — not a boy, mind you, a young white man — named Christian Roberts. This was in Kinnear Park, and Christian Roberts must have been just entertaining himself hanging out with the pack of homeless kids Randolph and I had taken up with. Maybe thirty years old, Christian was a hard guy with a prison record. He both scared and flattered us by keeping company with us, involving us in little scams, purse snatching, shoplifting, small-time theft. He wanted us to treat him like a teacher, and we did. He taught us skills at low-risk, small-time crime; he improved our living standard. Then late one evening he handed Randolph Pendleton a pistol, nodded over toward a liquor store, and told Randolph he didn't want to see him again until he'd liberated the contents of that store's cash register. Christian then showed Randolph a second pistol and told him he'd cover him, no sweat, there was an old Japanese guy in there clerking by himself, anyway. He told Randolph he knew for a fact that there was no weapon in that store. He told Randolph it would be the easiest five or six hundred dollars he'd ever make.

"In the streetlight shadows, Randolph Pendleton stood and faced Christian Roberts for more than a full minute. It was so quiet we could hear both of them breathing. Randolph was taller, heavier, and younger than Christian, but there was no question about who held the power in that stand-off. This was in a parking lot across the street from the liquor store, and there were maybe a dozen of us out there watching the two of them. The others were people Randolph and I had known before Christian Roberts had ever showed up. Before this evening, Randolph and I had never seen a gun in that crowd. So Christian Roberts was doing his teaching again. And the stakes were suddenly way higher than they'd ever been before. Armed robbery. As Christian had described the mission to Randolph — in front of us all — it sounded almost innocent. As if Randolph would be doing the old Japanese store clerk a favor by removing that money from the cash register. 'That old Jap sees that pistol in your hand? He's gonna open his cash register, lay all that money out on the counter, and tell you to help yourself.'

"Christian Roberts's voice had a sweetness that we'd gotten used to and that could make you think life on the street was really just playing around. But we knew him to be a ruthless person. Kids said they'd seen him take a purse away from an old lady, throw her down and kick her in the face. I know every kid standing in that parking lot knew that things were about to change for us in a big way.

"'No thanks, Christian,' Randolph finally said very softly. 'I don't want to do this.' He tried to hand the pistol back to Christian.

"Christian kept his hands at his sides and grinned at Randolph. 'Take it, young fellow,' he said in his sweet-sounding voice. 'Do what I ask you to do. Otherwise I might think you don't understand who's talking to you. And I'd hate to have to teach you.'

"Randolph shook his head like he was trying to shake off a bad dream.

"But Christian wouldn't take the gun back.

"The two of them faced each other there for another full minute before Randolph very carefully set the pistol down on the concrete in front of Christian, took two steps backward, gave a little nod that was almost a bow to Christian and said, 'Come on, Sally.' He and I walked very, very crisply away. We didn't look behind us, we didn't slow down, and we did some hard city walking for at least half an hour. We jaywalked, we took short cuts, we zigzagged though strange neighborhoods. When I expected us to turn toward the park where we'd been staying and Randolph didn't take the turn, I asked him where we were going. All he said was, 'Let's just hope we get there.'

"In the early morning hours, Randolph Pendleton and I bought tickets, boarded a Greyhound, and finally started breathing normally when we took our seats and figured we probably weren't going to get shot now that we were on that bus. The next afternoon we were home in San Francisco. He went to his parents' place, and I went to my mother's house.

"I'd worried that maybe it wouldn't, but my key to the house still opened the door. She wasn't there, but I knew where she was. My sisters were there, and they were excited to see me, wanted to know where I'd been, asking questions a mile a minute. I looked at the clock and figured that my mother would be home from her walk in about ten minutes. This was back in the day when she still had some youth left in her, and she wasted no time on her walk. All of a sudden I couldn't get enough hugging from my sisters, and I kept telling them lies and half-truths and jokes until she walked in and saw me. She opened her arms, and when I stepped into them, neither one of us seemed to want to let go. It'd been years, really, since I'd accepted a hug from my mother, and that was a good one. That one just about made up for all the hugs I'd turned down in my devil days.

"I wish that was the end of my story. I really wish it was.

"The end came two nights later. Randolph came over to visit me, and we were out on the porch with my sisters, the two of us sitting in the glider out there, with Eileen and Clarice peppering Randolph with questions and flirting with him in such funny ways we were all full of laughing. It was late summer, a warm evening, and, oh my, for a while that was such a dear time we had out there on that porch."

Sally stops talking, and we can tell she's stopped seeing us staring at her from the seats where we're crowded together all the way to the back of the bus. We're so completely with her there on the porch in the summer night with Randolph and her sisters that at first we don't mind her stopping. We want to stay right there with her. After a minute, though, Emily can't stand the tension. Her voice is very soft when she speaks for us all. "And?"

"And then a car drove by at a slow speed. I'm pretty sure it was a car that had come by a few minutes earlier. This time it slowed almost to a stop. From both front and back windows on the passenger side, hands — "

Sally's voice catches, and she closes her eyes. We wait for her.

"—those hands held pistols extended out toward us. It felt like slow motion, even though this all happened in just a few seconds."

This time when Sally stops speaking she keeps on looking at us, her eyes sweeping over our faces as if she's trying to bring us into focus, as if she desperately wants to see us. She takes a deep breath before she goes on.

"Twenty-six shots. That was what the police report said. Twenty-six. Seven of them hit Randolph. Three of them hit my sister Eileen. She and Randolph were dead in a second. One shot hit me. In the foot."

Her eyes are closed, and tears are streaming down her face, but she stops only a moment before she lets the rest of the words tumble out.

"Which is why to this day I walk with a little limp. My mother was inside the house, in the kitchen, and she was not hit by a bullet, but she went crazy for a little while. She started running toward us, and she was hollering even before she got out onto the porch. 'I wish I'd known they wanted to shoot somebody at this house!' she yelled out to the street. 'If I'd known they wanted to shoot somebody, I'd have come out here and let them shoot me a hundred times if they needed to shoot somebody!' She walked all the way out on the street hollering like that before she came back to the porch and made herself look at who'd gotten shot."

WE'RE SUBDUED AS OUR FATHER NAVIGATES

the bus into Washington traffic. He and Dr. Lawson and Dr. Prendergast and Sally Anderson spent all of yesterday afternoon working out the arrangements for us to park the vehicles and transport our mother into the museum and into Gallery 50C of the West Main Floor where "The Girl with the Red Hat" lives. We like saying it that way—she lives there — as if this painting our mother wants to see is a real girl we're going to visit. As if this girl just happens to live in a big house on Constitution Avenue in the District of Columbia. Our mother brought with us a big book she purchased years ago when she visited the National Gallery of Art — and we've been passing that book from one seat to the next ever since we left Goshen.

If our mother weren't so focused on this visit to "The Girl with the Red Hat," we might have fallen into making fun of the painting or the girl. But as it is, we stare at her page in the book and we speak of the girl as if she's a legendary aunt or a cousin, someone who married royalty or starred in a movie or had a career as an opera singer or a ballet dancer. Tony, however is not having any of the grandeur we want to assign to her. "You know what?" he says. "You can see plain as day she's just a peasant girl that old Vermeer brings in to his studio one day and dresses up in this kimono, or whatever it is. Then he paints up her face and puts earrings on her, and a minute before he's ready to start painting the picture, he pulls out this crazy hat he's seen in a window in a shop in Amsterdam and just had to have, and right that minute, he decides how he wants the painting to look. It doesn't matter who the model is whose head he puts under it — he's not even thinking about her. He could put that hat on almost any girl walking by on the street, and it would look about the same as it does in this picture."

It's not often the girls in our family gang up on one of the boys, but this time when it happens, it's like the jolt of energy we need to survive this part of the journey. The truth is that ever since our father and Dr. Lawson got into the fight on the beach at Cape May, we've all been dragging ourselves around like we were the ones who had cancer instead of our mother. Now it's with some animation in her face that Emily tells Tony his problem is that he lacks the discernment to tell a truly worthwhile person from a stoner girl. "You need to work on it, Tony," she tells him, "because in a few years you're gonna marry some girl who can't spell her own name."

"Which is not even to mention what you don't know about art," Sarah Jean tells him. "If you knew what you were looking at, you'd understand that there was only one girl in all of Europe who could have put that hat on and made it look right, and Vermeer found her."

Colleen — who reads all the time but who, in the family, is known to make things up just to see if she can fool somebody — announces that Vermeer found the model for the painting about a month before he found the right hat for her. "Read a book or two, Tony," she tells him. "Then you might know something."

Tony takes the book away from Patrick, who's been staring at the painting and not paying that much attention to the conversation. Both boys are careful not to tear a page or hurt the book, because it's our mother's from when she was in college. Tony is about to mount his counterattack on the girls, but then he gets distracted by the picture. "Why's she got her mouth open like that?" he asks. "What do your books say about that, Colleen?" She gives him a smoldering as-if-I-would-tell-you look. Then he says, "Her lips look like Molly Ringwald's." Then he shuts up and starts reading about the artist. This is how it is with Tony—or with a lot of us Faulkeses: we're distractible. Our father says it's because a Faulkes goes where his mind takes him. Our father acts like it's a good personality trait. But in this case, Tony has just let the girls make a fool out of him, and he doesn't even realize it. "I know why she likes this painting!" he suddenly announces. He looks around at us like he's just discovered a new planet. "Vermeer had eleven children!" he says. "That's what got her interested," he says.

We don't think so, of course, because back when our mother saw this picture, she didn't have any children, but it's not really worth saying. Tony seems to be feeling pretty good about what he's found out.

Colleen is reading a book about Mary Cassatt, but she looks up and says in her best schoolteacher voice, "Eleven children was about average for European families in the seventeenth century. Everybody knew at least half of them would die off before the parents got old, and they needed to have some children still alive to look after them in their old age." She goes back to her reading, which is how Colleen acts when she's made up a story — as if she couldn't care less whether or not you believe her. In this case, though, we're not sure. It's worth puzzling over.

Tony goes back to studying our mother's art book. We don't know what he's reading or looking at, but evidently he's going where his mind is taking him.

Our mother is down to only one or two words at a time. She gestures with her hands a little bit but not much. She's also notably weaker and so stiff she hardly moves at all once she's sitting or lying down. She can't walk even a step or two on her own. The girls — all of them — have started taking turns helping her dress and undress, helping her to the bathroom, giving her massages to make her feel better. These changes have come about just since we left Cape May — and though it was only a few days ago, it feels to us like it's far back in time that she could talk to us and move around on her own. Shocking to us, however, and even to strangers who look carefully at her, is that her face has become more expressive. Any slight movement of her eyelid, her nostrils, her lips tells us how she feels or what she wants. At first we didn't notice how strange it was that we were responding without her speaking aloud, but now we see that most of us seem to be able to communicate with her. From paying very intense attention to our mother's face, we can understand what she wants to tell us. The one who understands her best, of course, is Jane (who studies her constantly), though we hesitate to call on Jane to interpret for us. We very much don't want Jane to have another breakdown.

The issue we're still dealing with is our mother's transportation into the National Gallery. She doesn't want a wheelchair — which is what the administration of the museum would like her to use. Testimony to the fire still flickering within our mother is that she's not having any of a wheelchair. "She says take her out on Constitution Avenue and leave her in the middle of traffic," Jane tells us with a grim smile. And then says softly that she's sure our mother doesn't mean it. But when we look at our mother's face, it assures us that she does indeed mean it. She makes a little waving gesture toward Constitutional Avenue just to be sure that we get it. Meanwhile her face tells us silently but clearly, "NO WHEELCHAIR." This conversation is taking place in the big parking lot, just to the side of our bus. Our mother now sits in a camping chair we've brought for her to use once we get her in front of the picture. We're all crowded around her, with Jane and Sally Anderson and our father and the two doctors hovering over her. We've reached a crisis point.

"But you understand we can't take your traveling throne in there, don't you?" This is Dr. Lawson, who's knelt down beside her and now speaks very softly. We know he's even more frustrated by the situation than we are. He's the one who was on the phone yesterday afternoon speaking with the museum officials about our situation. We'd be impatient with Dr. Lawson now except that his voice makes clear how much he adores our mother and how much he wants to make it possible for her to have her encounter with "The Girl in the Red Hat."

"I wouldn't mind taking her in there on that throne," announces Tony. "I say put the throne together out here in the parking lot, load her up and march up to that entranceway, then just walk right in like we're transporting the Queen of Mars, step aside ladies and gentlemen, kiss the floor if you feel inclined, but please don't get in our way."

Nobody asks how many of us are in favor of playing chicken with the admissions people over Her Majesty's Traveling Throne, but every one of us raises a hand to show solidarity with Tony's plan. Fact is, we're all feeling simultaneously exhausted, bursting with energy, depressed over knowing our mother's death is coming to us soon, and excited over being on the verge of finally seeing the painting. We'd welcome some spirited conflict right now, an occasion for raising our voices and maybe even throwing a few punches. Which of course we all know is out of the question for a Faulkes family outing. Except for our father's recent outburst at Cape May, we're not a violent family.

In the solid stillness that follows Tony's rebellion speech, we notice, one after the other, that our mother's head — bare and winter white now in the August sunlight of Washington — is turned toward our father and his face is tilted down to meet her stare. After a few moments, he says, "Your mother and I have worked it out."

Dr. Prendergast carries the camp chair, and Dr. Lawson leads the way toward the main entrance. Jane and Sally Anderson walk close beside our father. He carries our mother in his arms. The sight of them shocks us. Her head shines against his chest, and she's hardly bigger than a toddler. But evidently this is what we need to see right now. Entering the Main Building, we're calm and orderly — and awestruck — as we step into the huge round room with a fountain in the middle of the building. There's a moment when Dr. Prendergast is asking one of the museum guards for directions to "The Girl in the Red Hat" and the whole Faulkes family is staring up into the enormous dome over our heads.

"I EXPECTED IT TO BE BIGGER."

So many of us say this when we enter the gallery where she lives that we might as well have spoken in unison. The painting itself takes up very little space, so they've put it in this frame that probably doubles the size of the actual picture. But even that frame is plain black and modest. Its companion, "Woman Holding a Balance," is equally small, and the other paintings in the gallery seem oafishly large compared to the petite Vermeers. We Faulkeses fill the room and begin taking turns moving forward to view the little painting, then moving back to let others have their turn. We pay almost no attention to the companion picture because we've held "The Girl in the Red Hat" in our minds for so long. It takes a while for all of us to have a proper glimpse of her. And that glimpse has a discernible effect.

Even before you face it at a distance of about six feet, you feel energy emanating from that hat. It's as if there's an apparatus behind the wall to which the painting is wired, so that it generates a magnetic field. As you step up to it — and it's really *her* we're talking about — you're pulled forward so as to be able to take in more detail about her. Your eyes are greedy for her. Then you blink because the intensity of life in that girl's face is so tangible it almost pushes you backward. Once you're close enough to really see her face, it feels almost too intimate. Maybe once or twice you've felt something like this emanating from a real person, a girl in your eighth grade homeroom in a moment of startlement or fear or sudden happiness or embarrassment.

What's in this painted girl's face is an intensity of composure: in this moment she's perfectly herself. And the hat —that extravagant angled whirligig of a hat—takes its fire from the state of mind directly beneath it. Her hat, her spinning orange-red flame that as you approach seems to be the great news of the picture, now, up close, reveals itself to you as merely an accessory. Those dots of light—on the girl's earring, her eyes, the lower lip of her open mouth, even the little bubble of light between her lip and her teeth —are the subtlest of signals. Herein burns a life! You step away having received two truths: Three hundred years ago that girl was once powerfully alive. And though the girl's bones must by now have dissolved into nothingness, this painting is a living thing.

Out in the great hallway our father has waited, standing beside our mother, her head bowed, huddled into herself, sitting quietly in the camp chair, with Sally and the two doctors hovering nearby. There are others out here, too, who are waiting to enter the gallery because there are so many of us Faulkeses crowded in there. In our maneuvering forward and backward in turns, we must have appeared to these strangers to be organized like a tour group from some special school. Our father steps in to catch Jane's eye. Jane nods at him and lifts a hand to signal us that our time is up. As we file out, our father lifts our mother from the camp chair, Sally picks it up to carry into the interior. Like Secret Service officers, the two doctors lead the way for them to enter the gallery.

From out in the hallway we take turns looking in.

Sally places the chair at what she guesses to be the right distance from the picture, then our father gently lowers our mother down into it. In that moment her body — the little that's left — appears rag-doll limp, so that Sally and our father arrange her feet on the floor and place her hands on the arms of the chair. Even as they move her arms and legs for her, our mother's face begins to show light and animation, as if she were catching sight of a beloved friend from years ago. While Sally and our father fuss over how they've arranged her, she trains her face slightly up toward the painting. Her hand moves ever so slightly to let them know she wants to be closer. She's so light that it's no trouble for them to scoot the chair forward. She moves her hand again to let them know when they should step away.

In the gallery regular museum-goers navigate around her. One elderly fellow steps directly in front of her, but our mother appears untroubled by his blocking her view. She waits for him to move away. The white bulb of her head remains perfectly still. Anyone observing her in these moments might surmise that our mother has the power to see directly through any human obstacle. Or that she's in such a deep trance that she would see "The Girl in the Red Hat" even if the room were dark. Or even if the painting had been loaned to another museum. Or even if it had never been here in the first place.

Out in the hallway, we try to make ourselves visit other paintings—and some of us do succeed in wandering a little distance away, stepping for a moment or two into nearby galleries. But we can't concentrate on other paintings, and soon we're back at Gallery 50C, peering in through the doorway at our mother and the painting. Our father and Sally sit on the bench in the center of the room. At a side wall Drs. Lawson and Prendergast stand together, speaking in low tones while they stare up at Pieter de Hooch's "The Bedroom."

"She's sitting forward in that chair, isn't she?" Sarah Jean whispers to the little crowd of us peering into the room. "I think so," says Emily. Tony pipes up to ask what she's getting from staring at that painting like God is speaking to her from it. Nobody answers Tony. Then Emily says, "There's something going on with her!" Emily keeps her voice low, but we can tell she's stirred up. "I see it, too," says Pruney from behind us. "It's just the skylight letting in a little sun," whispers Tony. "I could've sworn her face got brighter," says Emily. "Like she's plugged into a wall socket." "I didn't see any skylight in that room," says William. "But there is one—trust me." Even when Robert whispers he sounds like a know-it-all—but we did notice on the bus a while back that he was reading the museum book very carefully. "Sun came out from behind a cloud," says Tony. "That's all it was." "I think she's sitting back now," Emily says. "Yes, she's kind of slumped back in the chair now," she says, and Sarah Jean says, "Whatever she wanted from that painting, she either got it or she didn't." "We've been studying that woman for so long we can't even see her anymore,"

Delmer Junior mutters from back there with Pruney. Then, like a bird chirping we hear, "It wasn't the painting, it was the girl she wanted to see." It's Isobel in her tiniest voice. Tony can't let that stand. "So she's dying and she wants to come all the way to Washington just to see this girl in a picture?" He makes his voice harsh. "Painting? I can understand that. Girl in a painting? I don't think so." Tony's voice tells us he has no doubt. There's about half a minute of silence among us. Then Isobel murmurs again, just loud enough for a few of us to hear her, "I know so."

Our mother and father and Sally and the two doctors have been in that room for maybe as long as half an hour. Then our mother lifts a finger that Sally notices, because she's been watching our mother for the whole time. Sally stands up and says, "She's ready to leave now." The strangers in the gallery give Sally a look as if she's a crazy woman to speak aloud in such a way in this room. Then the strangers look away when our father lifts our mother out of the chair into his arms and her head rests against his chest. She seems almost instantly asleep.

Our father is telling us this —

it's unusual for him to volunteer a story, but he says it's time we heard this one:

"There was a period in your mother's life, a couple of years or more, when she was pretty close to crazy. She'd say so herself. She's already told you about that boy, Johnny Crockett, and what she did to him after school that day. So you probably think that was the story about how she got over Johnny Crockett. Not so. She got deeper into obsessing over him. Nobody at school knew what was up with her. People did keep an eye on Johnny. He was very handsome, and he was kind of a fourteen-year-old saint. Friendly to everybody, not attached to any particular group of kids, didn't have a best friend or anybody he hung out with on a regular basis. Extremely decent fellow. I think what made your mother focus on him was that she saw how, in spite of all the socializing he did and how much attention he got from everybody, the kid was a loner. Which is what *she* was. He'd just figured out a way to protect himself. Be friendly — to everybody equally.

"Your mother thought she understood Johnny Crockett pretty well, and she hoped he had some understanding of her as well. As you know, she'd definitely gotten his attention on at least one occasion. Or we have to assume she did, because of what she told you she did. But he never showed it. Never showed that he even remembered it happening. Your mother knew better than to throw herself at him because girls did that on a daily basis. Johnny had a way of letting them chat him up and flirt with him, then sending them on their way. He was noncommittal to all invitations. Said he'd have to check with his parents, and then he never got back to the inviter. So your mother knew she had no choice but to be subtle. Keep her distance. Smile, say hello, make small talk with him if the occasion called for it, but be sure not to threaten the boy in any way. After her one big intrusion into his life, she had to make him see that she wasn't going to crowd him. Wasn't going to try to 'close the space' between them any more. But of course if she wanted to get anywhere with him, she had to do more than just act normal whenever she was around him. Doing nothing wasn't going to affect him one way or the other.

"What you may not know about your mother is that she has some skill as an artist. Or she did in those days. She could draw, and she had a touch with watercolors, which not everybody does. But you probably do know this about your mother — she's a good storyteller, and she's even better when she writes her stories down instead of just telling them. You'd have no way of knowing this, but by that time in her life — fourteen, going on fifteen — she'd come to understand that she had these talents when other people didn't. So she figured out that her one chance with Johnny Crockett was to show him what she could do. A kid thing, right? Except it was also very grown-up of her. Especially since it required discipline of a kind that doesn't come easy when you're that age.

"She set herself the task of making illustrated stories for an audience of one. She set up a schedule for herself to produce a story every two weeks. She'd draft up the written part of it the first week, then spend the next week making the illustrations. She'd fuss with both parts, adding things, taking things out, changing this or that about it, rearranging where to put the drawings on the page, and polishing up the whole book. Because that's what it was — a real book, even if it was short. And hand-made. And one-of-a-kind. On Saturday morning she'd hand-stitch the pages together — they were anywhere from six to a dozen pages long — and she'd put that little booklet in a manila envelope, and she'd walk it to the post office, buy some stamps, address it to Johnny Crockett at his parents' home, and drop it in the box. No return address, no note or letter along with the story — but she always very carefully put her initials in tiny letters somewhere on the watercolor that was the cover for the story. She wanted him to have a slight chance of figuring out who was sending him these little booklets.

"This was your mother's secret through her sophomore and junior years of high school. And I do mean secret, because she told no one, and Johnny Crockett never mentioned it to anyone, not even your mother. In fact, he never gave a sign to your mother that he'd received the envelopes. No one in her family knew she was doing it; she never showed the stories to anyone, never worked on them in anybody's presence. Her secret. You think about that, and you understand that her state of mind was at least close to crazy — and not necessarily in a bad way. But the person who does something like that carries around this huge and invisible — *knowledge*, I guess you'd call it. It made your mother different from who she was before she started doing this secret thing. It was a little like knowing she was

Wonder Woman but also knowing nobody else knew that about her.

"This is where I come into the picture. I know it's strange for me to be telling you this story that's really all about your mother. But as you'll see, it's about me, too. And you might even say it's about you, too — every one of you — because if this story hadn't turned out the way it did, then you all wouldn't be here. Or I guess some of you might have made it into the world, but you wouldn't be Faulkeses. You'd be Joneses or Fairchilds or Stootses or part of some other family. This is the story of how your mother and I came to know we were supposed to get married and have a family.

"I come into the picture because I picked up on the difference in your mother. I don't mean that I figured out what she was doing with making those illustrated stories and sending them to Johnny — I found all that out later. I didn't even realize that Johnny Crockett had anything to do with what I was picking up. What I got was something like a musical tone. *There is something going on with this girl.* That's how it came to me when I'd see her in the hallway. It was in her walk, in her face, in her clothes, even in how she'd extend her pinky when she drank her water in the cafeteria at lunchtime. It was all over her. But — so far as I know — I was the only one in the whole school who was picking up the signal. I was the only one on that frequency. I can't believe Johnny Crockett himself wasn't aware of how intense your mother's presence was in those days, but your mother says he gave no sign that he was. Or she says that if he was aware, he did an impeccable job of ignoring it.

"So you can understand the dynamic I'm describing to

you. Your mother feels this powerful attraction to Johnny Crockett, she's pouring out her artistic soul for him, and he's not responding in any way. But I'm picking up on the energy it calls up in her, even though she's giving me no signals that she has more than a polite interest in me. This goes on for month after month — the three of us are like this off-balance and invisible three-person apparatus tumbling around the school's hallways, ricocheting off lockers, falling down the staircases.

"Years ago I used to pester your mother about what was in those stories. She told me a little. She put a bird in each story, a different one each time, cardinal, titmouse, chickadee. Also a tree and sometimes a lot of trees. And a rhyme, though she said most of the rhymes were not ones you'd notice. Each story had to have something in it about a nap — a parent got waked up from a nap, or a kid fell asleep in Algebra, or a dog went to sleep by a boy's or girl's feet in the living room. When I thought about your mother going to all that trouble for Johnny Crockett, it woke something in me, I tell you. By the time I found out about it, I was sweet on your mother anyway, and so it was like finding out that this person I thought I knew had climbed Mount Kilimanjaro or saved a kid's life or found a million dollars and returned it to its rightful owner — and that she'd never told anybody.

"I felt jealous of Johnny Crockett, of course, because I hadn't been getting any illustrated stories coming to me in the mail. But mostly I just felt admiration for her. Not just for what she did but for the fact that she did it entirely on her own, with nobody knowing anything about it. And I may be the only person she ever told about those stories.

"When she was a junior and I was a senior, I asked your

mother to our high school prom. She said yes. From her point of view it made sense, because we did know each other from some time back — remember, I told you about that visit she and I made to the graveyard — and over the years we'd occasionally fallen into some very pleasant conversations. But both of us understood this was a kind of prom-date of convenience — I wasn't dating anybody, and she wasn't either. Truth be known, I was pretty smitten with her by this time, but I also understood very clearly that I was no more than a friend to her. And I further understood that the fastest way to end the friendship would be for me to confess to her that I had a romantic interest in her. This was fine with me — I'm a Faulkes after all, and Faulkeses are generally inclined to appreciate what they have and not to dwell on what's out of their reach.

"Our prom-date started out as a very sweet evening — the gym was done up to be a Paris café, my rental tux fit me better than any of my own clothes did, and with her mother's help, your mother had made her own dress — a black silk sheath — in which she looked just smashing. For a corsage, she'd asked for a single red rose, and we survived the awkward occasion of my pinning it to the dress. We received many compliments from our schoolmates, who'd never seen the two of us together or either one of us dressed up. And you know how your mother looks when she blushes — she's very appealing in her embarrassment.

"She and I were dancing to 'Omaha Nights' when Johnny walked into the gym — the moment is like a hot spot in my memory. We both saw him make his entrance. We both instantly figured out that he'd come by himself — such a nervy act that only he would have the confidence to get by with it. He wore a white dinner jacket, and he had these patent leather shoes that caught the light with every step he took. Of course he was all smiles and *hello* and *don't you look wonderful* and *hey, man, great tie and cummerbund*. At the same time, he managed to be Mr. Modesty. By his senior year, just about everybody in that gym had come around to accepting him — which essentially meant that we'd gotten over wanting to hurt him because he was so perfect. That evening kids greeted him like he was our mayor or our ambassador to the grown-up world. That part of it seemed all right to me.

"In those first seconds, however, I didn't realize what I'd just found out or even how I'd found it out. But before the minute was up, I got it. Your mother and I had been slow-dancing in what I'd call a prom-enhanced manner — nothing inappropriate or lewd, but with some warmth and intimacy. Which is to say that I was holding her close. And there'd been some fluency to the way our bodies were moving. By that time in the evening, we were relaxed, having a good time, enjoying the music and each other. When Johnny walked in, your mother's body instantly turned into wood. All of a sudden I was trying to dance with a coat rack. Of course we were both distracted by Johnny, but I remember kind of laughing about the change in her — so sudden and extreme that I must have thought she was joking. I was about to try to say something funny, but when I looked her in the face, I saw this stricken expression that made me just shut up. I was still kind of rocking in time to the music, and she still had her arms around me, but the life had gone out of her.

"So that's when it hit me that your mother's feelings for Johnny Crockett were far more intense than anything I'd ever felt for anybody. And while I stood there doing my polite rocking back and forth and your mother stood there rigid as a scarecrow, my brain carried out a background search and a review of our entire high school history, so far as I'd experienced it, and offered up a conclusion: *She's had this secret crush on him all this time.*

"Okay, that hurt. Jolt of surprise pain. But as I said, I'm a Faulkes. Another young man would have turned on his heel and left your mother standing there on the dance floor in her paralyzed state. A Faulkes boy waits for her to recover herself and carry on with the evening. A Faulkes believes that tomorrow is a day worth waiting out, and my sitting here telling you this story is proof of the practical value of that gospel. This Faulkes said, after few moments more of mannerly rocking, 'Are you okay?' It was like I'd snapped my fingers and waked your mother from a deep trance. She looked around, took note of the dancing couples on all sides of us and the fact that we had our arms around each other, blinked a couple of times, managed a nod, and tried to move her body in time to the music.

"We finished the dance — we finished moving stiffly together out on the floor while the music played. Then we took up sitting stiffly at one of the little café tables and trying to appear to be having a good time. For different reasons, she and I were both in hell. When I get to the real hell, I won't be surprised if it's a high school gym decorated to look like a Paris café and filled with dressed-up high school kids who are mostly dancing and having a good time. I knew not to ask her to dance again. And after a while, I figured we might as well put an end to our misery. 'Ready to go?' I asked your mother, and her face told me she'd been ready for quite some time. So we stood up.

"He must have been keeping an eye on us, because

that's when Johnny came over to our table. He asked me if it was okay to ask your mother if she'd like to dance. When I said sure, he turned and asked her. She nodded without looking at him. When they headed out to the dance floor, she glanced over her shoulder and gave me what I interpreted as a terrified look. And she said, 'Wait for me?'

"I didn't say yes. I said, 'Sure thing.' I said it with some conviction. Because that's what I felt. If she and Johnny had walked out the gym door and driven across the state line and gotten married and bought a house and had kids, I might still be waiting right there at that little café table for her to come back. Because she'd said, 'Wait for me?' And that meant everything. I don't think it meant what your mother intended—which was something along the line of I-may-suffer-severe-trauma-from-this-dance-I'm-about-to-have-with-the-object-of-my-passion-and-I'll-need-somebody-to-drive-me-to-the-hospital-when-I-come-back-to-this-table. But the way I took it was that your mother cared enough about me to want me to know she wasn't abandoning me.

"Johnny led her some distance out into the crowd of dancers, but not so far that I wasn't able to watch them, Johnny in his white dinner jacket and glistening black shoes, your mother in her black silk sheath with the single red rose pinned to her chest. The rose was like a beacon to me. And what I saw was reassuring even if it wasn't pretty. Their dancing was awkward. He looked like he was practice-dancing with a mannequin. Your mother couldn't seem to look up into his face, so his efforts at conversation were directed toward her hair, which her mother had helped her put up in a French braid earlier in the evening. Out there on the dance floor, your mother actually accomplished something no one else could have — she made Johnny Crockett look clumsy and inept. When he escorted her back to the table, his face was flushed, and they were both tight-lipped. When he thanked her she nodded, still without being able to meet his eyes. He nodded to me and walked away.

"I waited a moment or two before I asked your mother if she was ready to go. She shook her head. She said nothing. She stared at the table. Then she said, 'He wants me to pick up something from his car. He says he's left it unlocked, so we can just find the package and take it out. Is that okay?' I told her that it was, and we left. We left during a rousing song — 'Let There Be Light' — that had almost everyone in the building either dancing or watching the others dance. So in making our way out, we managed to be noticed by almost nobody. It felt eerie, like we were invisible to our schoolmates. And we had almost nothing to say to each other until we were in my dad's car, and your mother was directing me to the spot where Johnny had told her he'd parked his car. We found it. I stopped. She got out, opened the passenger door, lifted out a brown box about the size of a grocery bag. I got out to help her with it, but she wouldn't give it over to me. So I opened the door for her, and she arranged herself in the passenger seat with that box in her lap. It was pretty big box, and it looked all wrong for your mother to be holding it in her lap, but I wasn't about to try to convince her to put it in the back seat. When I got back behind the steering wheel, she asked in a very small voice, 'Do you mind taking me home?' I told her I didn't mind at all.

"As you all know — or will know soon enough — the after-prom hours are an opportunity for, shall we say, 'youthful adventure.' From the beginning, I certainly hadn't counted on having any kind of adventure with your mother, though we'd been invited to an after-prom party at somebody's house. But I didn't mind taking her home instead. In fact, that box in her lap and the sorrowful mood she was in seemed to me clear evidence of a disaster between your mother and Johnny. So — remember, I'm a Faulkes and therefore look at almost everything from a practical point of view — that was in my favor. What wasn't in my favor was her silence. It was extreme, and though I knew it wasn't personal, it felt humiliating. I might as well have been the driver of a taxi taking her home.

"So here's what I thought in the hours and days that followed prom night. She'd had her heart broken. It would take her a while to recover. And the longer I could wait before I tried to make contact with her, the better my chances would be. In the hallways at school her face stayed expressionless as a zombie's. She gave no sign of even seeing me. So it wasn't a problem keeping myself from speaking to her. Or even saying hi.

"Then one afternoon near the end of school, just after I left the building through the main entrance, she fell in beside me as I walked toward the parking lot. I thought about saying hi, but when I took a careful look at her very serious face, I figured hi would be a stupid thing to say.

"We walked an uncomfortable distance together without saying anything. We got all the way to my dad's car, which he'd been letting me drive to and from school almost every day now that I was in the final months of my senior year. I stopped in front of it and faced her. She faced me, too. And I do mean faced, though I could almost feel her willing herself to do it. She met my eyes, though it did cause her to wince. And to tell you the truth, her face looked so full of hurt that I probably flinched from the sight. 'I need to talk,' she said. She didn't add 'with you,' but I assumed that must have been what she meant.

"I said okay, and we got in the car. She didn't say about what, or where, or how long we'd talk. After a moment or two, I figured she was leaving the where to me. After another moment or two, I decided on the place. I knew my dad needed the car after dinner, but that gave me a few hours. So I was lucky in that regard. I was torn about this talk your mother wanted to have, because pretty clearly I was going to hear a sad story, and I doubted my ability to be of any comfort to her. We hadn't gotten close enough to each other for me even to give her a hug. I imagined myself patting her hand and telling her something like 'Time heals all wounds.' I don't have to tell you that a Faulkes is generally not one for emotional conversation anyway. Okay, let's say that I was having some very cowardly thoughts as I steered the car out toward the countryside away from school. And your mother was hunched over next to the passenger-side door like she thought I might be taking her to the psych ward to commit her. Like she maybe even hoped that was where I was taking her.

"Where I took her was Hewitt's Cove, which as you know is the reservoir and the water supply for about half a dozen towns in our part of the state. It's also a state park, with a big picnic area and an expansive view out across the lake. I parked, we got out, and I led the way to a picnic table off to itself. Nobody was around to eavesdrop on us anyway.

"We took our seats across from each other at one end of the table. First she looked at her hands folded in front of her. Then she looked up — not exactly at me but more or less at the trees behind me. 'Okay,' she said. Just saying that much seemed help her a bit. She sat up straight and looked all around the picnic area, the mountains, the lake, all of it. It was sunny and clear with a breeze that had a cool current in it. Your mother breathed it in and surveyed the several hundred square miles of the outdoors that were directly in front of her. 'Okay,' she said again. 'I apologize for using you this way,' she said — and that made me stiffen my back and sit up straight. 'Sorry,' she said. 'I mean right now you're the closest to a best friend that I have, and I really, really need to get this out of my system. You've probably guessed that this is all about Johnny.'

"I told her that I had guessed as much. I didn't have anything else to tell her for a while. She didn't tell me then what she told you about what she did to Johnny in that school room her freshman year — I didn't get that story until after we were married. She started with telling me about making the illustrated books for him. And every two weeks walking one of them down to the post office to send to him. And what lengths she had to go to in order to keep it a secret. Once she started into the details of how she'd make the books and how she scheduled her days around that project, the words tumbled out of her so steadily that listening to her was like watching a movie. But the thought did occur to me that maybe she didn't need me there at all. I mean she could have borrowed her dad's car and driven out to Hewitt's Cove and sat down at this picnic table and just started talking into the breeze.

"'Here's the thing,' she said. 'He and I had never spoken more than about five sentences to each other, but somehow I got it into my mind that Johnny *knew* about me. Like he knew that I'd make silly remarks to the rabbits that came out into our backyard just before dark every day. Like he knew if I sneaked a pudding out of the refrigerator that my mom had been saving for my dad's dessert. And if I had one of those stupid dreams about losing my homework and looking everywhere for it — he'd know that, too. It was this completely made-up relationship I built up in my mind — right now I know that very well, but I didn't really know it when I was doing it. You see, because Johnny was so nice to everybody and because I watched him so carefully I knew all kinds of details about him — like how he keeps his shirts tucked in perfectly and how he writes his name with a little flourish under it on his papers just before he hands them in and how he speaks to each one of the lunch ladies every day in the cafeteria. He was so nice it seemed okay for me to get all involved with him in my mind. I wasn't doing anything wrong, right?'

"Of course I nodded to her when she asked me that, because the fact was your mother hadn't done anything wrong. Her only mistake was getting carried away in her own thoughts — and that hurt nobody but herself. I was about to tell her exactly that, because I thought at least I could assure her that she'd harmed no one by what she'd done. And to tell you the truth, I thought it was pretty sweet how she'd so carefully made those books for Johnny and sent them to him. Anybody else would have gone to more trouble to give him clues about who his secret admirer was. But something was gnawing on the edge of my brain when I started thinking in that direction.

"Just about that time we got some company. A hefty lady — sort of grandmotherly looking, with her salt-and-pepper hair loose enough that the breeze was blowing it all around her head — started toward us from the parking area. She had a bag on each arm — not a shopping bag but the kind of bag people use to carry around books or supplies or sweaters — and she had this very friendly expression on her face as she walked toward us, almost as if she knew us.

"'How are you all today?' she asked, and before we could say a word she stationed herself beside our table and went on. 'I hope I won't bother you out here. You know, I come here almost every day,' she said. 'I usually sit right over there.' She pointed. 'And I do some writing. That's what I do over there.' She pointed again to a table. 'It's beautiful out here, don't you think?' The lady didn't look to us for an answer; instead, she cast her eyes up into the trees and out toward the lake. 'I just sit right over there, and I do my writing.' She pointed again to the table a couple of tables over from where your mother and I were sitting. 'I promise you I won't bother you. I just come out here and enjoy this place, and I do my writing. Sometimes I leave a little something I've written for the guys up there in the office.' She pointed up toward the building where the rangers stay to keep an eye on the place. 'But I don't want to be any trouble to you young folks. I know you need your time out here just like I do. I'll go over there, and I'll do my writing, and I won't be any trouble to you.'

"The whole time this lady's talking to us — and smiling in this very friendly way — your mother's got her head turned the other way, looking somewhere else, totally ignoring our new friend, and so I know it's up to me to make the manners for both of us. I assure the lady that we're happy to share this place with her and that we won't be a bother to her either. So the lady stands there and sways and smiles and hems and haws, but she does finally walk on over to her table. She gives us a wistful goodbye look, like what she really wants to do is to sit down with us and tell us the story of her life. But she leaves, and her table is far enough away that I don't see her being a problem.

"I wait for your mother to go on with what she was telling me, but she doesn't. Evidently the friendly old lady put a cork in the bottle of your mother's story about her one-person relationship with Johnny Crockett. I wait so long that I have to call up the reserves of my Faulkes patience to keep myself from saying anything. Then from her table the friendly old lady calls out, 'I'm not bothering you, am I?' I call back over to her that she's no bother at all. But I'm getting annoyed at myself for being so influenced by the lady's friendly smile.

"Your mother's lips tighten. 'I know her,' she says. 'She was my preschool teacher.' Her voice sounds pressurized, like she's keeping it down when what she'd really like to do is bellow.

"I let some silence go by. Then I say, almost in a whisper, 'I don't think she recognized you.'

"Your mother lifts her head and looks all around, like a bird that's just about to fly away. 'Can we go?' she asks.

"I say yes. We slowly rise from our places at the table. But now the lady is plodding over toward us. 'Wait,' she says. 'I just have to show you this.' When she reaches us she's a little out of breath. 'Here,' she says, extending a book-sized tablet toward us. I don't take it from her hand even though I know she'd rather I did. It's a still-damp picture of some trees around the picnic area with the blue water of the lake on the far side of the trees. The colors have been crudely dabbed on with a brush, but the scene is recognizable, and I'm grateful for that. 'Very nice,' I say. 'It's a watercolor, isn't it?'

"My response seems to make her happy. 'Oh, yes,' she says, 'it's a watercolor. I didn't have any water with me, so I used my tea.' She giggles modestly. 'I bring a thermos with me. But this is what I do when I'm out here. Sometimes I paint these pictures — just very quickly, you know — and I do some writing, and I just enjoy this beautiful place.'

"Your mother is moving up the path now, not looking back. 'Thank you for showing us your picture,' I tell the lady. 'Maybe we'll see you out here again,' I say, but I'm already on my way up the path, following after your mother.

"'Oh yes,' the lady says. 'You'll see me all right. I'm out here almost every day.' She waves as I hustle on up the path after your mother.

"In the car it's warm and quiet. But your mother is sitting upright as a two-by-four, with her fists clenched, breathing hard, and staring straight out the windshield. So I don't start the car. I'm pretty sure something else is about to transpire here. My thought is that if we just sit here long enough, she'll relax. But that doesn't happen. Her fists clench and unclench. Her breathing gets louder. All of a sudden she squeezes her eyes so tightly shut it's like she's trying to lock them permanently closed. 'I — burned — those — books!' she rasps out, stomping her foot hard with each word, and each word so pained and furious it hurts me to hear them. But now I see the part of the story I'd witnessed but hadn't understood.

"'In that box,' I say.

"'He gave them back to me,' she says. 'Every single one of them,' she says. When she turns her face to me, tears are welling up.

"'So he—'

"'He said he read them at first. But then a few months ago he figured out it was me sending them to him. So he stopped reading—he said it seemed wrong to him—and just left them in the envelopes. Without opening them.'

"Your mother's tears are flowing pretty steadily now, and I have to say that it is one of those moments when I know something is called for, but I think it probably isn't the obvious response, which would be to scoot over in the seat and give your mother a hug. Or pull her into my arms and make her submit to a hug. Because when I think about it, I'm pretty sure that's how it would have to go. She might be okay with a hug, but I'm fairly sure that isn't really what she wants. She's probably in the same state I'm in, knowing something should happen, and the obvious something is a hug—but she can't persuade herself that that would do her any good. But, then, what? Well, I know for certain she doesn't want me to say that I'm sorry. I figure that would make her open the car door and get out and start walking home. So a thought comes to me, and I take a chance.

"'Do you remember any of those stories?' I ask her. I keep my voice even.

"She looks at me for at least a minute but doesn't say anything.

"'Because they're all gone now, aren't they?' I say, a little softer.

"After almost too much time she nods.

"'So if you can tell me one—' I don't really know how I'm going to finish that sentence. But I don't have to, because she nods.

"'Do you have a handkerchief?' she asks me.

"Well, I do have one, and I dig it out of my hip pocket

—a little wrinkled but unused—and hand it to her. I'm not sure where the idea came from originally, but my mother had passed it down to me that carrying a handkerchief is generally a good idea. Maybe she anticipated that one day I'd be in a situation just like this, sitting in a car with a girl in tears and no tissues to be had. Your mother accepts it, turns away from me, and applies it to her eyes, her nose, and her face in general. 'I'll wash this and give it back to you,' she says.

"'Not necessary,' I say.

"'You're going to think this is silly,' she says.

"'I promise I won't,' I say. 'Even if it's silly.'

"So she snorts in what I take to be a kind of half laugh. And right there, right exactly there, I know we've made a turn. And something in my chest makes a racket that tells me the turn might be in my direction."

"'It was about a hurt bird,'

she says. She stops and puts the handkerchief to her nose a moment.

"'A hurt bird.' I shape the words but I don't say them aloud. I make a little humming noise—you've heard me do it a thousand times. It means *I'm sorry this is sort of painful for you and please do go on with what you're about to tell me.* Or that's what it meant on this occasion.

"'And the boy,' she says. 'The boy in this story. Took a lot of walks. He liked to walk beside a creek that was near where he lived. He liked looking at birds or turtles or sometimes even just leaves that caught the light in a certain way. He was a boy who was greedy to see things. And from taking those walks, he figured that out about himself. It worried him a little. He liked it better being out there by himself than he liked doing things with his friends. This boy — ' She stops and applies the handkerchief again. 'I hate hearing myself tell it like this,' she says. Her voice is suddenly nasal from the handkerchief pressing the side of her nose.

"'But I like it,' I tell her. I wait a minute. Then I say, 'When you tell it, I can see the writing. I can see the illustrations.'

"She takes a deep breath and keeps staring out the windshield. I'm not sure if she'll keep going, but I know better than to say anything else. I can tell that your mother feels very precarious. Like she's walked out on a tightrope across something that scares her.

"'So this boy also figured out he wasn't really normal. When he was out walking in the places where he walked, he loved being the way he was. Even if it felt like his eyes were eating up the world. Everything he saw — and especially the animals and birds and the water in the stream — told him it was fine to be that way. It was only in school or with his family or any other people that he worried about how he felt. Like he wanted to be somewhere else. So at school and with his family he practiced acting normal. He got good at it. He had friends. His family respected him. He asked for a camera for Christmas, and his parents gave it to him. A really good one, better than he'd even asked for. The camera made him act even stranger — made him look really carefully at everything, to see if it might be a picture he wanted to take. He felt like his eyes might set whatever he was looking at on fire.'

"She glances over at me to see how I'm taking it. I nod. I'm not pretending. 'I'm with you,' I say.

"'This is the really silly part,' she says. 'I even thought it was silly when I made it up. The boy was out walking in the late afternoon. He'd decided to walk into the meadow on his way to the creek where he usually went. But on this day, he noticed how the grass had grown up high in the meadow and how down in the grass there were buttercups and clover blossoms and some tiny blue and purple blossoms. So even though he knew he'd be stepping on some of those wildflowers, he wanted to get out into that high grass. He just walked over into it some distance away from the trail. All that green stuff was so thick it wasn't easy walking — the way it resisted his feet reminded him of fresh snow. But still he liked being out in it, a different world from what it felt like with his feet on the dirt trail. He tried focusing his camera down toward the places where the blossoms made a pretty pattern in the green stuff. But then he couldn't find exactly the right place — or once he'd found a place that seemed right, he'd notice another area that seemed better. So he kept wandering randomly in the meadow without taking even a single picture. All of a sudden he saw a bird flopping around in the high grass, maybe a couple of yards away from him. Really close to him. It was a peculiar little bird with long legs, big eyes, and a white collar — and this one had somehow hurt its wing. The boy stepped toward it. His first thought was to try to take a picture.'

"She gives me another glance. 'It was a killdeer,' she says.

"'Okay,' I say. I hope she won't ask me what I know about killdeers, because the answer to that question is nothing whatsoever. I just now found out for sure that a killdeer is a bird. I take a chance anyway. 'Aren't they shorebirds?' I ask. 'Don't you usually see them beside the ocean?'

"'Yes,' she says. 'That's right.' I see a little smile shadowing her face, as if I've demonstrated unusual intelligence. 'But they like fields and meadows for nesting, even if they're not near the ocean. Anyway, the boy didn't know what kind of bird it was when he saw it flopping around in the grass. He only found out it was a killdeer after he went to the school library the next day and looked it up. What he knew right then was that the little creature was struggling to get away from him, in spite of its hurt wing. So at first the boy just wanted to take its picture. But then of course he wanted to catch the little thing and take it home and put it somewhere so its wing could heal and it wouldn't get caught by a fox or a hawk. Suddenly that was what the boy wanted more than anything — he even had this glimpse of himself with a pet bird that appreciated his helping its wing to heal so much that it would ride on his shoulder whenever he went out for his walks. The boy could see that just so clearly — people asking him about the bird on his shoulder, and him telling them. So he put his camera down in the grass and went walking quickly after the hurt bird in a sort of careful way, wanting to swoop down and catch it but also not wanting to frighten it too much.

"'The bird led him out to the trail he usually took to the creek, led him down that trail maybe twenty yards or so, and then suddenly flew away. Both its wings worked just fine.

"'The boy stood there with his face hot from his effort and from feeling like a complete fool. A bird had played a trick on him, one that had definitely worked. He laughed out loud, because there wasn't anybody nearby to hear him or to have seen what had happened. "Okay for you, bird," he said aloud before he turned back to get his camera.

"'He wasn't sure exactly where the bird had led him out of the grass and onto the trail, so he just guessed about where it was. Then he looked for something like the footsteps of crushed grass he must have made with his wading through the stuff. It was crazy trying to follow his own tracks out there in the meadow.

"'A half hour later, it was getting dark, and he still hadn't found his camera. The boy wasn't a crybaby, but if he had to go home without that camera, he was pretty sure he was going to cry. He'd probably cry, too, when he had to tell his parents that he'd lost the camera they'd given him. "Darn bird!" he said aloud. He would have said worse except that he thought it would be bad luck to curse the bird the way he wanted to. He'd be punished by never finding his camera.

"'That was when he almost tripped over it. He hadn't really kicked it with his foot all that hard, but he wouldn't have found it if his foot hadn't knocked against it. He picked it up and turned it every which way to be sure it was okay. He almost cried then because he was so glad to have the camera back in his hands. He didn't waste any time, he headed straight back home, because he knew his parents were probably already worried about him.

"'Dinner was on the table, but his parents hadn't started eating. They were just sitting there when he walked in. "Where have you been?" they asked him, one voice echoing the other and both a little too loud. Their faces were so worried it hurt to see them.'

"This time when your mother looks at me, her face has changed. *She likes her own story.* That is the news that comes to me, and I'm pretty thrilled. Now that she's told it to me, it doesn't seem silly to her anymore. So I really like it that she's changed her mind about her killdeer story. Something in me wants to take credit for it — *See how I've helped you feel better?* I want to say. The minute I think of it, I hate how it sounds. Instead, I say, 'I bet he doesn't want to tell his parents what happened.'

"She nods. 'He doesn't quite lie about it,' she says. 'And this is the really interesting part of the story. That he doesn't lie to them directly but he also doesn't tell them what actually happened.'

"'He wants to keep the story for himself,' I murmur. I don't know how I know this is what your mother is thinking, but I do. She nods again.

"She goes on. 'He tells his parents, "I was taking pictures of birds, and I kept following one bird and another and not watching where I was going. I got a little bit lost." They're quiet a moment or two, sitting there with their arms crossed, so that he's worried they're going to ask him more questions. He knows they can get it out of him — what actually happened — if they really press him. But he also knows that if he tells them it will somehow kill it for himself. They glance at each other and then try to smile at him. "We were just so worried about you," they say.'

"In the car my voice sounds way louder than I want it to, but I'm excited that I know how your mother's story went. 'And I'll bet that boy can hardly wait to get to his room to play through that story again in his mind,' I say.

"She nods at me, and I look at her. You might even say we beam at each other. 'Seeing the killdeer,' she says soft as a song. 'Setting the camera down in the grass. Following the killdeer out onto the trail. How startled he was when it flew up like a little rocket ship. How he looked for his camera for a long time. How he found it and turned it every which way. He thinks about it all again and again,' she says. 'All the way into going to bed, turning out the light, and falling asleep,' she says. After a while, I ask her if she's ready to go, and your mother says she is."

"Sometimes you'll see her

out on the back porch steps catching the late morning sun on her legs. It's not like she sneaks to do it, but she's always out there by herself."

"Do you think it's possible to know everything about somebody—like we do her—and still feel like you're missing something really important?"

"I never think of her on that porch without smelling the petunias she planted in those boxes on either side of the steps."

"She likes the hummingbirds more than she does the flowers."

"All that gardening she did, and I don't think she ever asked us to help her—but then last fall, she asked me to dig the holes for the daffodils, and I did, but then she wanted to put the bulbs in herself. When I asked her why, she just laughed at me."

"She's like a teacher who knows you don't know the answer and then just thinks it's funny that you don't."

"Have you ever had her get mad at you? I mean like really screaming mad? The one time I did, I'd accidentally knocked her tea cup out of her hand so that it spilled all over her lap. I saw her widen her eyes at me, and her mouth start to open. I was about six, and that was the scardest I'd ever been until then. Then she just turned her back on me and went upstairs to her room and closed the door."

"I know she knows all the bad words, but the only one I ever heard her say was the S-word. She'd dropped a carton of eggs out of a grocery bag getting it out of the car. She thought she was by herself when she said it — and even then she didn't really say it, she said, 'Shhh' and put a soft little 't' on the end of it."

"Not a single one of us will ever be able to fit into the real world."

"Ever notice how she has to have the light in a room a certain way? She'll open blinds or turn on one light and turn off another one. One time we were at Aunt Beatrice's house, and she raised the blinds in the living room. Aunt Beatrice just laughed at her."

"Let me ask you this. Do you really think she wanted us? I mean all of us?"

"She knows she's not a good driver. One time she told me she just thinks she hasn't met the right car. 'If I had the right car, I'd be fine,' she said."

"And what is it with her and sleeping? Used to be, I'd wake up at two in the morning and find her reading downstairs in the living room. Or down in the basement ironing and watching some godawful TV program."

"I asked her one time what she really liked. You know what she said? 'Work. And you all.' So I asked her if that was it. She thought a while, and then she said. 'Singing with the car radio.' 'That's it?' I asked her. She thought another little while and then nodded."

"Not cooking. That's interesting. She must have fixed about twenty thousand meals since we've lived in that house."

"Maybe I'm the only one who ever thought this, but do you ever notice how she is after she's been reading upstairs or out for one of her walks by herself? More than once I've seen her face, and it's like she's been on the other side of the planet. Like when she's stepping into the kitchen, she has to remind herself who she is and who all these people are in her house."

"Mistake to talk to her about a book. I tried it one time for a book report I had to write. About five minutes into the conversation she said that I'd better read the book again. I told her I'd read it twice already. Which was true! She did that twirly little thing she does with her finger in the air. So I read the book again."

"I asked her one time who she'd rather be if she couldn't be who she was. She laughed at me. 'Water running over rocks,' she said. 'That's not somebody,' I said. 'You're a very bright girl,' she told me."

"Not great at helping with the homework. That just has to be said. Dad's a lot better, even though the only class he ever taught at school was shop."

"'What's the most scared you've ever been?' I asked her one time when she was ironing. 'My wedding day,' she told me straight off, not even looking up from what she was ironing. 'You mean you were scared of what married life was going to be like?' 'No,' she said and snorted and turned around to face me. 'Not at all. I was scared your father wasn't going to show up.' She started laughing, and I did, too. It actually was pretty funny."

"Okay, I'm going to tell you this. I think she sneaks and says the Now I Lay Me Down to Sleep prayer. One night I came downstairs really late. The only light on was the one in the kitchen over the stovetop. I was barefoot so I wasn't making any noise. When I stepped into the kitchen she was sitting over in the breakfast nook with her head bowed and her hands crossed under her chin. And she was whispering. I could swear I heard the words *my soul to take*. So I asked her very softly what she was doing. 'Nothing,' she said. But that was it. I got what I wanted out of the refrigerator, and she stayed where she was. Didn't move, as far as I could tell. I said good night as I headed out the door. She said good night back to me."

"SHE'S NOT A PARTICULARLY GOOD COOK.

But she's not a bad one either. And that apple cake she used to make is to die for."

"The part she doesn't like about cooking is having to make everything ready at the same time. She's very much a one-thing-at-a-time person."

"Well, I guess we're a problem for her, aren't we? Because there are so many of us she can't possibly deal with us one at a time."

"You know the funny thing about it is — I think she does deal with us one at a time."

"Maybe that's her secret."

"She's got more secrets than that."

"Name one."

"That stash of Hersey's kisses in her underwear drawer."

"Name two."

"If she can't sleep sometimes she comes downstairs and has one of those small brandy glasses about half full of cognac."

"That's not a secret. We all know that."

"It's a secret anyway. Do you know how she drinks it?"

"How?"

"She throws it back and takes it down like medicine she doesn't like the taste of."

"How do you know that?"

"I watched her do it one time."

"Little spy. That's your secret, not hers."

"So let me ask you. Has she ever embarrassed you? Made you wish she wasn't your mother sometime when you were out in public with her?"

We all have to think about that for a while.

"Doesn't know a single song all the way through to the end, but she'll sing along anyway."

"Not great about commiserating with the neighbors when somebody dies or gets sick."

"She used to be strong. I mean physically really strong. I saw her take a jar away from dad that he was trying to open and couldn't. She just twisted the lid off like it was nothing."

"Every now and then I'd see her watching me like she was seeing something she'd never noticed before. I'd say, 'What?' She'd shake her head and grin and say, 'What?' right back at me."

"Okay, we all know her thing with the car keys. She loses them, and then they're almost always in her purse."

"She used to say she was healthy as a horse."

"And she was."

"SOMEBODY WHO USED TO COME THROUGH HERE

years ago wants to visit you folks," our father says into the pay phone at the rest area where he's parked to make this call. "Yes, sir. She always stopped at your place on her way between college and home. She says it's the only restaurant in America she wants to visit one last time. Then his voice drops down very low. "Yes, sir," he says, "she's pretty ill." We've been heading north on I81, on our way to Hollywood's, last stop on the tour. Our father's timed it so that we'll be there for breakfast. He's called ahead to tell them we'll be there in about half an hour. "Thank you, sir — it will mean a lot to all of us."

We left Washington this morning before the sun was up. We've been gone only a little more than a week, and the tour has deeply affected us. We blink and smile at each other, and feeling wells up in us, especially when we first see our mother at the beginning of the day. We're baffled by our own feelings because they're such a swirling mix of sorrow and exhilaration, of being comforted by the constant presence of each other but nevertheless alone in our thoughts. Most of us aren't sleeping well, and we're not getting anywhere near the exercise we ordinarily get in our everyday lives.

And now our mother — whom Sally tends minute by minute — has entered a stage of sleeping through long swatches of time and waking only intermittently. When she wakes, her eyes seem to come forward in their sockets and shine with awareness. Then they gradually fade back toward unconsciousness and deeper and deeper sleep. When one of us comes close to her during her waking stage, our mother's eyes eagerly take in that son or daughter, and her lips move to shape words that we imagine to be *I know you*. It's almost too much for us to take, and yet we seek it out — that moment of her waking and seeing us with an intensity we can hardly stand.

"In a way, it's a relief that she can't stay awake very long," Colleen says. "I feel like there'd be nothing left of me if I had those eyes shining on me for more than a minute or two. I'd get hollowed out like a locust shell."

We reach our mother's third

and final destination, Hollywood's Restaurant — an extended and upgraded 1950s roadside diner in Hamlin, Pennsylvania — toward the end of breakfast on a mild and sunny morning. When we walk into that place our father carries our mother in his arms, as he carried her into and out of the National Gallery of Art. The clothes she wears to cover up how little flesh still covers her bones may weigh as much as her body does. When our father lifts her down out of the bus, she's rising up to consciousness, then sinking back down into semi-sleep. But once he carries her through the door of Hollywood's — and as he does so, he whispers to her, *We're here, love* — she's like a flare, one of those phosphorescent rockets an army patrol will send up at night to illuminate a landscape. Her face suddenly becomes animated, full of wonder at everything she sees; she might have just risen from death rather than being on the verge of surrendering.

Greeting us just inside, holding the inner door open for us, stands Jeremy, who was the first person to befriend our mother years ago when she stopped by here on her way to and from college. Jeremy is the one our father spoke with on the phone. Weeks ago, before we began the tour, our mother told us Jeremy would be thin, full of banter, quick on his feet, poised and sociable, eager to wait on us but ready to stand and chat, too. She told us that in the years she knew Jeremy he was the youthful father of a son, he was a student in EMT courses that would qualify him to lead ambulance crews, and just before she graduated college and stopped driving past Hollywood's, Jeremy became a father for the second time. "Two boys," she told us. "I don't know if he has more than that or not — but he loved children." She told us that Jeremy would stop what he was doing to show her the latest snapshots of his sons. She told us that Jeremy was kind to everybody and alert to every human current flowing through the restaurant at any one time and that he was never without an errand of some kind, carrying plates of food, glasses of water, clearing tables, running the cash register, greeting customers, taking orders, saying goodbye-and-come-back to people at the door. "He was in a dozen places at once, forever busy, and never anything other than cheerful."

"Karen Seifert," Jeremy says, when our father carries our mother through the door of Hollywood's and stops for her to speak to Jeremy while she's still in his arms. Seeing them as we do, it's hard for us not to imagine our father presenting a new baby to an old family friend. Jeremy extends his hand to our mother, and she extends hers, though you can tell she's worried that her little bundle of bones may freak him out. Jeremy doesn't flinch, he just takes that hand, looks straight into her face, and says, "My Lord, Karen, you're still the prettiest woman who's ever set foot in this place." We hear her murmuring thanks to him, a sound like the human version of purring.

Comes forward then Cathy of the matronly figure and Bobbi the fitness fanatic and April the mother of twins and Heather the former part-time college student and Caroline whose boyfriend had been a disgrace and Mattea who looked after her nephew who was no doubt a grown man now. Also Mark, the owner, who our mother told us always tried to speak personally to every diner in the restaurant whenever he was there. "Two things to know about Mark," she told us — "he's an insane Notre Dame football fan, a personal friend of Lou Holtz, and he's also a right winger that you don't ever want to get started talking politics with." This she knew from Jeremy about Mark's politics because she herself had never brought it up with him. "He was as kind to me as my own uncles were — he always asked me about my classes and gave me advice, though it always seemed to me bad advice. Once he told me that the best way to prepare for an exam was to riffle the pages of my notes in front of my eyes before I stepped into the room. He said my brain would pick up what it needed to remember from those pages even if they were moving too fast for my eyes. That was when I became so suspicious that I asked him what he'd majored in at Notre Dame, and he'd laughed at me. 'I didn't go, Karen,' he said. 'I never went to college. But I never failed an exam, either.'"

All these folks who wait tables at Hollywood's and whom our mother knew years ago now hover around as our father carries our mother in and sits her at the middle table of the special dining room they've opened up and prepared for us when they learned we were coming for breakfast this morning. Because they know they don't look the same as when our mother knew them, they say their names to help her remember them: "Karen, this is Bobbi," and "Karen, this is Heather," and they touch her and look at her with such sweetness it's as if they're seeing the college girl our mother was those years ago and not the mummified creature around whom our father and Sally are arranging cushions in the camp chair Sally has carried in for her.

Of course we introduce Sally and Dr. Lawson and Dr. Prendergast to the Hollywood's staff, and Jeremy strikes up conversations with the two doctors, and Cathy and April and Mattea bring in coffee and juice, and soon there are platters of pancakes and sausage and ham and bacon and scrambled eggs and bowls of grits and fried apples and homefries, and it's as if all of us, we Faulkeses and Hollywood's staff people, have somehow been trained in beehive behavior — there's a chaotic but wildly elegant turmoil all through the dining room they've given over to us, as well as over at the regular counter and in the other dining room, with Jeremy as the impresario, chattering and working like Kali, the Indian deity with half a dozen arms and hands and feet and legs. Cathy and Bobbi and April and Heather and Caroline and Mattea were young women when our mother came here those years ago, and of course they've gotten older, but somehow they've stayed strong and cheerful and agile. They move like dancers or acrobats in sync with each other, all the while carrying on at least two different kinds of conversation, mostly having to do with which tables get this order and what that table needs but doesn't yet have. Then another conversation springs up among them about what to name the baby that is on its way to the new girl at Hollywood's — Portia, blushing and vastly pregnant, who now sits behind the cash register and also participates in this conversation about her forthcoming baby's name. The conversation itself floats all through the restaurant into parts well beyond Portia's hearing. The staff members call out girls' names known and favored by Cathy or Bobbi or

April or one of the others, and April wants the baby named after her, because she's never had a baby named for her, but the others want Calista, Francine, Yvonne, Lindsey, Bess, Molly, Heloise, Missy, Pauline, Casey, Charlotte, Marianne, and Annemarie — all these names are called out and commented upon aloud. Sally speaks up to request that they consider Sally, because it has been a very durable name for a number of years. And we Faulkeses are included in the conversation, because Mattea and Mark ask our names and write them all down and take them back to Portia for consideration. Boys' names are not out of the picture — Portia sends word to us — because the doctors have seen the ultrasound pictures of the unborn baby, and they know the baby they saw was a girl, but they've also seen a shadow they think might mean there is another baby in there, a twin — and that unseen one could be a boy. This is when Dr. Lawson and Dr. Prendergast enter the conversation to offer their suggestions: Apollo, Siegfried, Klaus, Sergio, Umberto, Thomas, and Harold.

And, oh, how that grand stream of chatter circulates all through Hollywood's as little currents of wind blow through a section of woods or a stream meanders through a meadow. All the while our mother brightens and shines and even seems to speak, though for what she says we have to depend on our father, whose translations are utterly undependable. "Alphonso, Cicero, Cranstonian, Woodrow, Josephine, Jefferson, Fortunato," he claims she has offered, which of course causes both our parents to smile and amuses all the staff of Hollywood's Restaurant.

And then our mother's light begins to fade. We knew this moment would come. She's had a tiny bite of scrambled eggs, a little corner piece of toast — this just to be polite and to recover the taste of the food she loved here decades ago—and she fights the drowsiness coming down on her, but we can see it, and we can also sense that she's even happier now than we've seen her in days. The visit to "The Girl in the Red Hat" was actually kind of solemn and grim, and the visit to Cape May was scary, with our father and Dr. Lawson fighting on the beach. Now in the restaurant, we can see how this happiness of food and kind people working hard has lifted her up but is now gradually easing her back down into the sweet darkness that more and more wants to claim her. Our father scoots his chair nearer her camp chair, so that she can lean her head against his shoulder. The two of them appear to us so content in their settling into each other that we keep on with our talk and our eating, but we also turn down our volume. Though they still move with speed and efficiency, the Hollywood's folk seem to tread lighter.

And so our breakfast comes to an end. Dr. Lawson and Dr. Prendergast step over to the register to pay the bill. Our father lifts our mother to carry her out to the bus again, and with all the Hollywood's staff, even the cooks and dishwashers from the kitchen, coming out to say goodbye to her, Cathy and Bobbi and April and Mattea lingering around her, and Jeremy and Mark telling us all to come back soon, they'd love to have us again. "Any time," Mark says, and Jeremy says, "Just give us a call — even if we're closed, we'll come down here and open up the restaurant for you." Their voices are cheerful, but their faces tell us what we're about to go through.

And our mother might even be dead then — we know that, we know it very well as we watch our father carrying her and notice that, yes, something has changed in his face.

When he sets her in her seat on the bus, he does it so slowly and gently, we think maybe her spirit is no longer there in her body, but he turns to Peter and Jane and Sally and the two doctors and says, "She has a heartbeat. But it's slow and faint. I can hardly feel it."

Dr. Lawson is visibly upset—after all, he isn't a Faulkes, and it's all right for him to get choked up and blinky. He has to stand off to himself and leave it to Dr. Prendergast to explain how the medication our mother is taking will very likely keep her heart going in this decelerated mode for some hours to come. "She's still here," Dr. Prendergast says, his voice deliberately loud enough for most of us to hear him. "But we can be almost certain she won't regain consciousness."

This news comes to us in the bright sunlight of the enormous parking lot around Hollywood's. Hollywood's serves mostly as a truck stop, and the big trucks of America need such a field of concrete. By then it's full morning, ten o'clock or so, with the sun warming everything. We have monitored and discussed and defined and changed our feelings about our mother's dying for such a length of time that in this moment we can only stand near each other, stare at our feet on the hot pavement, and try to fathom what is transpiring in our hearts. We can't even meet the eyes of our brothers and sisters because every face is hellishly vivid in this blast of light. Our Faulkes hearts seem to have opened out into too much space for us to get our bearings. If it's possible for a person to be lost within him- or herself, that's what is happening to each one of us. So it is somewhat comforting to have all our bodies in close proximity, even if our faces can't bear much scrutiny. What we see is a kind of mirroring of our own confusion. Comforting as it might be to know that our brothers and sisters are equally adrift, we feel the beginning of panic rising in us. Jane rubs her eyes. Desi squats down on the concrete. Peter begins pacing. Our father stands with his hands in his pockets, staring out toward the interstate with its incessant traffic. C.J. steps away from us and begins smacking the side of his head. Emily picks at the cuticle of her thumbnail. Colleen crosses her arms and faces the sun with her eyes closed. Since our minds aren't able to instruct us about our feelings, evidently our bodies are going to do their best to take in the news, even if it means that Emily will pick at herself until she bleeds and C.J. will knock himself into a deep headache.

"You'll be all right," Sally tells us. One by one. So quietly and so softly. By now she's been through so much with us that she has no qualms about coming up to each of us and putting an arm around us or hugging us or placing a kiss on a forehead or a cheek. "You've already been through the really hard part, my dear," she says. "You can do this, and it will be all right." And when Sally speaks to us and touches us like this — which takes a while, because she doesn't hurry from one to the other — she is so patient that one or two of us push her toward another brother or sister who seems more in need of her. When Sally does this for us, she sets us right. Each one in turn. Though we know it isn't exactly true, it nevertheless feels like Sally saves us — not only from despair but also from the spiritual humiliation, the God prank of whisking our mother away from us. All this time it has never occurred to us that a Faulkes would need saving.

Here is what we do — and it's Sally who thinks of it. Our father lifts our mother from her fantastic seat on the bus, then moves her back to Sally's old seat. He and Sally place the cushions around her and fix the covers around her, but they leave her face open for us to see. Or for her to see us in case she opens her eyes again. Our mother's heart still beats — we know that, as we imagine we will probably sense it when her heart finally stops. Then Sally takes our mother's former seat, and our father returns to the driver's seat. And Dr. Lawson and Dr. Prendergast walk back to their minibus. And we begin the last leg of our journey home.

While our father drives north at seventy miles an hour with the deep summer world gliding past the bus's big side windows, our mother's heart goes on beating ever more slowly. So little talking is there among us now that we might be listening intently, trying to synchronize our many heartbeats with each one of hers. The bus windows beam midday light over our faces, broken now and then by the quick shadows of trees, ledges, or mountainsides. We might feel awful, we might all be keening in our grief, if not for the rhythm of taking turns sitting with her. Patrick has calculated the time — so many hours from Hamlin, Pennsylvania, to our home in Goshen, multiplied by sixty, to give us a total number of minutes, divided by the number of Faulkes children who will take a turn. Every single one of us wants his or her allotted time, and we pay attention right down to the second. Each Faulkes face lightens in the presence of our mother. Near enough to touch her, we can almost feel her heart's grave cadence. Now and then we glance over to study her still living face.

Other books from Tupelo Press

Fasting for Ramadan: Notes from a Spiritual Practice (memoir), Kazim Ali

Another English: Anglophone Poems from Around the World, edited by Catherine Barnett and Tiphanie Yanique

Moonbook and Sunbook (poems), Willis Barnstone

Circle's Apprentice (poems), Dan Beachy-Quick

The Vital System (poems), CM Burroughs

Stone Lyre: Poems of René Char, translated by Nancy Naomi Carlson

New Cathay: Contemporary Chinese Poetry, edited by Ming Di

Sanderlings (poems), Geri Doran

The Posthumous Affair (novel), James Friel

Into Daylight (poems), Jeffrey Harrison

Ay (poems), Joan Houlihan

Nothing Can Make Me Do This (novel), David Huddle

Darktown Follies (poems), Amaud Jamaul Johnson

Dancing in Odessa (poems), Ilya Kaminsky

A God in the House: Poets Talk About Faith (interviews), edited by Ilya Kaminsky and Katherine Towler

domina Un/blued (poems), Ruth Ellen Kocher

Phyla of Joy (poems), Karen An-hwei Lee

Engraved (poems), Anna George Meek

Boat (poems), Christopher Merrill

Lucky Fish (poems), Aimee Nezhukumatathil

Long Division (poems), Alan Michael Parker

Ex-Voto (poems), Adélia Prado, translated by Ellen Doré Watson

Intimate: An American Family Photo Album (memoir), Paisley Rekdal

Thrill-Bent (novel), Jan Richman

Vivarium (poetry), Natasha Sajé

Calendars of Fire (poems), Lee Sharkey

Cream of Kohlrabi: Stories, Floyd Skloot

The Perfect Life (essays), Peter Stitt

Swallowing the Sea (essays), Lee Upton

Butch Geography (poems), Stacey Waite

Dogged Hearts (poems), Ellen Doré Watson

CPSIA information can be obtained at www.ICGtesting.com
Printed in the USA
LVOW12s1458161014

409091LV00001B/19/P